MY FRIEND SANDY

J Paterson
16 Smith Ave
Inverness
1963

By the same author in P A N Books

MY FRIENDS THE MISS BOYDS
MY FRIEND MURIEL
MY FRIEND MONICA
MY FRIEND ANNIE

MY FRIEND SANDY

JANE DUNCAN

UNABRIDGED

PAN BOOKS LTD : LONDON

First published 1961 by Macmillan & Co. Ltd.
This edition published 1963 by Pan Books Ltd.,
8 Headfort Place, London SW1

TO ISABELLA

Printed in Great Britain by
Hunt, Barnard & Co. Ltd, Aylesbury,
Buckinghamshire

Chapter One

At the time when the events which I am going to record in this book took place My Friend Sandy was a small boy of eight years old and I have given the book his name because, when I look back to that time, he seems to be the only one of us whose words and deeds form a memory that is not marred by foolishness or worse. He was just an ordinary small boy – in so far as any human being can be described as ordinary – but, like every other person, he had a few tricks of behaviour and a few quirks of mannerism that were peculiar to himself, and I happened to find these likeable rather than otherwise. I became very fond of Sandy – and still am, for that matter.

One of Sandy's conversational phrases at this time I am telling of was: 'Look here, I'll tell you a thing —' This phrase had come down with him from his earlier childhood when, his mother told me, his imagination caused him to tell not only things but, frequently, 'absolute whoppers'. Maybe the telling of the whoppers was a fey characteristic in him because he was his mother's seventh son, but, if so, he had outgrown it by the time I came to know him. However, he was still haunted by the days of the whoppers, for when he had some intelligence to impart that seemed to him to be very extraordinary he was always afraid that he would not be believed, and the conversation would go like this: 'Look here, Missis Janet, I'll tell you a thing. . . .'

'What, Sandy?' I would say.

Then he would scratch his red head, rub his freckled nose, look at me very solemnly out of his round blue eyes, and I would know that the information was, to him, extraordinary and that he feared to be accused of whopping. Then, in an apologetic sort of voice, he would say: 'You won't hardly believe this, but it's quite true. . . .'

'*How* true, Sandy?' I would ask, because I had heard his mother take this precaution and I liked his reply, which invariably was: 'As true as my name's Sandy Maclean, Missis Janet!'

Well, to quote Sandy, you won't hardly believe this story that is in this book, but it is as true as my name's Janet Alexander, and if I had not lived through it all myself I would never believe that people could behave in the way that the people in this book did.

A story, they say, has to have a beginning, a middle and an end, but I defy anybody to say where any story that is about life had its beginning. One has to choose some arbitrary point and begin from there when relating a series of events like this, and the point in time which I am choosing is the spring of 1950, when my husband and I were getting ready to go out to the West Indies on business for a year, and the point in space is Reachfar, my home in Ross-shire, where we were spending a few days before going on our journey.

From Reachfar, on our last Saturday night in Scotland, my husband and I and my brother Jock had gone a couple of miles down the hill to Poyntdale to have a parting drink with my friend Monica and her husband, Torquil Daviot. My husband is an engineer called Alexander Alexander, but he answers to the name of Twice if it is spoken in the right tone by the right voice, and when he and Monica get to having a parting drink it takes quite a number of drinks, in the plural, to part them. I mention this only because, perhaps, if they had parted at the third drink, none of what is to follow would have happened to me, for it was at the fourth drink that my brother Jock, who is a scholarly, absent-minded sort of type, said: 'You know, ever since you came back from being at this St Jago place the last time, I've felt it rang a bell.'

'Were you there with the Navy in the war?' somebody suggested.

'No. No, if I'd *been* there I'd have remembered,' Jock assured us solemnly.

Sometimes I think that he is a little wanting, but universities and scholastic circles seem to think quite highly of him, so maybe it is just that he has a different kind of mind from mine.

'No. I've never been there myself, but it's where Don Candlesham is.'

'You don't mean Don *Can*dlesham, Jock?' Monica squealed. 'Not Don *Can*dlesham?'

'D'you know him?' Jock asked.

'*Ev*erybody knows Don Candlesham!'

'*I* don't,' said Twice, who always keeps his feet on the ground even at the tenth parting drink. 'Who is he?'

'Some people said he was One of Those,' Monica said to Jock, 'but that was a calumnious lie.'

6

'Undoubtedly,' said Jock. 'Don was definitely the parish bull in a naval officer's clothing during the war, but I liked him – especially as long as there were no women around. *I* know what, you two. . . .' He turned to Twice and me. 'Don's keeping a boarding-house or something. You want to go and stay with him.'

'Oh no we don't!' I said.

Sometimes I think I have a touch of The Sight, being Highland, but I never remember to take any notice of its warnings until it is too late.

'Why should we?'

'Look here,' said Monica, 'you've got to stay *somewhere* out there until this house you are getting is ready.'

Now, some people get all mellow and wobbly and generally amenable at the fourth drink, but not my friend Monica. In general character she is always fairly cussed and difficult, and the odd drink merely makes her more so, so she tossed back her red hair and swung into her stride.

'You know perfectly well that you've got to go to a hotel out there for a bit because you're going earlier than you said, and your house isn't ready, and I think it's pretty stinking going giving the money to somebody else and not patronising old Don's boarding-house when he's a friend of Jock's and mine and everybody's. What have you got against him? Oh, I know a lot of people said things because he *would* have his uniform tunics lined with pink satin, but in the war people had to do *some*thing for a change, and it wasn't Black Market – it was only the old curtains out of Lady C.'s boudoir after the London house was bombed, and I think it's pretty rotten of you — '

'Let's all have one for the road!' said Torquil, who is a peace-loving soul who handles Monica with great tact and smoothness.

'I don't mind if I do,' said Monica, and, of course, one would have thought that the matter would have ended there, but not with my friend Monica.

On the following Tuesday, Twice and I boarded our aeroplane at London airport and the stewardess handed Twice a fat orange envelope.

'Monica!' I said.

Twice ripped the thing open, the normal four sheets or so which is one of Monica's briefer telegrams burst out and I read over his shoulder: 'Been in cable contact with Don would not wish anything closer stop he has heavenly place near Jago Bay all mod con excellent food cultured company terms reasonable to recommended guests stop have instructed him hold suitable rooms basket flowers dressing-table if not delivered please cable stop suspect him of petty dishonesty nothing serious stop Twice left presentation sola topee here children using it accouchement white mice love Monica.'

'Cultured company! Accouchement white mice! Honestly, what will the Post Office think?' Twice asked.

'Never mind the Post Office!' I said bitterly. 'What about *us*?'

'Oh, we don't have to *go* to this place!' he told me airily.

That is what he thought. In spite of being very fond of Monica, Twice does not know her as I know her – he did not share a tin hut with her all through the 1939-45 war in the Women's Air Force as I did – and I know that when Monica arranges anything it takes a lot of trouble – if not an actual lawsuit – before it can be *dis*arranged.

In the reliable way that aircraft do – although I can never believe in it when I step into them – this aircraft duly set us down on schedule on the blistering tarmac of the one airport in the island of St Jago, which lies about two miles outside of the capital, Jago Bay, or simply 'The Bay', as the island metropolis is commonly called. We came quickly through the Customs, for our heavy baggage had been sent out by sea, and walked out of the wire cage to look for a taxi that would take us to the Palace Hotel with which we already had some acquaintance. As we came into the main hall, an ethereal vision in a peach-pink shirt, claret-coloured trousers, suède shoes to tone, the whole offset by a lime-green suède belt and watch-strap *en suite*, flitted up to us on tiptoe and said: 'I say, you *are*, aren't you? *Do* say you are – the Alexanders, I mean!' He darted a glance at the label on Twice's suitcases, clapped his hands, jumped a dainty foot or so into the air and crowed gleefully: 'Oh, you *are*! Darlings, what Heaven! I win ten shillings! Oh, *how* d'you do! Don said you were those two over there. . . .' He lowered his voice. 'The woman with the hips, so *fe*cund, but I bet him Monica would *never* recommend those hips! Don! Don! I win! I win!' He executed a dashing pirouette on one suède-shod toe. 'See how I win! Look! . . . Now, Don, it's only ten shillings! *Don't* be cross! *Quite* the reverse!'

Towards us, through the staring crowd, walked what I am quite sure is the most handsome man I have ever seen. He was somewhere around thirty years old and perfect, physically, to the last fine dark hair on his sculptured, muscular forearms. Even in its physical form humanity is seldom perfect, so seldom that, even when seen, it is difficult to believe. Automatically I looked for the malformed ear, the dropped arch in the foot, the mis-shaped fingernail, the false tooth or the impediment in the speech, but none of them were there.

'I'm Don Candlesham,' he said in a pleasant rich voice, smiling, holding out a hand. 'This sliver of embarrassment is Sasha de Marnay. Actually he's completely harmless. Shake hands like a gentleman, Sashie!'

'I am not at all, of course,' said Sashie, extending to me a limp, apparently boneless hand, 'at all a gentleman – quite the reverse – but how *do* you do?' He bobbed a dainty curtsy, one foot behind the other. '*And* you, Mr Alexander – such *rugged* charm!'

'Sashie, behave yourself!' said Don.

'I beg of you, *don't* quarrel before the customers, Donald!' Sashie said, 'And — ' as the eyes of Don followed the neat hips of an air-stewardess across the hall – 'do *try* not to lust openly after those great strapping wenches in uniform!'

I hiccupped out a silly giggle because I could not help it, with which Sashie said: 'I beg of you, don't encourage him! . . . You *are* coming to our place, aren't you? Don't say No! Quite the reverse!'

'As a matter of fact,' said Twice, making a desperate stand, 'we are booked at the Palace. We didn't know Monica was doing —'

'Dear Monica, so monstrously managing! As for the Palace – Ike, the owner, you know, *so* co-operative and understanding. He will *adore* it if you come to us and then we'll take you down to him one night for drinks and he can tell all his American commercial-traveller friends – so exhausting with all their ice-boxes and slide-rules and things – about how we are the Beoble from the Beak, zo egsgluesiff.'

'Sashie, stop being a bitch and come *on*!' said Don.

'I'm *not* being a bitch! Ike *does* have intestinal blockage of the nose, poor sweet, due to chronic overdevelopment, I think. So *very* Levantine, but a perfect *gem* under the grease!'

'Mrs Alexander,' said Don solemnly, 'in spite of all obvious disadvantages, will you step into our car and come to our hotel for a drink before lunch, even if you don't stay with us? Next time,' he added, with a vicious glance at Sashie, 'I will not bring the cook to the airport with me!'

'Yes!' said Sashie with a fresh burst of enthusiasm, 'I am the cook! And the lunch? My dears, a dream! *Do* come!' and, picking up Twice's briefcase, he skipped off towards the exit.

'He's quite amusing, actually,' said Don, as we followed the cavorting Sashie to the station wagon which was painted brilliant blue, with 'The Peak' scrawled along its side in gold paint, but I looked at Twice's frozen face and made no comment.

The lunch, served in a long, low, whitewashed room, hung with some very pleasing modern pictures, was indeed a dream, and, when it was over, Don came to us and said: 'Monica indicated you'd prefer a small house, really. They just *aren't*, in the ordinary, rentable way, actually. The local houses, if you could rent them, which you can't, start at six bedrooms and go on up. But Sashie and I are trying a stunt here, actually. . . . Come across the garden, this way. . . . It's all a bit of a mess as yet,' he explained when we had passed through a gap in the hibiscus hedge that led to a green slope above the sea, 'but that one's finished.' He pointed to a small white building. 'Cottages – meals back in the main house,' he explained. 'This island is in for a tourist boom in my opinion, so – by the way, how are you on sex, actually?'

'Actually,' said Twice belligerently, 'what the hell do you mean?'

'Just a minute — ' I broke in hastily, but Don waved a shapely hand, grinning at me.

'You must forgive the actually, actually,' he told Twice. 'I started saying it to pay out Sashie's 'quite the reverse' and it's become a habit. . . . What I mean about sex is, are you fearfully Presbyterian and Lutheran about it, and wishful to nail theses to church doors or throw stools or anything?'

'No,' I said. 'We regard it as everybody's private and nobody's public affair. Why?'

He smiled down at me. I am a tall woman, unaccustomed to being smiled down at, and I found it disconcerting. 'Well, speaking privately of everybody's public affair,' he said, '*in re* this tourist boom – we're going to get a mass of Americans in here – we are only four hours away by air. The way I see it, where you get Americans, you get sex; where you get sex, you want privacy to some degree – hence the cottages. Love-nests under a tropic moon, if you follow me.' He waved the shapely tanned hand at the completed cottage and eleven others in various stages of building. 'A considerable capital investment. Come and have a look.'

We followed him into the completed cottage, which consisted of a long verandah, already shaded by a quick-growing, trellised creeper, with, behind it, a sitting-room, a bedroom and a bathroom. The furniture was good, the bathroom and light fittings pleasant and practical, the curtains and upholstery of good quality and in excellent taste. 'On the whole, far too good for its purpose,' I told him after we had looked round.

He shrugged his shoulders. 'We're out for the diamond and platinum trade,' he said. 'Ike can provide for the bread-and-butter people down at the Palace. The point is, Alexander, can you run to twelve guineas a week each? Say twenty-five quid for the two of you? That would cover everything, of course – cottage, meals, personal laundry and the odd drink. Of course, if you want to get into a polluted alcoholic stupor *every* night of the week, it would cost a little more.'

Twice is almost painfully honest, 'You're a fool, Candlesham,' he said. 'You'll never make out on your investment at rates like that in this island.'

Don grinned. 'This has no relation to our normal rates,' he said. 'The fact is that it would suit us to have you two here for a bit. The tourist trade is seasonal, you know – January to May, actually. We want to fill the place up in between. I want a hard core of Island connections, as it were.'

'I see.' Twice was still doubtful. 'Well —'

'We've got another English couple in the house,' Don said. 'Hugo and Miranda Beaumont – they are opening up a tourist shop in the town – arty-crafty stuff, you know, straw hats and baskets and nightmare knick-knacks carved out of native wood. They and you would form a nucleus, as it were. . . . Give it a thought. It would suit us if it suits you. Keep Sashie busy too. He's not such a fool as he looks, actually.'

'There certainly was no fooling about the lunch,' I said.

'Best caterer in two continents.' Don smiled. 'Makes a pound of butter stretch a mile while giving people the impression they are simply wallowing in it. . . . You haven't met Miss Poynter yet?'

'No.'

'She gives the place a rather eccentric air.' This caused Twice and me to stare at one another in alarm, for we felt that the air of the place was already eccentric enough. 'But she is madly useful. We bought the old house and land from her actually, the last remains of the old Poynter Plantation. Then we found that we had more or less bought *her* as well for the time being until she can find the kind of place she wants. She insists on staying in that little house down there – used to be the Headman's house for the property, nice little place – and acting as housekeeper.'

'Is she old?' I asked, for I am always interested in personalities and family histories and such things.

'The rudeness!' said the voice of Sashie behind us. 'The dretful, incredible rudeness, mentioning *age* like that! Janet – I'll call you Janet because when *I* do it it doesn't matter – Janet darling, Miss Poynter is *age*less, but ageless, to the last henna-ed hair. . . . I say, you *are* going to take Number One, aren't you? Do, *do* say you will!'

'Well, Flash?' Twice asked me.

'I like it,' I told him and he turned to Don.

'All right, Candlesham. Your cottage is let. You realize that we won't be here for very long, though?'

Don nodded. 'Days, weeks, months – delighted to have you. Sashie, tell them to send the baggage over.'

Sashie skipped away, singing, across the grass between the piles of bricks, lumber and flooring tiles.

I have come to the conclusion that I am over-susceptible to influence from other people. I do not mean, by this, that a drug-addict has only to look at me and I will be led by him by the hand into eating – or whatever one does with it – heroin, in large quantities. What I mean is, that if a drug-addict looked at me I would tend to feel just as he did, either hopped-up or depressed-down according to whether he had had his daily dollop or not. What this comes to is that I can feel like a drug-fiend without benefit of drug, without any desire or will on my part to feel that way at all. It simply comes over me.

Being like this, I had not been staying at the Peak for forty-eight hours before something was coming over me although I was not sure what it was. Even now I am not sure. Twice, being a working man, left Number One at seven in the morning and did not re-appear until about five in the evening, and everything was very strange and foreign and permeated by an extraordinary, exotic luxury. The breakfast bowl of fruit – oranges, grapefruit, bananas, paw-paw, pineapple, star-apple, passion-fruit – was lavish and garnished with a spray of beige orchids; the flaring scarlet of the poincianas, the deep blue of the jacarandas, the heavy pink of the frangipanis, the funeral white of the daturas combined in an assault on the eye and nose that was as exotic as their names to the ear; the sea of subtlest shadings of deep blue to pale green rolled, always, in lazy, limpid waves on to the glittering white beach, and woven through all this were the unpredictable personalities of the handsome Don and the fantastic Sashie. It all combined, in Twice's absence particularly, to give me the feeling that I too was living inside the iridescent bubble which Don and Sashie inhabited, so that I felt that I too – the mundane Janet Alexander – was being swept and bounced along on the sparkling air-current which seemed to surround them.

Except for a little typewriting for Twice and my normal correspondence with the people at home, I had nothing to do all day and, always being interested in any enterprise of any sort, I naturally took an interest in Don's and Sashie's activities in the development of their hotel. I conferred with them on the building and the furnishing of the cottages; I made suggestions about the planting of trees and shrubs; I interfered with their book-keeping arrangements and, in general, became a third, non-financial partner in the business rather than a hotel guest. Don and Sashie amused me, and when I was in their company my susceptibility to influence made me speak in their idiom, so that by custom and daily usage the strangeness they had, at first, had for me was rubbed away and I began to regard them as just one more norm of this unusual country. It contained people like Don and Sashie; it contained other people like the negro staff; it contained exotic trees and fruits and was ringed around by a sea that was always sunlit and calm. At first, I found all this strangeness amusing, but Twice, apparently, had more resistance.

'I don't understand how a bloke *gets* like that,' he said to me of Sashie one evening. 'And I don't understand Don Candlesham either. In fact, the whole damned issue is demented. . . . We should have gone to live at Ike's after all. I hope they'll soon be ready for us at Paradise.'

'Paradise is fairly demented too, come to that,' I said. 'Madame and Sir Ian, I mean. . . . Besides, I like it here. It amuses me. Twice, would you really like to move to Ike's?'

'Not really, my pet. This has all sorts of advantages and, after all, I'm away a lot of the week. As long as *you* are all right – but – don't get peculiar, will you?'

There was a strange note in his voice that I had never heard in it before.

'Peculiar, darling? In what way?'

13

'Just peculiar, among all these peculiar people in this peculiar place in this peculiar climate.'

'Twice, I don't understand.'

He moved his shoulders uneasily. Twice has big, heavy shoulders and this movement he made is difficult to describe – it had something animal and instinctive in it of the uneasy movement that a horse makes before the panic that leads to a shy gains complete control.

'I myself don't understand what I mean,' he said. 'I just have a queer uneasy feeling.' He stared at the wall for a moment and then laughed.

'Some of your Granny's witchcraft has got into me, I suppose. . . . Flash, what *about* Don Candlesham? What do you think of him, really?'

'Quite honestly, Twice, I don't know. He's interesting to me – he is like one of these fearfully modern books written in a foreign language I don't understand and I know I wouldn't understand it and what it's getting at even if it were translated into English, but I have to keep on having another look at it. He seems to be having himself a hell of a time demonstrating a freedom that nobody in the world is trying to withhold from him.'

'He's certainly a free wolf among the women.'

'It's rather disgusting. Strickly coyote-like, as Martha would say.'

Twice giggled. 'Don Coyote, in fact!'

'You're dead right. Mind you, the women encourage him – and no wonder. His looks are astonishing and so are his swimming and his tennis – not to mention the dancing. As for Sashie – Don Coyote and Sashie Pansy!'

Twice and I rolled on the bed in a fit of those giggles to which, even at the age of forty, we were still regrettably prone.

'Sashie Pansy is just something you have to take as you find it,' I said later. 'To tell the truth, I don't believe he is a homosexual at all. I think he's just a sort of neuter who is not a bit interested either way. If he were a homosexual, he would resent Don and the women, wouldn't he?'

'Why ask me?' said Twice. 'It is a subject of which I have no knowledge.'

'No, but wouldn't you *think* so?'

'I never think about him – it – anyway, Sashie, if I can help it. Mind you, he can be damned amusing.'

'He makes a study of it, just as he does of catering. When you think of it, the two of them are just a couple of modern pirates

14

of the Spanish Main, except that they don't even have the risk of the high seas. I think every single thing they do is directed towards making a success of this hotel. They certainly create an atmosphere about the place and pull in the customers.'

'Still, they're not everybody's cup of tea.'

'This isn't a cup-of-tea hotel, remember. Think of that first day – Don and the platinum and diamond trade. There are a lot of real diamonds and hunks of platinum in the provinces of America these days in the little towns, and provincials will pay good money to see Life with a capital L in the form of Sashie. As for Don, I think maybe he is just a cold-blooded, money-grubbing brute at heart.'

'You could be right at that,' Twice admitted grudgingly.

Our lives were not spent entirely enwrapped in the atmosphere of the Peak, of course. Twice and I have a world of our own, which has its own ambient air, and which we can transport with us wherever we go. This atmosphere of ours, our own norm, prevailed in Number One, our little bungalow, and was impervious to the frequent alarms and excursions without, which were the scenes between Don and Sashie themselves, and Don and Sashie and all servants, builders, tradesmen and gardeners. Also, Twice in his capacity of consultant for his engineering firm made many friends about the island, mainly on the sugar plantations whose processing factories contained a large percentage of the island's industrial equipment, and we spent many evenings 'in the bush', as the urban people of the Bay called any place that was outside the city's limits.

The largest plantation on the island was 'Paradise', where we were to go when our house there was ready. The dominating 'Great House' of Paradise Estate lay at the centre of a valley, about an hour's driving over rough inland roads from the Bay and the Peak Hotel. A few months before, Twice and I had made a preliminary visit to the island and had found ourselves, quite by chance, the guests of Paradise for the duration of our stay. We had realized at the time that the Estate, and the Dulac family who owned it, were a survival from the past, but it was not until we had lived against the background of the Peak, Don and Sashie, for a few days, and then drove out to Paradise to spend our first weekend in the island that we realized just how far back was that past, or how remarkable was Paradise as a survival. That motor journey of an hour's duration was a journey from one world into another.

Paradise marked itself in many ways as being different from other estates and plantations in the island, but one of the most striking differences lay in the fact that it was still in the private ownership of the Dulac family who had been growing sugar there since the early eighteenth century. Most of the other sugar plantations were running on a company basis, on overseas capital, under the management of boards of directors and employed managers. But not Paradise. Paradise was running on Dulac capital, under the immediate, plump, beringed little hand of Madame Dulac, a Scotswoman born in Edinburgh eighty years before, who was ably assisted by her Scottish manager, Rob Maclean from Perthshire, who had been putting up with her eccentricities and smoothing out her difficulties for over thirty years.

Madame had come to Paradise as a bride, in 1890, in the heyday of the Victorian era, and she had steadfastly refused to recognize the march of time or history for the last sixty years, unless the march of time or history happened to please her. It pleased her to accept current fashion to the extent that women's skirts should no longer sweep the ground; she was not pleased to accept negroes in any position of authority. Consequently, she wore skirts that exposed her ankles and no more, but would have no direct dealings with the local parochial board whose members were coloured men. She approved of the advance of education and would subscribe large amounts for the establishment of village schools, but she disapproved of the fact that the editor of the island newspaper in 1950 was a negro. She approved of scientific advancement in general and of the airmail in particular, but she did not approve of aeroplanes bringing tourists and holidaymakers to St Jago. 'It will ruin the fundamentally agricultural economy of the island,' she said.

Like most other people, Madame Dulac was neither all right nor all wrong, but she had, in a marked degree, the Victorian conviction that the British flag *could* not be wrong and that Madame Dulac, as one of its strongest supporters in St Jago, was imbued with much of its divine rightness. She was an extremely cussed old woman, in brief, with enough of the power that wealth can command in a commercial age, to constitute herself a law unto herself and indulge her cussedness to the top of her bent. She ruled Paradise and everyone in it openly, with an iron hand, and she ruled half the island and its population with an iron hand only barely concealed. She reminded me very strongly of my grandmother, whose name I always tend to write as 'MY GRANDMOTHER' with capital letters and underlined, for that is how the memory of her stands in my mind.

The heir to the broad lands of Paradise and all its wealth was Madame's son, Sir Ian, who had retired after a distinguished career in the Army and Colonial Police and was living at home on the estate. In January, when Twice and I had made our preliminary trip to St Jago, Sir Ian and little Sandy Maclean had been travelling by the same plane, and thus began the connection between Paradise and us. We had stayed at the Great House for the month of January and, when Twice's firm had decided to send him back to St Jago for a year or so, Madame decided that nothing would do but that we should return to a house on her estate.

'It's coming along nicely,' Marion Maclean told me when we drove out from the Peak on our first Saturday in the island. 'Another fortnight or so should do it. Let's go over there now. . . . Are you men coming?'

'Hi, Mother, can Sir Ian an' me get comin' as well?' Sandy asked.

'All right. Come along.'

As we drove across the valley, I found myself – not for the first time – studying Sir Ian and Sandy. Every moment of the day, except for a few morning hours when Sandy had to do lessons with his tutor, Sir Ian and the boy were together and they reminded me, nostalgically, of my own childhood friendship with my friend Tom. Sir Ian was about sixty, with a ruddy, genial face, an abundance of silver, well-barbered hair, and a spirit as youthful as that of his eight-year-old, carrot-haired, stubby-faced companion.

'This house is going to be extremely useful to us, now that we've got around to repairing it,' Rob Maclean said when we got out of the car. 'We get so many visiting agriculturalists and engineers and odd bodies that Marion and I and the rest of the staff are sick of never being able to call our homes our own. When you are finished with this place, Janet, we'll put a housekeeper in here and use it as a guest house. All the plantations in Cuba and Peru have them.'

'Excellent idea,' said Sir Ian, 'specially for fellahs that ask for ice in their port like that fellah last year. . . . Sandy, my boy, you and I will have to get this garden cleaned up for Missis Janet. Let's see now — '

Sandy and Sir Ian went off on a tour of inspection of the overgrown garden.

'We thought of putting up a new modern bungalow,' Marion said, ' — it would have been just as quick and cheaper if anything, but so many of the old buildings in the island have been torn down that it seemed a pity to destroy one more. . . . This will make a nice drawing-room.'

I looked round the beautifully-proportioned room. 'I think it's beautiful, Marion.'

'The furniture will be a job,' she said. 'The store-rooms at the Great House are chock-a-block with stuff, so you and I will have to go round there with a labour gang next week and pull out what we want.'

'Sir Ian and me's got some things marked out already, Mother,' said Sandy through the window. 'A table an' chairs an' a sideboard thing — '

'That stuff that came from the sale at Retreat,' Sir Ian explained. 'That tree will have to come down, boy – it's dangerous.'

'They're right,' Marion said, 'about the furniture. That Retreat stuff is all Regency.'

For lunch, after our tour of the house, Sir Ian and Sandy went away to the Great House, while Twice and I went back with Rob and Marion to Olympus, itself a great house of a former estate which was now part of the Paradise lands.

'Marion,' I said, 'I suppose you are used to the lavishness of this place, but it is a bit stunning to me to see a house and masses of Regency furniture being conjured out of the air, as it were.'

'I know.' Marion laughed. 'Thirty years ago, when Rob and I came here, I felt much as you do now. I know exactly what you mean, but one does get used to it.'

'But where did all that furniture in the store-rooms come from in the first place?'

'Part of it is stuff discarded from the Great House from time to time, but most of it is just Madame. She is terribly acquisitive and she never throws anything away.'

'These damned store-rooms are a sort of repository of island history,' Rob said and turned to Twice. 'My time here has seen a kind of revolution in the sugar industry. When I came out to Paradise in 1919, Olympus here still had its own little factory, and so had Pleasant Valley and Orange Grove and a dozen others. Then it got to the Get-bigger-or-get-out stage. Processing equipment became more efficient and more costly, but only those who could afford to install it could carry on. Those who installed it could process more cane, so a spiral got working. Paradise held on. In 1920, Boss Dulac and I decided to buy Olympus when it came into the market and, after that, we just went on buying until we had the whole valley. It was the only thing to do – *some*body had to do it. Boss Dulac was criticized and cursed for it – choking other planters out and so on – but it was a trend that could not be stopped. And it wasn't all fun for the Boss and me either.'

'I can imagine that,' Twice said.

'In the late 1920s, with sugar prices below zero, we were on the verge of bankruptcy, but the rum pulled us through. Madame hates the distillery because of the smell, but she would be a poor old lady without it.'

'And Madame didn't help any in those days,' Marion said. 'When a plantation was bought by Paradise, she *would* go to the sales of the household stuff and buy up the furniture and silver and so on. Mind you, she paid good prices, but she made a lot of enemies among the old owners. I suppose their resentment was natural. Anyway, that's where a lot of the furniture came from. All the staff houses are furnished with period stuff she bought at one time or another. Some of the young wives hate it – they would rather have modern stuff – but they have to put up with it. I like it myself – and everything has a history.' She laughed, nodding at a sideboard to her left. 'Rob and I call that sideboard The Unforgiven. Madame bought it along with a lot of other stuff at the sale at Riverhead, the property at the top of the valley – *that* sale practically led to a vendetta. . . . Do these ancient tales interest you?'

'We could listen for ever,' Twice said. 'Go ahead!'

'The Riverhead sale was long before our time. When was it, Rob? 1910?'

'Early '11.'

'In 1911, that's right. The land round the rise of the Rio d'Oro – the river in the gorge you cross on your way to the Bay, you know – was all owned by the Denholm family, but it was divided into two plantations – one of them a hill property with cattle and pimento, called Mount Melody, and the other a sugar property called Riverhead. Round about 1870, the Mrs Denholm of the time gave birth to twin sons rather late in life – they were her only children – and around the turn of the century she and her husband died, and the will left Mount Melody to one son and

Riverhead to the other, and all the other family stuff was more or less equally divided. It was all perfectly amicable, but the boys were two of the biggest drunks and gamblers that this island has ever seen, and it has seen a few. The Mount Melody one, Toby, was a little more sober than the other and married to a strong-minded woman, which checked him a little, but Oliver, the one who got Riverhead, was a bachelor with no check on him of any kind. In no time at all, he had got through his share of the capital, and in 1911 Riverhead itself came up for sale. The land marched with Paradise at the top of the valley, so Mr Dulac bought the land, but Madame went to the sale of the household effects, of course. You've noticed the Georgian tea-things at the Great House? That was among the stuff, and that sideboard over there and a lot of other things – Denholm family stuff – and Mrs Denholm of Mount Melody was also at the sale.'

'This is where you have to visualize the two women,' Rob broke in. 'Madame Dulac, daughter of an Edinburgh Writer to the Signet of some standing, aged about forty, and Mrs Denholm, about ten years younger, of a leading island family and very wealthy in her own right.'

'Mrs Denholm wished to buy in the family silver, Madame Dulac wished to acquire it, and Oliver, bottle of rum in hand, wanted the money and stood beside the auctioneer and egged the ladies on. In the end, Mrs Denholm gathered up her skirts and swept out to her carriage and the stuff was knocked down to Madame at a fantastic price. After that, no tea was taken between Paradise and Mount Melody, and for years this island was split into two factions – Paradise and Mount Melody.'

'And is it still?' I asked.

'I suppose it would be, but that in 1923 Mr Denholm of Mount Melody died, and Mrs Denholm went off to the States.'

'And the place was sold? Did Madame go to the Mount Melody sale?' Twice asked.

'That's the thing,' said Rob. 'Mount Melody *wasn't* sold and neither were any of the effects, so Madame didn't get a chance.' He laughed. 'I always thought Mrs Denholm meant to come back, but it doesn't look like it. The pasture-land is let, of course, but the Great House has been lying empty for years. It must be in pretty shabby repair by now.'

'Were there any children?' I asked.

'Yes.' It was Marion who answered. 'One son, and as different from his father as chalk from cheese – used to drive out paying

20

formal calls with his Mama. I came out here in 1920, a year after Rob – David Denholm was about twenty then and a source of fury to the island dames. They were all after him for their daughters, and he wouldn't leave Mama's apron-strings. He'll be around fifty now and married long ago, but it all seems like yesterday. I can still feel my hands sweating inside my gloves when Madame and I used to drive up to Mount Melody to call.'

'To *call*?' I said. 'But I thought you said that after the sale — '

'My dear, you don't know the grand dames of this island! It would never do to have a public rift between the members of the plantocracy as they called themselves and have the coloured people knowing all about it. . . . The coloured people knew all about it all the time, of course. . . . It was in the veneer over the rift that the fun came in – the frigid bowings at church or garden parties, the duty conversations at dinners at King's House, the stiff-necked duty dances at the local balls, the duty calls and the returning of them. The Dulac-Denholm feud wasn't the only one – there were about a dozen feuds running at the same time. It made social life extremely complicated.'

'Not half!' said Rob. 'And some of the Committee Meetings at the Club in the Bay would have curled your hair. But the women were worse than the men. . . . I don't know, but the modern women seem to be different. They have rows, of course, but not on the same grand old scale. Thank God for it too, although sometimes I miss the old characters. Madame isn't unique, you know. In fact, she's not a patch on some of them. Remember old Mrs Poynter of the Peak, Marion?'

'*She* wore a bonnet tied with purple ribbons under her chin until she died, just before the last war,' Marion said. 'She must have been about a hundred. She outlived all her children. And she always carried a great big black fan – it looked as if it was made of crow's feathers – and if anyone disagreed with her about anything she would clout them over the face with it. "Fanning people" she called it. Dreadful old woman. That's her grand-daughter who's working at the hotel at the Peak now.'

'Listen, are you people *still* eatin'?' said Sandy, coming in with Sir Ian.

'Good God! Soon be tea-time!' Sir Ian said.

Rob laughed. 'Marion and I were telling Janet and Twice about some of the old people who used to be around – the Denholms and the Poynters and so on.'

'Splendid old crowd!' Sir Ian pulled out a chair and sat down.

21

'Practically drank and gambled themselves to death to the last man, 'cept for Pickerin' o' Castle Cardon. *He* died of blood-poisonin' after his pet alligator bit him.'

'Pet alligator?' I said.

'Certainly. Lot of alligators round Castle Gordon in those days. Pickerin' caught this one when it was young an' reared it – used to share his rum with it at nights. The brute used to get drunk an' quite dangerous – bit several o' the servants an' that – but Pickerin' claimed it contained the spirit of his great-grand-father. Anyway, his great-grandfather bit him in the end, an' he died of it.'

'What happened to the alligator?' I asked, fascinated.

'Oh, Pickerin's brother got a chance the followin' mornin' early an' took a pot at it with his gun – killed it all right – but one o' the shots went wide an' hit the kerosene lamp an' burned half the house down. Old Pickerin's corpse was quite badly scorched here an' there by the time we got him out.'

'Great days, sir,' said Twice.

'Oh, yes. Was only a youngster myself at the time – must be about fifty years ago. The Pickerin's were regicides, of course.'

'Regicides?' I said.

'Certainly! So were the Poynters – oh, I see, Missis Janet. I beg your pardon. Local idiom, ye know,' he explained. 'The island was a Spanish possession, ye know that, of course. We annexed it around 1630. Then there was that fellah with the wart on his nose, Whatsisname — '

'Cromwell, sir,'' Sandy supplied.

'That's the fellah! Never can remember his name although I can see his ugly face as plain as a pikestaff! Never been good at names. What was I talkin' about?'

'The Poynters, Sir Ian,' Sandy prompted.

'Oh, yes! Well, this fellah Cromwell got this idea of beheadin' the King but, of course, he just couldn't go an' do a thing like that all on his own, so he got up a what-d'ye-call-it? A paper thing, ye know, an' you get all sorts o' rascals to sign it, like the suffragettes were always doin' — '

'A petition?' Twice suggested.

'*That's* it! A petition. That's what he did and a lot o' fellahs signed it – about forty o' them, with their seals an' everything. Copy of it down there in the Court House in the Bay – ask that clerk fellah down there to show it to you sometime, very interestin'. What was I sayin'? Oh, yes. One o' Maud's – Maud Poynter,

22

ye know – ancestors signed it, ye see – name wasn't Poynter, forget what it was – but anyway, that's why we call them regicides. The Denholms o' Mount Melody were another lot and so were the Forrests o' Honey Valley. We – the Dulacs – we didn't get our land like that. We just stole the first bit round Paradise in the ordinary way. Bought the rest of course.'

'Oh, I *see*! The Poynter and Denholm lands were awarded to them by Cromwell for their collaboration in the Civil War and the regicide and so on?' Twice said.

'Certainly! Ain't that what I been tellin' you? *Regicides*, the whole bloody – beg your pardon, ladies – lot o' them. Funny thing, blood, ye know. You take these regicide families – the original ancestor, the bloke that signed the thing for old Wart-on-his-nose, was usually a bit of a wart himself. I suppose there were some quite decent fellahs in his army – dammit, *what's* his name?'

'Cromwell, sir, and the Roundheads were his army.'

'*That's* it! I suppose there was the odd decent Roundhead, but the decent ones didn't want to come out to a pest-ridden hole like this was in those days, so the ones that *did* take these land grants from old Roundhead were a pretty poor lot, morally speakin' I mean. Physically, they were all right – must have been, or they'd never have survived the malaria an' yellow fever an' everything. But morally, in every generation o' these families, you get at least one rotter if not more – can't depend on 'em. What d'ye expect? Descended from chaps that killed their king? Don't hold with that sort o' thing myself – bound to lead to trouble. . . . Here, are you people goin' to sit here all day? The boy an' I thought we'd go an' look into this furniture question for Missis Janet. Like to come?'

'Count us out, Sir Ian,' Rob said. 'Twice and I have to look at something in the factory.'

'Stinkin' hole. An' it's Saturday – but please yourselves.

'Well, ladies?'

'Yes, please,' I said and Marion rose too.

'And I'll tell you a thing – you've forgotten after all, Sir Ian!' Sandy said.

'What, boy?'

'Madame's invitation.'

'Bless my soul! Yes. Mother says will you all come to lunch tomorrow, Missis Marion?'

'Yes, thank you,' Marion said. 'And remember to tell her – or shall I write a note?'

'D'ye think I'm half-witted? Anyway, if I forget, the boy will remind me. Come along. Stop hangin' about! Time's passin' and we've got to go to Mount Ararat for dinner, ye know!'

Chapter Two

FROM EARLY childhood, I have always been interested in words in general and in place-names as a particular area of the word-world, as it were. I think this may have begun because our own small, isolated farm in Ross-shire, and its immediate environs, was for eight years the entire world that I knew, and its name 'Reachfar' became symbolic to me of the wide views that extended in every direction from its hill-top situation. As my world widened, and the surrounding farms came into my ken, their names – Poyntdale, Dinchory, Shoremills, Overnewton, Seamuir – represented other worlds as yet undiscovered, but whose character could be imagined from their names, and they had about them an aura of romance. As a child, I wrote poems about these places —

Looking northwards from Reachfar, you see Poyntdale Estate,
A big place with a mansion house and tall wrought-iron gate,
And east from there along the shore, Shoremills is by the sea,
Its water-wheel goes round and makes oatmeal for Tom and me —

— and so on, and, at the age of forty, although no longer a poet, place names still had a fascination for me.

From the time of my first visit to St Jago, when Twice and I had first plunged into the life of the Paradise Plantation, the island place-names had held me in thrall and were, indeed, my main reason for reading at all the island's one very badly-composed, execrably-printed, ill-informed newspaper, *The Island Sun*. It amused me to find in it items such as: 'Friendship Village. In the course of a cutlass fight over a woman here last night, Hezekiah Montgomery was severely wounded and taken to hospital at Wait-for-Me, while Obadiah Jones was arrested by the police and removed to the gaol at Freedom.' To know that this was an actual report of an actual series of occurrences at actual places in the island was one more factor that contributed to the unreal and fantastic quality that the island held for me.

The place-names, after a while, seemed to settle into six categories, but this did not in any way reduce their romantic appeal.

(a) Names of biblical character – Mount Ararat, Canaan, Paradise, Manna plains.
(b) Names of Spanish origin, dating from the Spanish occupation, confined nowadays to main physical features such as St Jago, the name of the island itself; Rio d'Oro, the name of its main river, and Sierre Grande, the name of its spine-like mountain range.
(c) Names of nostalgic quality, such as Edinburgh, London, Wensleydale and Glenshee.
(d) Names of an escape-to-another-world type, such as Retreat, Content, New Hope, Olympus, Parnassus.
(e) Names topographically or agriculturally inspired, such as The Peak, Pimento Hill, Honey Grove, Pasture Plains, Ginger Valley and Cinnamon Springs.
(f) Names purely whimsical, that trying quality, always lurking like Puck to the danger of taste, such as As-We-Like-It, Blue Heaven and Hidey-Hole.

This last category, I would mention, was rapidly being expanded by wealthy Britons and Americans who were building seaside houses around the island for winter use.

With my particular type of mind, it was impossible for me to say: 'I am going to Heaven's Gate for the weekend', or 'I am going to dinner at Utopia', without being overcome by a dream-like sense of living in an unreal world and, in a similar way, it was impossible for me to listen to Sir Ian's tales of regicides and keepers of pet alligators without feeling that I had, like Alice, stepped through the looking-glass. This island, to me, was a place where, literally, anything could happen and in which I, in turn, might, without being aware of it, behave in a way, as one can in dreams, that has no relation to real life.

Paradise itself was the most unreal wonderland of all. During my working life, I had had a little contact with wealth, but I had never been in the midst of wealth as it existed at Paradise. In the married life of Twice and myself, every household possession in our Scottish home at Crookmill represented some earning of our own hands or brains, and we were now being given what in Scotland would be a small period mansion house, to be equipped, apparently, to the last linen pillow-case and silver saltspoon. When, in the Great House cellar store-room, I protested at this, Marion Maclean said: 'We don't usually give plate and linen to the staff but in your case it's a little different. To start with, you're not staff and it's only for a year, unfortunately. And to end with, you appreciate good stuff and can look after it, which the average staff wife can't.'

'But, Marion, by the time you're finished, this house will be worth a fortune!'

'What of it? The stuff might as well be in decent use for a bit instead of rotting in here.'

'I feel I am being spoilt.'

'People who went through the war at home are due a bit of spoiling from us – people like Twice and you are on the conscience of people like Rob and me. . . . Give me a hand with this chest, will you? I'd like to get at that sofa in there.'

'Marion, why is this house we are having called Guinea Corner?'

Marion straightened her back and pushed the hair back from her forehead. 'Lord, *I* don't know. The questions you ask – you're as bad as Sandy!'

'By Jove!' came the voice of Sir Ian from the far end of the big cellar. 'That's old Aunt Maria's mandoline! Hi, Missis Marion, the boy's found old Aunt Maria's mandoline!'

This was followed by a few twanging, off-key notes and then a sadly out-of-tune version of the first phrase of 'God Save the King'.

'You take it, boy. Get it strung in the Bay and play the odd chune on it when you're sick o' your guitar.'

'Gosh! *Thank* you, sir!'

'Another means of noise!' said Marion. 'Oh, well.'

Sir Ian and Sandy came over to us and Sandy sat down on a mahogany commode and began to dust the mandoline with his handkerchief.

'Old Aunt Maria's mandoline!' said Sir Ian. 'Imagine that! Before your time, of course, Missis Marion. Was only a boy myself when she died, but I can remember her though! Awful-lookin' old woman an' mad as a coot. Aunt of the Guvnor, really – my great-aunt, ye know. My Aunt Flossie was here at the time too – the Guvnor's sister, ye know – an' young Stooie

26

Malcolm o' Harmony Vale was courtin' Flossie. The Malcolms were from Argyllshire – fine people, but damnable slow to make up their minds about anythin' an' Flossie was gettin' pretty sick o' Stooie comin' an' sittin' about an' keepin' the other chaps away an' yet not *doin'* anythin' about it. An' the old Guvnor, my grandfather, that is, was gettin' pretty sick o' Stooie too, but Aunt Maria was all for Stooie. "Very well, Maria", the old Guvnor said, "but make him understand he either has to pee or get off the pot" – there was no beatin' about the bush or dilly-dallyin' with the old Guvnor. "I'll bring him to the point with my mandoline," says Aunt Maria an' that night, when Stooie came an' was hangin' about in the drawin'-room with Flossie, Aunt Maria gets in a cupboard with the mandoline an' starts strummin' like billy-ho an' singin' that thing called "Juanita", all full o' stuff about Stooie askin' his soul if they should part an' all that. Aunt Maria had a voice like a perishin' corncrake an' ye know the size o' the drawin'-room an' the thick mahogany doors an' that an' no electric light in those days – anyway, Stooie gets the idea the place is haunted an' runs for his perishin' life. . . . Married one o' the Thomsons o' Thunder Hill in the end. . . . But the thing was that what with the humiliation an' that, Flossie starts cryin' an' runs away to bed an' Aunt Maria spent the night in the perishin' cupboard!'

'Was she all right?' I asked.

'Well, no. Of course, she never *had* been all right, but she was loopier than ever after that. You'd have thought she'd had enough o' cupboards, but there was somethin' contrary about Aunt Maria. She took to doin' nothin' else but playin' her mandoline in cupboards – frightened the wits out o' a woman we had stayin' once when she went up to bed and found Aunt Maria an' her mandoline sleepin' in the perishin' wardrobe. . . . You have the mandoline, boy, but don't play it in cupboards and frighten your mother.'

'By the way, Sir Ian,' Marion said, 'Janet was asking why her house is called Guinea Corner. Do you know by any chance?'

'I can't think why we're sittin' about in this bloomin' cellar,' said Sir Ian. 'We're finished for now, ain't we? Let's go outside. Guinea Corner? Sit down here, Missis Janet. Guinea Corner's a fairly new name – dates from the old Guvnor, my grandfather, ye know. At that time, Guinea Corner wasn't part o' Paradise at all. The Paradise march went through where that big cotton tree is now, the one at the corner o' your garden. Missis Janet, an' your garden an' all these cane-pieces to the south an' east o' you belonged to the Priestlys o' Golden Guineas. We still call the cane-pieces Guinea One an' Guinea Two an' so on. The Golden Guineas house was up on that hill we call Guinea Hill, but it took a bad shake in the 1923 earthquake an' fell down an' it was part o' Paradise then an' we never rebuilt it. Used the dressed stone for these new buildin's at the factory. What was I talkin' about?'

'Guinea Corner, Sir Ian.'

'Oh, yes, an' the Priestlys. Now, the Priestlys as a family had a peculiar thing about them – can't explain these things – but there never was a Priestly that got married that didn't marry the damnedest, worst-tempered shrews o' women that were ever created. An' *live*? These Priestly women'd live for ever an' there was always an old tartar of a grandmother about if not a great-grand-one as well, so back about 1790 the Priestly o' the time got fed up with the rows in the house so he builds that house o' yours, right at the edge o' the property, an' sticks the old grandmother in it with a bunch o' slaves o' her own to stop her interferin'. . . . Got the paper with the names o' the slaves an' everything down in the office there – show it to you sometime, very interestin'. A dozen or so o' them there were, an' the old grandmother was to have the progeny bred out o' them during her lifetime, but at her death they were all to revei to Priestly.'

'So it was a sort of dower house?' I asked.

'That'd be the polite name for it. Wasn't called anythin' in those days though. On the paper it just says: "House slaves o' Amelia Priestly, relict o' William Priestly".'

'So your grandfather named it?'

'Yes. When he won it.'

'*Won* it?'

'Well, ye see, the Priestly o' the old Guvnor's time had the usual old grandmother livin' in the house, an' bein' as awkward as all the rest o' these Priestly women she had to choose to die on Easter Sunday an' the funeral had to be held on Easter Monday. Well, of course, Easter Monday has always been the race-meetin' o' the year here, down at the Bay, an' Priestly an' the old Guvnor an' Denholm an' Pickerin' an' the rest all had horses racin' an' here they were with this perishin' funeral on their hands. . . . No ice much, in those days – they had to get the old dame under ground. . . . So they get it all fixed up for ten o'clock on Easter Monday mornin' – couldn't have it earlier, for people were drivin' to it from all over the island – an' what with one thing an' another, by the time it was over an' they had sung all the hymns the old dame had left instructions about, they were all well up on their rum an' they go harin' off hell-for-leather to the Bay to hold the race-meetin'. The race-horses an' that had gone down the day before, of course. Now, these old boys didn't go much on actual money, ye know, except for things like cards and race-meetin's. It was all gold money an' dangerous to keep about the house an' they never knew how much they had in the bank either an' poor Priestly, with this old dame gettin' sick an' dyin' an' everything, there he was at the races an' not a damn' penny to bet with. Of course, everybody trusted him, but by way o' makin' the thing gentlemanly an' that, Priestly started bettin' so many guineas against his prize bull an' so many more against a certain coconut crop an' that. He an' the old Guvnor were great horse fanciers an' the race o' the day – the Governor's Cup – was recognized as bein' between Paradise Punch an' Guineas Galahad – it's one o' the historic races in the island. So the bets get laid an' the Governor o' the time is collectin' the bets in the Cup, like they did for that race in those days, an' apart from all the other bettin', the Guvnor an' old Priestly placed side bets – the story goes that they used the Governor's cocked hat. Can believe it, too – they were all as tight as fiddlers' b——s by this time, what with the funeral an' everythin'. The old Guvnor tosses a purse into the hat on Punch an' Priestly tosses in a bit o' paper on Galahad an' they go off an' have another drink an' then the race gets run. I wish I'd seen it! The Guvnor – he was only a youngster at the time – spoke about it till the day he died. Punch an' Galahad left the rest from the off an' came neck an' neck hell-for-leather round the course an' Punch just got home by a nose. Everythin' was fine until they looked into the bets in the Governor's hat. My old Guvnor must have been pretty tight, for when H.E. opened the purse he'd put in, it had nothin' in it but the pennies they'd used to weigh down the old grandmother's eyelids an' her rings an' stuff an' an odd sovereign that had been in there before an' Priestly's paper said: "My old grandmother's house – God rest her soul – William Priestly." Got it framed in my office downstairs. . . . What started me on this yarn? Oh, yes, that's why we call the house Guinea Corner – my old Guvnor got it for what was in the purse. He felt pretty badly about it at the time, but everybody thought it was a great joke, especially Priestly an' H.E. The old Guvnor gave Priestly

29

back the rings an' stuff, of course, but Priestly wouldn't take the house back for any money. Said his son would have an excuse for shippin' the old woman – Priestly's own wife, mind you – back to England when she got old an' a damn' good thing too. Great sportsmen they were in those days. . . . Well, what about some tea? Let's all go up to your place, Missis Marion. Mother's havin' a bunch o' these old hens up from the Bay for tea an' bridge an' they'll talk our perishin' heads off. Can talk a bit myself, but nothin' like they can. Come, boy, we're goin' over to Olympus.'

When Twice and I were going to bed that night, I said to him: 'Listen, I ought to put on record that I am not quite myself and should not be reckoned entirely responsible for my actions.'

'What d'you mean?'

'What with Don and Sashie at the Peak, having dinner on Mount Ararat and listening between times to Sir Ian's sagas of old St Jago, I am in a complete dither.' Twice laughed. 'It's all completely through the looking-glass.'

'Are you enjoying yourself, Flash?'

'I'm loving it, but my head does go round a bit at times. Don't be worried if I stagger occasionally and make the odd queer noise. It's like drinking champagne – one has to get used to the bubbles.'

The Great House of Paradise is one of St Jago's more impressive houses, basically Georgian in character as to dimensions of rooms, character of windows and other details, but its front, which is to the north and the cool side, has been modified to suit tropical conditions, with pillars rising from a verandah-terrace at ground level to support a long verandah on the first floor. The house has, as it were, two main entrances, one on the ground floor under the wide stone staircase which leads up to the first-floor verandah, and one on the first floor at the top of the stone staircase itself. The vast dining-room is on the ground floor and, at midday on Sunday, Madame Dulac and Sir Ian were waiting for us in the cool alcove below the stone staircase which, being on the Paradise scale, is as large as many a drawing-room, and green with Madame's collection of tropical ferns, and jewelled with orchids in hanging baskets.

It is impossible, I think, to look at Madame Dulac without automatically thinking of Queen Victoria, and I find it impossible to be in her presence without thinking of my grandmother. This, if you know your history and if you had ever seen my grandmother, is a formidable combination. My grandmother was tall and spare, and a woman of considerable force and determination. Madame Dulac is short and stout and so like the pictures of Queen Victoria that an aura of royalty hangs about her, on top of which her presence exudes as much force and determination as did that of my grandmother.

'Well, welcome back to Paradise!' she said to Twice and me now. 'Ian, attend to the drinks. You can't have gin, any of you – you know I don't approve of it. Rob, how are they getting on with Janet's house? They can't stay with Maud Poynter for ever.'

This was one of Madame's wilful blind spots – one of the modern changes in the life of the island that she chose not to see – that the Peak was no longer the property of the Poynter family but had been turned into a hotel.

'I hope she makes you comfortable. Maud was always a clever girl and quite pretty when she was young – I don't know why she never married. I knew her father very well – a clever man in cattle. The Peak was never a sugar property, of course. I never liked the Peak House – dreary big barren place on that hill with the northers blowing in from the sea all the time.'

'It's very cool, Madame,' Twice said.

'That's true. Of course, I don't like the coast. Yes, Ian, just mix me a rum punch. . . . Now, Rob, we had a letter from Edward yesterday. . . . Edward is Ian's boy, Janet, my grand-son, you know. . . . He says he can't be here with us before Christmas, which is most disappointing, but there it is. . . . Edward is in the office of our London brokers, Twice. . . . He is going over to the Continent, Rob, about something in connection with orders for rum and he told me to say that he would write to you as soon as he had full details. . . . Now, I think that is all the business. . . . Well, Janet, how are you? And all your people in Scotland?'

During lunch, the conversation veered back to Edward. He was Sir Ian's only child, I gathered, whose mother had died many years ago and Madame was obviously very fond of him.

'I hope he'll bring a wife back with him when he comes out this time,' Rob said.

'So do I, Rob,' the old lady agreed. 'But not from the Con-tinent. Oh, yes, Ian, I know the Dulacs were French originally, but France isn't what it was. Not that I ever approved of it, especially of Paris – so dirty. I hope that Edward will go sensibly to Scotland for a wife.'

31

'How old is Edward?' I asked.

'Twenty-five. Quite old enough to be married,' Madame replied.

'I was married at eighteen. We had sense in my day. Ian there — ' she looked scornfully at her son, – 'was over thirty before he married – of course there was the first war and he was abroad so much. Still, people are more irresponsible than they used to be. Fifty years ago, the people had a great deal more sense.'

'From what we were hearing yesterday,' Twice said, 'I think that is open to question, Madame.'

I would interpolate here that if Marion Maclean or I or any woman had dared to question a statement of Madame's, we would have received very short shrift, but a man she happened to like had all sorts of licence.

'And what were you hearing?' she inquired.

'About a gentleman who kept a pet alligator for one thing.'

Madame laughed. 'Oh, Ernie Pickering? But the Pickerings were all a little eccentric. Still, they *did* have children and keep the family going. . . . Bless me, Marion, that reminds me! I had the most extraordinary letter yesterday! Talking of Edward quite put it out of my head. You will never guess who wrote to me! Beattie Denholm!'

Marion's glance flickered towards me and her mouth tightened for a moment before she dared to speak. 'Mrs Denholm, Madame? Good gracious! So she's still alive?'

'That's just what *I* said! I should have thought she'd have been dead long ago.'

'Nonsense, Mother!' said Sir Ian. 'Beattie ain't all that old, ye know!'

'Don't talk rubbish, Ian! Beattie Denholm is seventy if she's a day!'

'Well, *you* are eighty, Mother, an' *you*'re still with us!'

'Ian, that is quite enough! And quite irrelevant!'

Rob, Twice and I were all staring down at our plates, leaving poor Marion to carry the burden of our suppressed amusement, which she did manfully. 'And what did she have to say, Madame?'

'She is coming back to Mount Melody. Utterly crazy, in my opinion – the place must be a ruin – but Beatrice never was completely balanced.'

'But why did she write to *you*, Madame?'

'You may well ask, my dear! To inform me that she has given

orders for the re-fencing of the property and presuming – *presuming*, mark you – that Paradise will bear half the cost on the marches in what she calls the usual way.'

'That's fair enough,' said Sir Ian. 'What's our Riverhead march like, Rob? You been up there lately?'

'Just last fall, sir. But we walled that march just before the war, you know. It was part of that labour relief scheme when we had a lot of walls built. You remember, Madame?'

'*I* remember!' The brilliant old eyes glittered. 'So Beattie must pay *us* for *her* share of the wall? I shall write at once and tell her so!'

'No, Madame,' said Rob. 'The labour was subsidized by the Government – all we found was the stone and I took a lot of that off Mount Melody.'

'Oh,' said Madame regretfully, but she quickly recovered, 'Very well, Rob. After lunch, remind me to give you Beatrice's letter and you will write and tell her about the new wall.'

'Very good, Madame.'

'And, of course, I shall acknowledge the letter personally as well. I do not understand why she wrote to *me*. She knows that *you* manage all the estate affairs. Perhaps her mind is failing.'

'It will be very nice to see her again,' plunged Marion.

'Oh, yes. We must call. Janet, you will come too. Mount Melody is a very interesting old house – the Denholms were regicides, of course.'

When Twice and I returned to the Peak and Number One that evening, the big white plate that is the tropical moon was hanging on the black wall of the sky to the landward side, the sea was like a black blanket scrolled with silver threads and our frail bungalow seemed to be perched on the air above it. I suppose that, to many people, it would all have seemed very beautiful.

'I'll be glad when Guinea Corner is ready, Twice,' I said.

'So will I. A lot of my work is at Paradise and further inland and I loathe that Rio d'Oro road. The emancipation of the negro is all very fine, but they should not have taught him to drive cars and lorries yet. . . . Like a drink before we go to bed?'

'I don't mind if I do. I'm not sleepy, are you?'

'Not a bit.' He fetched two drinks and we sat down on the verandah. 'You don't like this place, Flash? Are you miserable?'

'Darling, no! One can express a preference, surely, without being miserable? No. It's that I am a rooted sort of person, I think. There is something transient and temporary about this place – it's like being in a Nissen hut in the war all over again and going to the mess for breakfast and seeing a kitbag in the hall and hearing that old So-and-So's been posted to another unit.'

Twice laughed. 'Don Coyote and Sashie Pansy would not be flattered at that as a description of their love-nests under a tropic moon! But it's true, except that a service unit had the discipline. I don't imagine the male officers popped in and out of the ladies' rooms as Don does here.'

'No, they didn't. I find it rather disgusting. Is that prudish of me?'

'I don't think so. I don't find it prudish, anyway. He reminds me of a tom cat on the prowl on a fine night.'

'And the trouble is that all the nights in this country are fine. I wish we could have a nice, damp, foggy, cold November one and I bet he wouldn't leave the comfort of his own bed. . . . But it's not just Don and his capers, the he-goat that he is. The whole place and all the people in it have an air of upheaval and impermanence about them.'

'It's the aftermath of war, I think.'

'But the war was over five years ago!'

'But this is a beach in a far corner of the world. All sorts of people and things are going to get washed up on it for all sorts of reasons. Look at Hugo and Miranda Beaumont over there. Arty-crafty – never done a real day's work in their lives. What would they do in England? A little money, but not quite enough, and Miranda can't cook and has never washed a dish. As for Hugo – hanging about that shop of theirs, selling raffia handbags! Besides, I bet they were born plain Hugh and Mary!'

'Oh, Twice, they're not bad. They are very kind.'

'Oh, I know! . . . And then Sashie and Don – at least, they're quite frank. They are sick of the privations of England as Sashie calls the ration books and out to have a good time. I don't blame them, really, and I suppose they *are* supplying a need. This place is going to be popular – no doubt of that. But it's not for people like us. I think you are being very decent and patient about it, Flash. It's easy for me. I am out all day among blokes like Rob Maclean who have something real to do and are trying to do it. . . . I ought to get you a little car and teach you to drive it so that you can get out on your own, but these roads are such death-traps and the native drivers don't bear thinking about.'

'Don't worry about *me*, Twice. I'm all right for another week or two. And anyhow, it isn't only at the Peak here that I feel that I've stepped through the looking-glass. There's a dreamlike air of magic about the whole island and not – not just ordinary magic, either.'

Twice grinned at me. 'What's the difference between ordinary and extraordinary magic? I didn't know there were degrees and qualities of it.'

'Well, there's *black* magic!' I defended myself, and went on: 'And talking of that, do they have voodooism here?'

'No. There's still some of it in Haiti they tell me. A few charlatans here go in for a thing called "obeah", sort of witch-doctor stuff they work as a swindle on the more ignorant people in the bush, but it's an indictable offence. They are doing their best to stamp it out.'

'It will be very difficult, I should think. The country – you think of that road down the gorge of the Rio d'Oro from Paradise – lends itself to the powers of darkness, the jungly bush with all those creepers writhing and whispering on one side of you and that thick muddy river coiling about like a serpent in the bottom of that black gully on the other. If *I* had been born here and brought up to believe in that obeah-black-magic thing, it would take more than the law to get it out of my system.'

'Oh, rot, Flash!'

'It isn't rot at all! The nature of a country has a lot of effect on the beliefs its natives develop, and if Central Africa is anything like the bush here – and I gather it is, only more so – I don't blame the negroes for having witch-doctors and voodooism and scaring themselves into fits over them.'

'Oh, you and your Celtic twilight!' Twice scoffed. 'It's merely the mystery of life sort of erupting in the primitive mind – another form of the old Druids in Britain, that's all.'

'The truth of the matter is that I have a more primitive mind than you, you old Lowlander, you!' Twice and I were born at opposite ends of Scotland and never allow each other to forget the fact. 'You can always pull a hair out of the whiskers of Old Man Reason to cope with anything, but me, when I am faced with the jungle, I forget Old Man Reason and tend to fall under the jungle's influence. . . . But, seriously, Twice, there is a feeling of violence, of ruthlessness about this island. The nature red in tooth and claw thing.'

'There's certainly that about this platinum and diamond, chromium and neon jungle at the Peak here!' said Twice. 'All right, I'm not laughing at you, really, and I know what you mean.

There *is* a feeling of violence and disrespect for human life about tropical countries, but having seen a bit of Africa and a lot of India and various places in between, I'm more used to it than you are.'

'It's not only the violence either,' I persisted. 'When I peer into that jungly bush, I get a feeling of something inimical, a sort of threat of evil, as if destruction were lurking behind those big screens of purple trumpet flowers that look so exotic and so beautiful.'

'So there is – a definite threat of destruction. Those big purple trumpet flowers are of the belladonna family and stinking with poison.'

'Reason again. But what *I* mean is that the feeling I get is that these beautiful flowers are a symbol of the other *bigger* evil that is lurking behind all the sunshine and blue sky and everything. Oh, I can't put into words what I mean, but I just feel that in a place like this, *any*thing could happen!'

'And it can, apparently. Pet alligators, forsooth!'

'The story I liked best was the one about Sir Ian's grandfather winning Guinea Corner on a horse race. It *is* a lovely house, isn't it, Twice?'

'You really like it? You think you'll be happy there, Flash?'

I nodded. 'I'm so sure that I am sort of sorry that it is only ours for a year. Talking of atmospheres, *houses* have atmospheres and Guinea Corner has a nice one and I don't believe all those old Priestly grandmothers that lived in it would be as nasty as Sir Ian made out.'

'Atmosphere works two ways,' Twice said. 'You *like* old grandmothers, no matter how queer and eccentric they are, so you would like the atmosphere they leave behind them. . . . Holy cow, Flash! You are extraordinarily persuasive with your nebulous twilight stuff about feelings and atmospheres! You'll have me convinced of this Highland Second Sight stuff yet! You've got me talking about Guinea Corner as if it were something more than stone, mortar and wood constructed to a certain – quite pleasing – design!'

'And a good thing too!' I laughed at him. 'I do believe that stone, mortar and wood can become impregnated with something of the people who live and breathe and think in their shelter. My enormous ego and my pride in that ego won't allow me to believe anything else! . . . And the feeling of ruthlessness and recklessness and violence and disregard for human life that is rife in this island is induced by its history of ruthlessness and recklessness and violence and disregard for human life. So there!'

I stood up and laid my glass aside. 'Come on! Bed!'

Twice also rose. 'As the apostle of reason in this family,' he said, 'I would point out that all your *feelings* about ruthlessness and violence and so on are sired by your knowledge of the history of the island out of your white man's guilt about the sin of the slave-trade. This is just one more tract of the earth's surface and has no magic, white or black, that you couldn't find on Hampstead Heath!'

'You are sticking your neck out,' I said. 'I wouldn't say a thing like that about any place. You'll get a fright one day, maybe.'

And, laughing, we went off to bed.

Chapter Three

FROM MY childhood days, ever since I could hold a pencil, I have written stories and 'poems' and, although I had never had any opinion of any of these efforts and had never imagined that anyone except my uncle George and my friend Tom would want to read them, they had always been a magnificent antidote to boredom. I had always been very secretive about this pastime of mine, because I was afraid that people would laugh at me, but Twice, of course, had discovered what I was doing and, being Twice, he had not laughed. Quite the reverse, as Sashie would put it. Twice had done all he could to encourage me, and my slight gift and bent for story-writing became one more of the many secret bonds between us. We seldom spoke of my writing, for I was still sensitive and easily embarrassed on the subject, an attitude, I think, induced by the fact that in my family, when I was a child, my scribbling had been regarded by most of its members as 'a waste of good time', but, tacitly, I think, both Twice and I had expected great things of this sojourn in a country where I would be free of the ordinary, everyday chores that take up the time of the British housewife. Here, I had no catering, cooking, cleaning or dish-washing to do, but – and this is demonstrative of the extreme cussedness which characterizes human nature as manifested in me, at least – I had no urge to write either. I do not attempt to explain the phenomenon. I merely state the fact. In Number One at the Peak, I had pleasant comfortable surroundings in an atmosphere of carefree peace and all I did was to yawn my days away in an excess of boredom or cavort about with Don and Sashie, waiting for the moment when Twice would come home in the evening and life, for me, would begin to move again.

I was very pleased, therefore, the day after our weekend at Paradise, when, in the middle of the afternoon, while I was writing what I felt to be some very uninspired prose, Sashie came capering up the verandah steps, struck a conspiratorial attitude in the creeper-hung doorway and said: 'Darling Janet, there is the *most* extraordinary old military party outside, in a Rolling-*Royce*, my dear, with a red-headed child with him. Do you *know* what he said to me?'

'No,' I said. 'What?'

'He said: "I say, my good fellah, is Mrs Alexander at home?"'

'I'm sorry, Sashie,' I said. 'What did *you* say?'

'But not at *all*! Don't be sorry – quite the reverse! . . . My dear, I bobbed a curtsy and said I would go and see. *Do* be at home to him, darling! I've never seen a fugitive from Poona before. Don't be a meanie!'

'Don't you be an ass, Sashie,' I said, tying on the skirt that turned my bathing dress into a frock of sorts.

'You are *so* right,' said Sashie, watching me. 'I am sure he doesn't believe that a woman has thighs during the daytime as well – the ladies, God bless 'em! . . . Oh, but you mustn't come *out*! Quite the reverse! *Do* let me buttle him in!' He danced away across the grass and in a short time returned, leading Sir Ian and Sandy.

'The gentleman, Mrs Alexander, Mum,' he announced, sketching another curtsy.

'Sashie, stop your nonsense at once!' I said. 'Good afternoon, Sir Ian. Hello, Sandy. . . . Sir Ian, this is Sashie de Marnay – he likes to play the fool.'

'How d'ye do, my boy?' said Sir Ian heartily, shaking the whole of Sashie through the medium of his hand. 'Charmin' place you are makin' here. I like it. You built these little shacks?' He strode to the door and peered into the bathroom. 'Excellent idea, Very nice indeed.'

'Thank you, sir,' said Sashie demurely.

'You said to come, Missis Janet,' said Sandy, 'so here's us an' we brought our bathin' things an' towels an' everything an' if you'll give us tea, then we'll take *you* out for a special treat!'

'Can we manage to give this boy tea, Sashie?' I asked. 'He eats a tremendous amount.'

'All our resources shall be strained, but *all*. . . . And, tell me, what is the nature of the treat for – er – Missis Janet?'

'We're goin' on board the sugar boat for Sir Ian to get a drink from the Captain at six o'clock and she is to *come*!' said Sandy.

'I *say*!' Sashie bent his faun-like glance on me. 'You be a good girl, darling, and maybe the Captain will give *you* a drink too! Well, I must be off.' He glanced at Sir Ian. 'Tea about four? And should you require anything, sir, no matter how extraordinary, just come to the door and shout – er – Ho, Varlet, or something.'

Sandy watched him skip away across the grass and then said dispassionately: 'My topmost brother, Donald, wouldn't care for him, but oh well, live an' let live. . . . May I change in your bathroom, Missis Janet?'

Silently and shaking with laughter, I pointed to the bathroom and Sandy went inside and closed the door.

'Sir Ian, that is one delightful boy,' I said.

'The little fellow?' The old man sat down. 'Yes, I'm very fond of Sandy. Excellent company – the boy's no fool, ye know. . . . What *is* that fellah – Sashie, ye called him?'

I explained Sashie's position as part-owner of the hotel and as caterer as best I could and ended: ' — There are some things, I find, that one can't explain.'

'Hah! The less said the better. Ye find a lot of it among the Sikhs – often they're gifted in unexpected ways. . . . Ah, there you are, boy. Off you go. Don't think I'll swim after all, would rather chat to Missis Janet. Don't often get such pleasant company,' he ended gallantly.

'All right, sir,' said Sandy agreeably. 'Call me when tea comes, Missis Janet.'

'I won't forget,' I promised.

Sir Ian and I sat on the verandah and watched Sandy make his sturdy way down to the beach, on to the little jetty, and dive into the clear blue water.

'He's safe enough on his own, I suppose, Sir Ian?' I asked.

'Swims like a fish. Been doin' it since he could walk. Got six elder brothers, ye know, all fine boys. Fine people, the Macleans.

39

Older boys are all over at home – school, university an' that. Donald, the eldest one, is a vet. in Edinburgh. Clever, the whole lot of them. . . . You have no children, Missis Janet?'

Some things cannot be explained. I married fairly late in life and became pregnant shortly afterwards, but I had an accident and lost my baby. I also lost the ability to have children in the future. This was a thing in life that I never discussed even with the most intimate members of my family – even Twice and I seldom mentioned it, for it seemed to be something that was better left alone – but I found myself telling this brusque old man all about it. As I came to the end of the little personal story which, to me, was such a sadness, I could not explain to myself why I had told it and I cannot explain the reason now.

'I'm very sorry, my dear,' he said when I had finished. 'Difficult to understand some things that happen. Thank ye for tellin' me. . . . Fine chap, your husband. Bein' a great help to us out at the factory. Tell me, where was he trained?'

I told him the details of Twice's career in engineering and then he said: 'Very interestin' – they don't train 'em like that now. Can't use their hands – not craftsmen any more – all on paper – drawin's an' that – office wallahs. I'm old-fashioned. Believe that the chap that designs the shaft should be able to turn it in the lathe as well if need be. Better that way, 'specially if you're handlin' native labour. Pretty poor lot we have here, these Africans. Not their fault, of course – savages when they were brought here in the slave ships an' never allowed to develop. Not like India. An' now they're startin' to run before they can walk – tearin' about in big cars. Bound to happen, of course. . . . By the way, Mother thinks I'm a fool.'

I was taken by surprise and was about to say: 'I know, Sir Ian', but had enough wits to say instead: 'I don't agree with her, Sir Ian.'

He laughed. 'Probably am in lots of ways, but not about people an' not about negroes. Mother thinks she can hold back the clock – *doin'* it too, on Paradise to some extent – but it can't go on. Got to let the negroes have their head before long. End of an epoch – might as well recognize it. Every old one of Mother's generation that dies off is another nail in the coffin. Say what ye like, these old ones had force, dignity – negroes respected them. The new lot comin' in aren't the same. What black man is goin' to take orders from that pansy in the pink trousers – Sashie, ye called him? Can't blame the negroes – wouldn't listen to him

40

meself. Far cry between that and my Guvnor an' my old grandfather, by Jove!'

'I have noticed that the negroes in the Bay are quite different from those at Paradise, Sir Ian,' I said. 'Is that the difference between the town man and the country man that you find everywhere?'

'Partly. In fact, very largely. This is the big city, the seat o' Government, an' the people here are in closer contact with the native politicians – a lot of them are pure smart-alecs, featherin' their own nests. But there's another thing comin' into these islands that's damn' bad for the negro, and that's this tourist trade. Oh, it's bringin' money in – I grant you that – but it's turnin' them into a bunch o' cunnin', lick-spittlin' thieves an' rogues. They all want to be waiters an' taxi-drivers an' get big tips. They don't want to learn a decent job an' work at it. The negro ain't a worker either by temperament or climate an' the tourist thing'll be the ruination of him. Only my own opinion, of course, but I believe the basis o' a country is the honest work o' its men's hands an' brains. A country don't get anywhere if its men can only slip their hands round the corner for the odd tip from a foreigner. An' the men who do it don't get anywhere either, except sink a little lower than they are already. The negro can't see that, of course, an' ye can't blame him. Thinks if he can sign his name he's an educated man an' if he can get a car to drive he's a gentleman. I'm not like Mother – tryin' to hold the clock back, ye know. I'm all in favour o' the negro takin' over this island and his own clock an' makin' it tick, but he's not old enough in his mind yet to see that a clock ain't goin' to keep good time or be a damn' bit o' use to him or anybody else unless it's sittin' level an' balanced an' all its parts workin' right. The negro thinks that if he can get rid o' the white man an' get the clock for his own, everything'll be fine. God will help him, he'll tell you. And God'll *have* to, by Jove! The negro feels he has been exploited by the white man and so he *was*, dammit, but not any more. When he gets rid o' the white man an' the help o' Britain an' everything, he's goin' to need an awful lot o' God. . . . I seem to be talkin' a great deal!'

'Go on, Sir Ian. I am very interested. When I look at the island I feel that I'm drowning in a sea of ignorance.'

'You spoke o' the difference between the Bay people an' the Paradise people. If we'd been given another hundred years o' the Paradise method o' bringin' the negro on an' up, *I* think we'd have turned out a very good, sound, civilized type o' man. Only my own opinion, of course. But we're not goin' to get that hundred years. Nothin' like it. The wireless can reach Paradise; the politicians can drive out there in their big cars. If they had to come on mule-back they wouldn't bother. They promise the people the Kingdom o' Heaven on a plate. Ye can't blame the people for believin' them an' preferrin' them to the like o' myself an' Mother that won't let them get away with any sloppy, slap-dash bit o' work. The people forget, when the politicians get talkin', that they already *have* all the benefits o' a welfare state on Paradise – our own doctor an' nurse an' schools an' all that. They don't see that all that costs money which has to be made out o' the sugar an' rum that they have to grow an' process. They see no connection between their work an' the doctor bein' there, an' their politicians do their best to *stop* them seein'. The politicians tells them *You* don't live in a big house like Sir Ian an' that's all they see. Can't blame 'em. But you wait till Paradise is national-ized an' run by civil servants an' see if they can make it pay well enough to afford its own doctor. *That's* when the Paradise negro is goin' to need the help o' God, poor devil. I've often thought o' —'

A sudden hard spatter of rain blew in through the trellis and bounced from the tiles of the verandah and Sir Ian leapt from his chair. 'Dammit! Where's that boy?' He sprang to the door. I followed him, wondering what had upset him, but I now saw a canoe some distance from the shore and I was appalled to see in it the red head of Sandy with, between us and him, huge white-crested waves where the blue millpond had been, and the grey, obscuring curtain of rain sweeping across. Sir Ian, tearing off his coat, ran for the beach.

'Sir Ian! Don't!' I yelled. 'Sashie! Don!'

Through the rain, I saw Don in bathing trunks running for the beach. 'Sir Ian, come back!'

'I'll get the old party!' Sashie called.

Three of the negro beach boys now also ran to the boathouse and, in a few moments, through the roar of the rain, I heard the engine of the motor-boat start up and then I ran down to stare into the grey wall of rain beside Sir Ian and Sashie. 'My God!' the old man kept muttering. 'Oh, my God!' and Sashie kept saying: 'All right, sir. All *right*!' but it seemed to be a very long time before, away to our left, I saw the brown arm of Don rise from the heaving water and could then descry Sandy's red head and Don's dark one.

'There they are, Sir Ian!' I shouted.

'God dammit, I'll *skin* that boy!' he said.

On the sand, Don, panting, hung Sandy head-down over one arm and squeezed upwards along his back with the other hand, at which the boy was violently sick but as soon as it was over he stared at Sashie with his huge blue eyes and said: 'I — I lost your canoe, sir.'

'Never mind the bloody canoe!' said Don. 'Any whisky in Number One, Janet?'

'Yes. Come on.'

Like drowned rats, and all shivering, for the sudden rain had been icy cold on the skin, we forced whisky down Sandy's throat and then all sat down with a glass apiece. Before we had swallowed twice, the rain had stopped, the sun was drawing it back to the heavens in steam from the earth and the beach boys were tying up in the calm water by the jetty with the canoe in tow. I stared, unbelievingly and balefully, out of the dripping doorway at the angelic blue sea.

'Of all the damned treacherous climates!' I said and burst into noisy, slobbering tears which ran down my face while my clothes and my long hair, that the sudden wind had torns from its pins, as wet from the rain as if I too had been in the sea, clung to my shivering body and dripped around me on to the floor. I rose to my feet and stumbled across the room, with some idea of taking my slobbering, embarrassing self beyond the sight of the people around me. My mind was in a muddle of the blessed sense of release I had felt in the unexpected telling of Sir Ian about my own lost child, of reaction from the panic fear I had felt on the beach while Sandy was in the water, of the out-of-my-element feeling which life at the Peak had induced in me and of gratitude to Don Candlesham for bringing the boy back to safety.

'Here, here!' Don said now, as I stumbled unsteadily across the floor and he caught at me so that I reeled against his still wet, naked body. 'Steady! Have a drink of — ' he started to say.

I am at a loss to describe what happened. The only likeness of a physical character which I can think of was the time I accidentally put my wet fingers on a damaged electric flex. I jerked away from Don Candlesham as if I had been stung and looked up into his eyes. They were wide open, so that I could see white both above and below the pupils and through my own tears they were magnified in some way so that I saw no other features of his face, only these huge eyes which seemed to be alight with a life of their

43

own. They were blotted out from my sight by Sashie, who stepped between us, took the glass from Don's hand and said: 'Janet, darling, *not* the vapours! So Victorian. Just have an eensy-teensy little swallow to please little Sashie!' I took the glass from him and as I swallowed a mouthful of whisky and water he looked over his shoulder and said: 'I wouldn't wish to behave like a nursemaid – quite the reverse – but *do* go, Don, and get dry and put on some clothes.'

Without speaking, Don went away towards the main building.

'Well, dammit, boy!' bellowed Sir Ian, who was reacting from fear, characteristically, into anger. 'What you got to say for yourself, hey? Scarin' the wits out o' Missis Janet an' all of us?'

'I'm very sorry, sir,' said Sandy contritely.

'Sorry! God dammit — '

'Not *his* fault,' said Sashie calmly. '*Quite* the reverse! *I* let him have the ghastly canoe. Let us just say no more about the entire affair, don't you think? All this drama, so embarrassing and exhausting. . . . Janet, I wouldn't wish to be ungallant – quite the reverse – but you *do* look quite extraordinarily homely, as the Americans call it. Could you go and comb the hair or something?'

'You don't look supremely elegant yourself!' I told him with a flush of anger. 'I wish to God you'd go and order tea and stop talking!'

'Please, darling, let us have no more angry passion. As for tea, certainly – at once.'

'And bring your friend, Don Whatsisname – back here!' Sir Ian commanded. 'I wish to see him!'

Sashie raised both hands to his forehead. 'Sahib,' he said, 'it shall be done!' and he backed down the steps into the sunlight.

'Bloody idiot!' said Sir Ian and strode into the bathroom, presumably to dry himself off.

'You all right?' I asked Sandy.

'Yes, thank you, Missis Janet. . . . Missis Janet, I am most terrible, *awful* sorry! I just didn't *see* that squall comin' up. Are you all right now?'

'Perfectly all right, Sandy, thank you. I'm just going to change. Tea will be here in a minute.'

'Goody. . . . I'll tell you a thing, Missis Janet – that Mr Don can't half swim!'

'I know,' I said. 'He's a very strong sort of person.'

When I came out of the bathroom, tea had been brought and

44

Sashie and Don, both clad in dry shirts and slacks, were back too. I was grateful, in an absurd way, for my own dress and high-heeled shoes and for the covering of all the sea-wet, naked skin. I was also grateful that Sir Ian had apparently completed his speech of thanks to Don and had put it behind him.

'Is Maud about?' he was asking. 'Like to see old Maud while I'm here, don't ye know.'

'Maud?' Don and Sashie looked at one another.

'Maud Poynter! Use to own this place!'

'Oh, Miss *Poynter*!' said Don.

'Come into the g-a-*ar*-den, Maud!' carolled Sashie, which made Sandy start to giggle.

'Shut up, Sashie,' I said and began to pour tea.

'Missis Janet,' Sandy said, 'we ought to have Mr Sashie in our next play we do!'

What play?' said Sashie rather crossly.

It emerged that, the previous Christmas, Sandy and Sir Ian had made something of a local theatrical success in a one-act play which had smitten them both with stage fever.

'Great fun it was!' said Sir Ian enthusiastically. 'Didn't give us enough scope, though – too short an' not enough action. Saw a proper play in Scotland once when I was at school in Edinburgh – *Rob Roy*, it was – clansmen yellin' an' fightin' all over the place – very excitin' – that's the sort o' thing we want. I'd wear that helmet in the dinin'-room, boy. Always wanted to wear that helmet, by jove!'

'Gadsooks and by my halberd!' yelled the irrepressible Sashie. 'And I would be the Court Jester, Janet darling, with a bladder on a stick and *tip* people in un*men*tionable places with it!' with which he flipped Don on the cheek, daintily, with a paper napkin. 'Avaunt, thou scurvy knave!'

I thought that Don was about to strike him, but Sir Ian said: 'By jove, the very thing! We'll have a play an' you *two* will be in it!'

I could not resist glancing at Don's sullenly astonished face and, seeing my ill-suppressed smile, he narrowed his eyes at me and said: 'Yes, and Missis Janet will write it for us. She *writes*, you know!'

It was my turn to feel murderous. I did not know how Don Candlesham had found out about my writing – I was sure that Twice had not told him and I certainly had not – and I was as angry and mortified as if I had been surprised at some secret

45

sin, so angry and mortified that I could feel myself shaking with the effort at concealment as I said: 'Oh, yes. *I*'ll write it! I've never written anything in my life but I could probably manage a touch of ham drama and – and Ho, Varlet!'

'Jolly good title!' said Sir Ian and then bellowed: 'Ho, Varlet!'

'Ya call, sah?' said a negro waiter appearing in the doorway.

'Service,' said Don, staring at me, 'immediate devoted service is our watchword,' and to the waiter: 'All right, Peterkin. Bring some more hot water.'

I was glad when tea was at last over and Sir Ian indicated that Captain Davey would be expecting us aboard his ship.

'If I'm not back, Sashie, when Twice gets here,' I said, 'you will tell him where I am?'

'Of course, darling. We wouldn't have him anxious for the world – quite the reverse.'

'And remember, my boy' – Sir Ian shook Don's hand – 'you'll be welcome at Paradise any time. You too, of course,' he added to Sashie with less enthusiasm.

'Ah, yes, of course,' said Sashie with a wicked smile and sketching a small curtsy. 'Thank you, sir.'

Sir Ian stared hard at him for a moment. 'Hum,' he said and then turned to Sandy. 'All right, come along, boy. Got your towel an' things?'

On the cool deck of Captain Davey's boat, listening to Captain Davey's familiar south Scotland voice, I wondered if I had dreamed all the absurdities of the afternoon from the sudden squall to the ridiculous talk of Ho, Varlet! but above all I was glad that the afternoon – and the dream – were over.

As is common in many of the West Indian islands, the Bay is not a deep-water port. Visiting ships cannot tie up at the piers and passengers and cargo have to be taken aboard by launch or lighter, so that the *Pandora* was lying out in the bay and we were looking across at the town, a fringe round the water's edge, dominated at one end by the Peak with the white buildings of the Peak Hotel on its seaward slope.

'It *is* a beautiful situation, the Peak, seen from here,' I said.

'Beautiful prices too!' said Captain Davey. 'I was up there this afternoon.'

'Dammit, man, *we've* all been there all the afternoon! Missis Janet is livin' there at the moment.'

'Did you want to make a booking at the hotel, Captain?' I asked.

'I had thought of it, but apart from the rates it wouldn't be suitable for a young girl on her own.'

'No, I don't think it could be,' I agreed with him.

'It's my daughter,' the captain explained. 'She got pneumonia the winter before last and it left a spot on her lung. She's been in a sanatorium in Aberdeenshire for eighteen months, but she's cured now.'

'Poor girl! How old is she?'

'Just eighteen, Mrs Alexander. The doctors recommend a warm climate for a bit – I thought if she was here I could see her occasionally. This is a bus run for me – I'm in the Bay here every three weeks or so. But you can't put a young girl on her own in a place like that and the Palace is worse, if anything.'

'Your wife could not come with her?' I asked.

'My wife died at her birth. Dorothy is all I have – it makes her kind of – well – valuable.'

'Good God, man, send her to us at Paradise!' said Sir Ian. 'Plenty of room, good climate – cooler in summer than the Bay here and not so humid, plenty of food. Hotels! Good God, the girl would go mad in a week in that place up there!'

'It's very good of you, sir — ' the captain hesitated.

'Send her to *me* at Paradise, Captain!' I said. 'My husband is out all day, I'm all on my own – I'd *love* to have her! Our house at Paradise will soon be ready and — '

'And Sir Ian an' me will look after her, sir!' said Sandy. 'Sir Ian an' me is very good with sick people. We wheeled Dad everywhere for months in a chair when he broke his leg in the fact'ry!'

The captain smiled. 'Dorothy isn't that sick now. She wouldn't need wheeling, son. . . . But Mrs Alexander, if you think you could — '

'Of course I could!' I told him.

As usual, I did not think of what I was doing until after I had done it, so that, that evening, by the time I had finished telling Twice about the arrangement I was a little shaky and quite breathless: ' — and there it is and she's coming on next Tuesday's 'plane, probably, and staying here till we all go to Paradise and what do you think?'

'My dear idiot, don't pant as if the Hound of the Baskervilles were after you!' Twice laughed at me. 'I think you've bought someting of a pig in a poke – the girl may have a hare-lip or model herself on one of the more tedious film stars or almost anything, but you seem to be committed now.'

'Twice! Captain Davey is such a nice man and he was so worried and wistful and I felt so sorry for him.'

'*Your* father is a nice man too. Fathers are no guide to their daughters. Go and mix us an evening drink and then I'll have a bath and wash the salt off me.' He sat down cross-legged on a rush mat on the floor in his wet bathing trunks and as I passed him I rubbed a hand across his shoulders. He looked up at me, his blue eyes very intent. 'Thank ye kindly,' he said and kissed my forearm lightly. 'I'm *not* cross about your Dorothy, if she's on your conscience. I think, in theory, she's an excellent idea, as long as in practice her personality doesn't drive you nuts.' I came back with the drinks and handed him one. 'Thank you. . . . And what else happened today?'

It was only now that I told him of Sandy, the canoe and the squall. 'I got a thorough scare, Twice. But for Don, anything could have happened. Sandy is a good swimmer, but you've no idea how suddenly that millpond of a sea blew up into a real storm.'

'I know how it can come up. Sashie is an irresponsible little brute – he should never have let him go out alone on the canoe in the first place. The sooner we get out of here the better – this place is doing you no good.'

'Oh, *I*'m all right, darling. But young Sandy isn't going bathing alone if he comes here again.'

There was no question about Sandy and Sir Ian coming to the Peak again – they arrived without fail almost every afternoon of the week and I was delighted to have them, although by Friday evening I had lost most of the skin from my shoulders and back through over-exposure to the sea and sun.

'You are crazy!' Don told me that evening when I was seeing Sandy and Sir Ian off after tea. 'Get back inside Number One and I'll bring you some lotion.'

I waited at the door of the bungalow until he arrived with the bottle in his hand. 'Thank you, Don. I'll go downtown and get some for myself tomorrow.'

'Get inside,' he said, not relinquishing the bottle. 'Go and have a fresh-water shower and then come out here.'

'I can cope, Don,' I said. 'It's not as bad as it looks.'

'Are you going to have that shower or shall I do it forcibly, service-delousing style?'

'Oh, all right.'

While I was drying myself, I heard Twice come in and, thankfully, I wriggled gingerly into a dry bathing-dress and came out on to the verandah.

'I ask you to look at her!' said Don, handing the bottle to Twice and glaring at me as if I had acquired the sunburn specially for his enragement. 'Here – coat her with this from top to bottom.'

'Great Heaven!' said Twice. 'What the hell have you been doing?'

I suddenly felt very ill indeed. My head felt as if it might split, my skin red-hot and as if it might burst in long tears like a fried sausage. I felt very sick and extremely sorry for myself. I began to cry, of course.

'It's Sandy!' I bawled. 'I can't let him go in there alone, can I? And Sir Ian was with Miss P – Poynter!'

'That's right!' said Don. 'Burn the hide off yourself and now have a fit of bloody hysterics!'

'You hold your bloody tongue!' Twice shouted at him. 'Flash Alexander, stop that bawling and lie down over there!'

'Flash is just the name for her! Red-hot all — '

'Don't you dare call me Flash, Don Candlesham!' I yelled.

'Don't you dare — '

'And what *is* going on in here if it is not too incredibly rude?' Sashie demanded from the doorway, and then his eyes came to rest on my scarlet chest and arms. 'Bless my liver and lights, the woman is a cinder before her time!'

Calmly, he took the bottle of lotion from Twice's hand and with gentle, impersonal fingers began to smooth it over my burning skin. 'Lie down and roll over on the tum, dear, and let's see the back. How quite abominable! Have you a thermometer, Twice?' Twice shook his head. 'Don, there is one in my room and send over some ice. . . . Don't worry, Twice, my sweet. She is far from well, but she'll get better.'

'Going to be sick,' I announced. 'Bathroom.'

'Help yourself, darling,' said Sashie. 'Do it right here. Nice tiled floor.'

'Bathroom!' I managed to insist.

'Pick up the body, Twice,' said Sashie and stood aside.

I was very, very sick indeed, but when it was over and Twice had deposited me on my bed, I felt a lot better.

'So help me!' he said. '*We*'d better take the next 'plane back to Scotland!'

Sashie poured some lotion on to my thigh and began to smooth it over the skin. 'Scotland may be a little extreme,' he said. 'I wouldn't wish to offend the customers for anything – quite the reverse – but I'll be so, *so* glad to speed you away from the Peak, darlings. . . . Oh, there you are, Don. . . . We won't bother with the temperature just now. She's been sick. Just some ice in a towel for the head. There we are. . . . We'll send your dinner over, Twice. If you are worried, just send for me and I'll come fleet as a tiny swallow. Don, isn't it time we opened up the bars?'

Vaguely, through the bumps in my head, I was aware of their going away.

I must have slept as if stunned and I do not remember anything more until the next morning, when I awoke to an awareness that I had slept much later than usual and that Twice, who would normally have gone about his business by this time, was sitting on the verandah, in bathing trunks, writing letters.

'Hi!' I called through the open window. 'Have you been fired?'

'No. I've decided I'm a platinum and diamond tourist for a day. . . . How do you feel?'

'Perfectly all right, thank you.'

'Sashie said you would. Are you hungry?'

'Yes. . . . Oh, damn!'

'Still sore?'

'Horrible.'

'My lord, what a mess! Flash, you *are* a silly ass!'

'But, Twice, I didn't *feel* it happening! Sandy and I were fishing and — '

'You never feel *anything* happening! I've warned you and warned you — '

'Twice, I'm sorry.'

'Oh, don't sit there with those big eyes like a kid! You're *forty* years old!'

'All right! And I'm *still* a bloody fool! Go on, say it!'

'Oh, shut up! What shall I order for breakfast?'

'I don't care!'

'Flash, be your age. Do you want eggs or anything, or just fruit?'

'Only toast and fruit and coffee, please. Twice, I am truly and sincerely sorry.'

'It's all right, darling. I'm sorry I was so short in the grain. . . . I was badly worried about you last night. . . . I'll order our breakfast.'

50

As soon as Twice had gone away across the grass to the main building, I was plunged into misery and every moment of that weekend that I was alone, with no other person to engage or distract my attention, the ready black wall of misery closed in about me. I tried to be sensible, I think; I tried to 'be my age' as Twice had admonished me and told myself that I had been on the verge of sunstroke and was suffering from the ensuing depression. I told myself all sorts of things, but I did not believe any of them. I have never been an accomplished liar and have never been able to deceive completely even myself, although it is simpler to deceive oneself than other people. I knew that I was telling myself lies and I also knew that I was afraid to face the truth, which was that I had somehow lost my moorings. The knowledge of this truth lurked at the back of my mind; I had but to strip aside the most tenuous of veils to expose it and face it, but I did not do that. I was too afraid, so I took the obvious, easy way out. I began to avoid spending a moment alone. I was very gay. Oh, yes, ever so gay. Sashie said he had no idea I could be so devastatingly amusing; Hugo and Miranda said that I had at last come out of my shell and Don said that, until now, my dancing potential had gone entirely unsuspected.

'Dancing,' Twice said in a cold, distant voice on the Monday night, 'is one of her minor gifts. As one who knows her, her unsuspected potential is absolutely terrifying. . . . Who wants another drink?'

We all had another drink and, the next morning – I felt dreadful and my cloud of misery was hanging over me like a cliff – we all went out to the airport, Twice and I to meet Captain Davey's daughter; Don and Sashie to meet three guests who were due to arrive on the 'plane from New York which arrived about the same time as the 'plane from England.

Airports always seem to me to be unreal places, to have about them a temporary air, as if the buildings were not solidly founded in the earth. When I look at a great old building – say Canterbury Cathedral – I feel that the spirits of men have conjured it out of the earth to aspire towards the sky, but when I look at an airport, I feel that some careless giant child, striding about the universe from one planet to the other as if playing at stepping only on certain paving-stones, has dropped the airport there having, momentarily, grown tired of his toy. When I look at Canterbury Cathedral, I feel that it will remain there, where it stands, as long as men, as I know them, retain their senses, but when I look at an airport, I feel that I may close my eyes for an instant and re-open them to find it gone. The giant child, in the seemingly reasonless way of children, may have remembered his dropped toy, have come back, folded up the cardboard runways, put them in his pocket and taken them away, sweeping up at the same time the silver-winged aeroplanes, the red petrol wagons and the radar-crowned control tower that he had left on the grass beside them. This giant child that strides about the upper air is not a creature that I understand. I am afraid of him.

All this was in my mind that morning and a great deal more. I had a sour, disgusted after-taste from the 'party' of the night before; I was full of regrets at having committed myself about this girl Dorothy, and I was unhappily aware that Twice was withdrawn to a distance, but watching me with his mind, as if to see all around me and estimate what I might do next. I could not understand this last thing and I felt resentful of it, so I took refuge in a silly, fretful self-pity. *I* was not going to do anything! God knows *I* did not want to do anything except go somewhere and crawl under something! Twice had no right to watch me like this, I snivelled to myself. I could have sat down on the blazing, glaring, white concrete and wept with misery and self-pity while all my forty years stood back and jeered at me for being a fool.

'Hi there!' said Sandy's voice. 'Here's us!'

His young, well-slept, enthusiastic voice clove through my head like an axe to be followed by the bludgeon of Sir Ian's: 'Mornin' all! Thought we could help you with the young lady an' the Customs!' before he strode away to suborn the Customs officers into showing favouritism by taking the baggage of our parties first.

The American 'plane was signalled and came roaring, ear-splitting, down to the far end of the runway and taxied up to the building. We all gravitated towards the Customs cage inside which Sir Ian was talking to the negro officers.

'What's the name o' your people, Don?' he asked through the mesh.

'Denholm, sir,' said Don. 'Mr Denholm, Mrs Denholm, Miss Denholm.'

'Hear that, Charlie? Got those?'

The Customs officer checked his list. 'Yes, Sir Ian, sir. American passengers just comin' through now, sir.'

'Right,' said Sir Ian and came out to join us. 'Denholm! Good

God!' he said. 'That'll be *Beattie* Denholm! Well I'm dashed! Why didn't you *tell* me?'

'I didn't know you knew her, sir,' said Don reasonably. 'But that will be right – the letter making the booking was signed Beatrice Denholm.'

'Well I'm blessed! I'm glad I came down! Fine to see old Beattie again!' and with renewed interested he went back to the barrier at the Customs cage.

'We left Mother at the Peak, Missis Janet,' Sandy said, patting my arm. 'An' I'll tell you a thing – you can get comin' to Guinea Corner today if you like! The 'lectricians worked on Sunday an' finished the lights because Dad wanted them for the fact'ry yesterday an' Sir Ian an' me got the furniture in yesterday, so there!'

'Why, Sandy,' I said as enthusiastically as I could, 'that's absolutely splendid!'

I felt that if I had to pack for Twice and myself and go to a strange place as well as take charge of this girl Dorothy today, I would lie down and die, and in this moment the 'plane from England came roaring in, rolled up to the front of the building and a new rush and bustle began. I wished I were home on the bare cool hill of Reachfar and thousands of miles away from all of it.

'You feeling all right, Flash?' Twice asked.

'Yes, fine, darling. It's hot, though.'

'Won't be long now.'

Sir Ian came towards us with a very erect, tall, slim, old woman in immaculately-tailored white linen, a broad straw hat on silver hair above a thin, proud face with brilliant eyes. 'Beattie,' he said, 'this is Mrs Alexander, a Scottish friend of ours. Mrs Denholm, Missis Janet.'

I felt utterly overpowered. Sheer personal force seemed to radiate from every pore of the tall woman's skin as she extended her white-gloved hand, and in my weak mental and physical state I felt I was being reduced – before my very own eyes, as my grandmother would have said – to a small rusty stain on the concrete floor.

'How d'you do, Mrs Alexander? My grandson, David — ' I shook hands with a dark, weedy-looking young man, ' — and my grand-daughter, Isobel — ' I looked at a tall, red-haired Amazon in tailored grey linen.

'My husband, Twice Alexander,' I said and passed them all

on to Twice, who brought Don and Sashie into play, but it seemed to be no time at all before Twice was before me again with a tiny little creature with frightened eyes beside him, saying: 'Flash, here is Miss Davey.'

This little girl looked so physically delicate, so nervous and so much as if she had just been rescued from an arena of roaring lions, that she had the effect of making me pull myself together and I found myself at the head of a large luncheon table at the hotel, taking, for the first time that day, a little interest in what was going on around me. Twice sat with Mrs Denholm on his right and Dorothy Davey on his left and, separated from him by Sir Ian, Isobel Denholm and Marion Maclean on one hand and David Denholm and Sandy on the other, I was less guiltily-conscious of his watchful eyes and mind. There were, however, other eyes.

'Janet, you don't look well,' Marion said. 'I don't think this place suits you. The sea air is much too strong.'

'Nonsense, Marion. I am merely paying for my own sins. I have a hangover. I was up dancing, smoking and carousing until three this morning.'

'Maybe, but there's more to it than that. You are not as well as when you arrived. . . . And I heard you got a touch of heatstroke the other day.'

I looked up the table at Twice. Had he been talking to Marion? If he had, I would not like that.

'It was nothing much, Marion.'

'Your skin isn't made for that sort of thing.' Marion nodded through the window towards the jetty where a crowd of people were splashing about in the water or lying in the sun. 'You're not a Hottentot.'

My mind swung dizzily back through the years to an evening when a country doctor in Scotland had used precisely the same phrase to me. 'And you weren't born to it, like Sandy there. You know what I think?'

'No. What?'

'After lunch, we'll pack you up and go right out to Paradise.'

I felt an uprush of panic, as if my mind had disintegrated like a broken glass at the thought of so sudden a move.

'But – we have a lot of stuff, Marion!'

'Not all that much.'

'Twice may have plans — '

'I've already spoken to Twice.'

So they *had* been discussing me. As I had promised myself, I did not like it. I felt angry and sulky.

'Oh, well. If you think so — '

'I *do* think so. Besides, that Davey child looks all in. . . . Sandy — ' She spoke across the table to her son. 'Did you and Sir Ian take those boxes of linen and silver down to Guinea Corner yesterday as I asked you?'

'Yes, Mother, and locked them in the pantry like you said.'

'And where are the keys?'

'On Sir Ian's ring in his pocket, Mother,' Sandy replied precisely.

'The Maclean organization is terrific,' I said, rather unpleasantly, but Marion did not seem to notice.

With what seemed to me to be remarkably little effort, she took charge after lunch and with Sandy and two maids to direct, she packed up Twice's and my belongings in Number One without herself moving from an easy chair in the middle of the sitting-room floor. In a desultory way, I took dresses and suits from the clothes cupboards and handed them to the maids, while in the intervals I packed my own dressing-case. Sandy, with concentration and neatness, packed Twice's brushes and shaving tackle and then passed on to the desk, packing the drawing instruments and then the papers in orderly fashion. Sir Ian and Twice had disappeared on business into the hot commercial depths of the town.

Throughout all this, Dorothy Davey lay on one of the beds in an exhausted sleep and if I stopped what I was doing to look at her, I would feel an uprush of tenderness which was almost a physical pain. She had no particular beauty or even prettiness, but she had an infinite pathos. She was so very small that every bone and feature seemed to be in miniature; the skin was pale and had a young vulnerability, but most heart-rending of all was the exhaustion – she seemed to be steeped and soaked, body and soul, in sheer weariness.

'Is that child still asleep?' Marion asked about four in the afternoon when I came out with my dressing-case and shut the door of the bedroom behind me.

'Yes. Sound,' I said.

'Poor little thing!'

'Let's have some tea,' I suggested. 'We're all set and we have to wait for Sir Ian and Twice anyway.'

'Mother, can I bathe?' Sandy asked.

'Yes, off you go.'

'The energy of that child!' I said enviously. 'I'll go and order tea.'

As I crossed the lawn, I found Don under the shade of a poinciana tree, leaning against the grey bole, staring down at the bathers on the beach. He was in the bathing trunks which he wore all day except in the dining-room or when he went out of the hotel premises.

'Beach guard!' I said. 'Our redhead is just going swimming.' He smiled a little. 'I'll be about.'

'Don, I'm sorry about this sudden departure. I – we – we're being railroaded a little. Financially, it – it will be all right.'

He waved a hand. 'Think nothing of it, Janet. It's been fun having you here.'

'And we'll see you at Paradise sometimes?'

'But definitely. There's the play, you know. The play's the thing.'

'Oh, yes, the play,' I said foolishly.

Sir Ian, Sashie and Sandy, during the past week, had talked of little else because, I think, it was the only subject that Sir Ian and Sashie could discuss on equal terms and without embarrassment, for, fundamentally, they each regarded the other not as a real person, but as a character out of some strange fiction.

I was aware now that I ought to go away about my errand of ordering tea, but Don stood there, shoulders against the tree trunk, arms folded across his chest, looking at me, strangely implacable.

'I'll have to get busy and write it,' I said.

'The play? Oh, yes, you'll have to write it. To quote Sandy: You *promised*, you know.'

'I *didn't*, actually.'

'He has the impression you did. That's what matters, the impression. What, after all, is life but an impression?' He grinned at me, mouth and eyes elongated and narrow, giving him an archaic, pagan look.

'Talking of impressions,' I said in a businesslike way, 'you got three unusually interesting-looking guests this morning.'

'The Denholms? You think so?'

At that moment, the tall, red-haired girl, Isobel Denholm, in a jade-green bathing dress jumped off the verandah of the main building and came towards us across the grass. There was a free-striding magnificence about her, a commanding stateliness,

56

but nothing of the woman. Nothing female. Nor was she masculine. It was rather that she seemed to be sexless. At the airport, in the grey linen dress, she had looked like a tall, slender, smartly-dressed woman, but in the exposure of the bathing dress the womanliness disappeared. There was little chest development and the legs and arms were long and straight, well-developed, but without a curve. Looking at her, I was conscious of little that was physical, but I was piercingly conscious of a mind, and I had the impression that it was a mind that worked in a dimension unknown to me, as did the mind of Sashie.

'You been waiting long?' she asked Don and tossed at me a: 'Hello, Mrs Alexander.'

'Hello,' I said. 'Mind the sun. I got a scorching last week and with your colouring — '

'I won't,' she said. 'In spite of the hair.' She ran a hand through her short-cropped red hair. 'I'm a pigmentation half-breed. . . . This man can really waterski?'

'I have to admit that he can – expertly.'

'Fine.'

'Where's Sashie?' Don asked.

'I come, I come!' Sashie skipped across the grass. 'Are you ready? Should one cause the engine to roar and tow forth the old murder-board?' He bobbed a curtsy to me.

'Goodbye, Mrs Alexander. Nothing is so unkind as woman's ingratitude.'

'Sashie, I have just been explaining to Don that I am being shanghaied.' I laughed. 'I had no intention of leaving you so soon.'

Don and Isobel Denholm had begun to walk away down the slope together. They looked very handsome and athletic and cool and in their own element of sunshine and water and I felt hot, overclad and outrée in my cotton dress and shoes and I also felt cross. I felt lonely, too – shamefully so – the shame being because there were so many people leagued together to befriend me and look after me and take me away from this nasty horrid place that gave me near-heatstroke. For two pins I would have sat down under the poinciana tree and have cried with pity for myself. At the water's edge, Isobel Denholm turned her high, arrogant head towards us and called to Sashie: 'Say, are you comin' or not?'

Sashie smiled towards her, waved an assenting hand, said 'Bitch!' in his gentle, musical voice and the zephyr breeze carried the word harmlessly away. I suddenly felt quite happy again and he smiled at me: 'It's been great knowin' ya, as our tourist guests say,' he said. 'May one call on your At Home day?'

'I shall be delighted, Sashie. Any day except every fourth Wednesday.'

'Go with God, my sweet, while I remain in the service of the flesh and the devil.' He moved away down the slope out of the shade of the tree into the glaring sunlight. There he began to skip. 'I come! I come! See how I come!' I turned away, went into the main building and ordered tea for six, for Twice and Sir Ian must soon come back now.

Chapter Four

UNDER THE soft-voiced but efficient generalship of Marion Maclean, our move into Guinea Corner was accomplished with remarkable ease; and after an evening meal at Olympus, Twice, Dorothy and I were able to drive over and go to bed as if we had lived there all our lives. The house was even stocked with basic groceries, and a cook, a housemaid and a yardboy were at the gate to welcome us as we drove in. I immediately took Dorothy to her bedroom.

'Dorothy, are you sure that you are all right?'

'Yes, thank you, Mrs – Missis Janet.' She smiled her shy smile. 'But I'm sleepy again. You – you see — ' She fingered the catch on her suitcase and then the words rushed out. ' — it was the aeroplane! I'm terrified of heights. Dad doesn't know. And that window in the hotel dining-room! I thought I'd fall into the sea from it! I – I've been frightened ever since I left London and it seems to be such a terribly long time!' Tears sprang into her eyes and she began to cry weakly and helplessly.

'My poor child!' I began to undo the buttons on her dress. 'Come, we'll get you to bed. You'll be safe here and in the morning everything will be better. Come now.'

Sobbing, she allowed me to undress her and put on her nightgown.

'Come. In you go. Never mind about any teethbrushing or anything. There's a girl.' I lifted her feet on to the bed. 'Through the bathroom there, on the other side, is my room and if you wake up you just come straight through, will you?'

'You are so kind! I won't wake up. I'm not frightened of *any*-thing – not the dark or anything – it's just that awful height — '

'Try to forget all about it — '

I sat down on the edge of the bed and talked to her, but after a few moments I suddenly realized that she was asleep. I laid her clothes over a chair, put her absurdly small shoes under it, propped open the door to the bathroom with another chair and went out on to the landing. Twice was standing there.

'I am glad that Dorothy Davey has come to stay with us,' he said.

I looked at him. 'I would not wish to be sentimental,' he went on, ' — quite the reverse – but I prefer Dorothy and Guinea Corner for you to react against to Don and Sashie and the Peak. . . . Shall we go down and have a bedtime drink to hansel us hame as they say in a chap's own country?'

'Oh, Twice, I'm *happy* to be here!' I said and threw myself against him in an intense, gripping way which, I was aware at the time, was unusual in me. After a surprised little start, he held me firmly, then patted my shoulder in a comforting way and led me downstairs.

'Isn't Dorothy pathetic?' I asked then, out of a need to say something but having difficulty in finding anything to say.

'At the moment, yes,' he agreed. 'But' – he took from the sideboard a bottle of whisky provided by the efficient Marion and broke the metal screw top open with a grinding noise – 'hear ye the words of Old Moore Alexander. In a day or two, when she comes out of her trance of exhaustion, you will find that she will be a very bonnie wee lassie.' He than gave minute attention to the pouring of two drinks, stood back and stared through narrowed eyes at the glasses and said: 'And, of course, when you have played your personality on her in your blundering way for a week or two, you will wake up one morning, all surprised, to find that she is your devoted slave.'

There was a queer, vague note of warning in his voice and a questioning quizzicality in his look and I shied away quickly from both voice and look by saying: 'Oh, nonsense! But talking of lassies, what of the Denholm girl? She and Don walked down to the beach together this afternoon to go water-ski-ing. I must say, they were a magnificent sight. I *do* enjoy good-looking people. I can just stare at them as Tom stares over a gate at the Poyntdale Aberdeen Angus herd!'

'The Denholm girl is striking-looking, all right, but I wouldn't put her in the lassie class.'

'You didn't take to her?'

'It isn't exactly that,' he said. 'It's that I couldn't find anything to take to or not take to. It was like talking to someone who had a helmet on with the visor down, if you follow me. She is all closed up inside herself. . . . I'll tell you a thing that struck me as odd. She and the brother are twins.'

'No! . . . Twice, they couldn't *look* more different!'

'That's what I mean. She is a big strapping wench — '

'And with that red hair — '

'And *he*'s like a little black weed. . . . But anyway, the old dame said twins and she should know. I gather she has brought them up, more or less. I suppose the parents are divorced or something.'

'I must say the old dame, as you call her, is quite something. I don't think I've seen a more handsome old woman. How did you get on with her at lunch?'

'Oh, well enough. I couldn't take much of her, though. She is very high and wide in her ideas, as well as handsome. She looked round the table at one point, let her eagle eye rest on Sir Ian for a moment and then told me the island isn't what it was – it was full nowadays of upstarts and tradespeople. I got the impression that Sir Ian represented the upstarts and I the tradespeople.'

'The old cow!'

'Darling, it couldn't be less important. That's what's so sad. The old order is changing and it is going to change in spite of her. She would be far wiser if she would swim with the tide – but with her brakes on, as it were – as old Madame does. . . . What did you think of the grandson, David, isn't it? You had him beside you.'

'I could hardly get a word out of him. He's a morose sort of type and Sir Ian was bellowing and – to be truthful, I wasn't taking in a great deal today anyway, Twice. Life, with a capital L, got the upper hand of me, rather, down there at the Peak. I can't put my finger on it. It just wasn't my element. I couldn't get a grip on things, somehow – it kept getting the better of me. *This* is different.' I looked round the cool, well-proportioned room. 'I feel I can take a hold on this – I suppose you will accuse me again of wanting to bring life to heel?'

He had once used this phrase of me and I had never forgotten it.

'Yes. But accuse is the wrong verb. To have life at heel – for want of a better phrase – is your true way of living. You aren't the spindrift type.'

'Spindrift,' I repeated. I love words. 'That's what Don and Sashie are – spindrift.'

'Don, yes. Sashie, I'm not so sure. . . . Flash, I'm sorry for Don Candlesham.'

'Don? Why?'

'I don't think things have ever gone well for him.'

'I don't see that,' I said. 'He has looks, health – he obviously has money. You don't buy a half-share in the Peak for chicken-feed and he has ability. What's gone wrong for him?'

'I don't know – there's something in himself – he's self-defeating, somehow.'

'All that's wrong with him is the way he whores around. It really is a bit much, even if your mind is as broad as a barn-door. I wonder how the Denholm girl is on sex – actually?'

'Quote: Where you get Americans,' said Twice, 'you get sex. . . . Unquote. They are probably in bed by now, together, the both of the two of them, as Tom would say. . . . And we should go to bed too – we are getting bitchy. . . . Darling, I'm glad you like Guinea Corner.'

'I do like it, Twice, and thank you for bringing me here.'

When I awoke about five-thirty, with the first light the next morning, I crept quietly out of bed, put on shorts, a shirt and sandals and went off to explore my new home, for it had been too dark to see anything the night before and there had always been too many other people present on my former visits. The house sat, like all the older island houses and the more sensible modern ones, on a slight eminence so that the grass, dotted with groups of flowering shrubs, sloped away on all sides to the surrounding loose-stone wall. At this hour, the grass was wet with dew and the shrubs and trees were wearing gossamer chains hung with dew-drops which were taking on the reds, yellows and blues of the flowers and the greens of the leaves and being struck to sparkles by the quick-climbing sun. Yesterday evening, I thought, between five o'clock and six, we had made the journey from one world to another, and this world was the one that I preferred.

I had been round the garden, into the kitchen to see the cook light the wood-burning stove and had told her of our weakness for early tea and was back at the front gate, looking out over the green sea of sugar cane in the valley bottom, when Sandy, accompanied by a young man, came riding up the road. He leaned down from his piebald pony and handed me a large basket of fruit.

'Morning, Missis Janet. Mother says that's to help out with breakfast. Do you know Mr Bertie?'

The young man dismounted and came towards me and as I noticed his empty left sleeve I remembered Sir Ian saying: ' — tutor, nice young fellah. Name is Yates. War casualty, ye know.'

'You are Mr Yates, aren't you? How d'you do? Won't you come in? There ought to be a cup of tea about by now.'

I opened the gate and they led the horses to a tree by the verandah and tied them to the rail.

'Hi, listen,' said Sandy, 'where's Mr Twice an' everybody?'

'Now, then,' said Mr Yates, 'it's only about six o'clock, you know!'

'Go up and tell him to come down, Sandy. He's in the room right above here. But don't wake Dorothy.'

Yates watched Sandy go into the house. 'Awful kid,' he commented with dispassionate affection. 'More energy than a dynamo and expects everybody else to be the same.'

'When do lessons start?' I asked.

'School opens at eight. As for him' – he jerked his head at the doorway – 'some days with me for only an hour or two, other days all day. In theory, I don't agree with it. I believe in discipline and regular hours and so on, but I suppose there's always the exception. He's brighter than most. Then there's Sir Ian – he goes about with *him* and that's an education in itself. The rest, though, have their noses to the grindstone from eight till twelve, Monday to Friday.'

'The rest?' I asked.

'European staff children from the Compound – got eleven of them besides Sandy.'

'Why, you have a proper *school*, Mr Yates! I didn't realize that. I thought it was only Sandy.'

'It was, to start with – I was engaged primarily for him. But the other kids were around and no school about and it seemed like a good idea. . . . Queer place, Paradise, Missis Janet. . . . Mind if I call you that? I'm afraid it's almost inevitable. . . . Things just grow and come to be here. I never intended to be a schoolmaster. I just came out here for a year or two because the Macleans wanted somebody for Sandy and I was at a bit of a loose end after the war. Now I am a schoolmaster and I like it.'

'Hi,' said Sandy, coming back with Twice, 'is that Dorothy a psychological case, sleepin' like that?'

'Psychological case yourself!' I said. 'What do you mean?'

'There must be *some*thing wrong with her,' he averred. 'I say, can I have a biscuit, please?'

'Help yourself.'

'Thanks. Now me, I don't have any psychology and what I think is that people that's got psychology has always got something wrong with them. Now, Ivor Cranston, *he*'s got psychology an' — '

'You shut up and eat your biscuit,' said his tutor in a friendly way. 'Good morning, Mr Alexander. We don't usually call at this hour but that's your bad luck.'

Previously, as I have mentioned, Twice and I had spent a month at Paradise, but it had been spent at the Great House and directly under the eye and hand of Madame, and I now came to understand that that was very different from life at Guinea Corner as, as it were, free-lance members of the Paradise staff. The Great House, in relation to the European staff and in a greater degree in relation to the native workers, had something of the nature of the throne of the god of the Paradise universe. Then, Olympus, the home of the estate manager, was in the nature of a secondary throne. Guinea Corner, containing Twice and me, was destined to fall into place somewhere between the Great House and Olympus, for Twice worked all the time with Rob Maclean and shared his office at the factory, and at the homes of Madame and Marion Maclean I was on the footing of a guest of the estate rather than on that of a member of the staff.

'The Compound' consisted of some eight bungalows occupied by the European staff of engineers, chemists and agronomists, and 'School Bungalow', the domain of young Mr Yates. In outward appearance, the Compound looked like the happy green valley in Paradise which geographically it was, but in inward fact it was a microcosm of this ugly, earthly world and rent this way and that by a thousand jealousies and discontents. Of all this, Madame chose to be completely unaware and, as Marion Maclean said, the attitude of Madame was the only sensible one.

'It's the women, of course,' said Marion. 'The men get on not so badly, except for the odd professional difference of opinion. Sometimes I long for the early days when there was no Compound at all – only us at Olympus. I used to get to feeling a bit isolated and like a crow in a mist, but it was better than having to listen to the Cranston hinting obliquely at the iniquities of the Milner.'

'I understand that someone called Ivor Cranston suffers badly from something called psychology,' I said.

Marion smiled. 'Sandy been talking to you? You want to keep Sandy firmly in his place, by the way. . . . Ivor is his natural enemy. I try very hard to take up a non-partisan attitude about Sandy, but have to agree with him about Ivor. Mrs Cranston and her four children are all sufferers from psychology. You see, Mrs Cranston *had* them – the children I mean – for what she calls a psychological reason – to aid in the re-population of the earth after the war by what she calls "the right sort". She'll tell you all about it herself, I am sure, when she calls on you.'

'Oh, Gawd!'

'I know. It's very trying. But don't be discouraged. You and Twice and this little Dorothy are being the greatest help to Rob and me, especially as the rains will soon be starting and the Compound is always at its worst in the wet season – difficult to get out, you know. Think of yourselves as martyrs. You are a wonderful diversion, and by the time they have all taken sides about you, quarrelled and made it up again, we should be getting along nicely towards Christmas. Christmas is always hell,' she added, and I stared at her. 'It's all the peace and goodwill, you know. It simply isn't *in* them. And Mrs Murphy – she's Irish and extraordinarily bloody-minded even for an Irish Protestant, which is what she is – *will* give Bobbie Gray, whom she likes, a nicer present than she gives to Ivor Cranston whom she doesn't like and then Mrs Cranston won't speak to Mrs Gray and then Mrs Gray will come to me – or *you* this year, I hope – and weep and say she doesn't want to be the cause of trouble and should she send Bobbie's present back to Mrs Murphy. Nobody knows a *thing* about Christmas if they haven't spent it on Paradise. . . . I am talking far too much, but what a relief it is. It reminds me of my mother undoing her stays. . . . Then there's the play. The play is a nightmare. The quarrels begin with the actual choice of the thing and go on right through to the degrees of applause at the end. They are still quarrelling about the last one right now, although this is the end of June. I put Sir Ian and Sandy into it last year, thinking they might help to keep the peace, but that was a mistake. Sir Ian made Mrs Cranston play the Cockney barmaid because, he said, she could do it to a T. She hasn't yet made up her mind whether this was a compliment to her acting or an aspersion on her appearance and accent.'

'Well, you needn't think you're going to keep Sir Ian and Sandy out of the play this year,' I said, 'because you're not. And I am supposed to write it.'

'Oh, my dear, *will* you? What a relief! You can put in bits for *all* of them and then they can't quarrel!' She took thought for a moment. 'They *will*, of course,' she added.

'Don Candlesham and Sashie de Marnay have to have parts too,' I told her. 'Sir Ian's orders. Sashie insists on being a jester, in cap and bells.'

'My dear Janet, what are you going to do?'

'Don't say that like that, as if it were entirely my responsibility!' I said. 'You've got to help, Marion. I am terrified of a lot of quarrelling women. . . . I think the best thing to do is have some sort of mediaeval nonsense, with bags of court and crowd scenes and everybody dressed in old curtains and it can all end up with Sir Ian's big fight.'

'Fight?'

'Sir Ian says the last play didn't have enough action in it and there's some helmet that he wants to wear.'

'Oh, lord! Well, all right. It can't be worse than last year. . . . But, talking of quarrelling women, what I really came to tell you this morning was that we are for Mount Melody tomorrow. I think myself that it's a mistake, but Madame *will* do it. Mrs Denholm will be furious because I'm sure the house is still being painted if not actually re-roofed, but Madame insists on driving up there. Sheer wickedness, of course. She wants to put Mrs Denholm at a disadvantage among all the dust-sheets and things.'

'Really, Marion!'

'I know. It will be horrible. But be ready at three tomorrow – hatted, gloved and poker-faced.'

I have never been a good traveller in a car or a motor-coach over long distances and, in St Jago, the heat and the corkscrew nature of the roads made my failing more marked. Also, the smooth, oily sway of the tonneau of Madame's Rolls Royce did not ease matters and when we turned out of the Paradise south gates, went along the road a little way and the chauffeur turned sharply to the right and pointed the nose of the car upwards at an angle of about forty-five degrees on what looked like a cart-track through dense jungle, I felt my stomach turn over and a flood of saliva induced by nausea submerge my back teeth. I set my jaw, fixed my eyes on the distance beyond the window and prayed that I might not be publicly humiliated by having to ask to get out to be sick.

On the right side of us, to make matters worse, there *was* no distance to stare into, for the writhing jungle sprang fully armed from the very verge of the track and, on the left of us, what distance there was was in a strictly downward direction, to the rocky bed of the Rio d'Oro at the bottom of its gorge, whose cliffs were hung with trailing vines which made them look like the heads of a thousand Medusas.

'Beattie must have this road attended to!' said Madame, as we followed the gorge round another sickening hairpin bend.

'She will find it difficult. The parochial board people are not interested in the roads to these mountain places.'

'We ought to have brought the smaller car, Madame,' said Marion uneasily as the chauffeur came to a bend too acute and reversed to take a second cut at it until I was certain that our rear wheels were separated from the waters of the Rio d'Oro by only a hundred and fifty feet of air.

'Are you all right, Janet?' Marion asked when we were safely round.

'Perfectly, thank you,' I lied. 'Steep, though, isn't it?'

'It was very hard on the horses in the old days,' said Madame. I am reasonably fond of animals, but I found it difficult, out of the nauseated blankness of my mind, to generate any sympathy for horses long since dead. After what seemed to me like an eternity, we turned away from the edge of the gorge into what looked like a foetid black tunnel but was really a gentle upward slope through a thick wood of heavy trees under which the jungle rioted and whispered and writhed.

'Well, we're up at last,' said Madame and gave herself a satisfied little shake.

I thought of Twice's oft-repeated truism that whatever goes up has to come down again, gulped and wondered if the beads of sweat were actually standing out like blobs of grease on my upper lip. My car-sickness and the cold perspiration which it induced quite apart, the steamy heat under the heavy trees was intense, pressing down on the brain, it seemed, until the eyes saw everything through a nightmarish, distorting lens.

'I think I hate this bit of road more than the hill,' Marion said. 'It gives me the creeps. It's like crawling through the intestines of an animal.'

66

'My dear Marion, don't be absurd!' said the practical Madame. 'Although it *is* extremely hot and uncomfortable.'

Even with the down-to-earth Madame's fat little hip bouncing against my side, I was rapidly coming to the conclusion that for some unknown reason I had become one of the condemned of the earth and that, abandoned for ever by the living and the light, I was to travel deeper and deeper into this turgid darkness until, eventually, some reptilian tentacle of evil would reach out from the undergrowth and suck me away into the heaving darkness of these haunted woods. Just as the tentacle was reaching for my throat, there was a sudden brightness and Madame said: 'Well, really, Beattie has the drive cleaned up already!' in an indignant voice and I opened my eyes to find that we were sweeping across a broad parkland, dotted here and there with enormous trees, and before I could phrase my inward thanks for this deliverance the car was slowing up at the impressive pillared north front of Mount Melody.

If Marion's estimate of Madame's motive behind our visit was correct, and I believe it was, Madame was disappointed. A white-coated houseboy came forward, opened the door of the car, led us into the house and ushered us into a nobly proportioned and nobly furnished drawing-room, where Mrs Denholm greeted us with a cool, unflurried grace and there was not a dust-sheet in sight.

'How very kind of you to call so soon, Lottie,' she said, taking Madame's hand. 'And Mrs Alexander – we met at the Peak Hotel, Lottie — '

'And Mrs Maclean, Beattie – you remember her surely?'

'Oh, yes. . . . How d'you do, Mrs Maclean? . . . I'm not in my dotage yet, Lottie. Do come and sit down.'

She led us to the far end of the large room, to chairs and a sofa in a huge windowed bay which looked out over a steeply terraced wild garden that dropped down to the rocky gorge of the Rio d'Oro. I now realized how apt was the name Mount Melody, for the cool room was full of the music of tumbling water, and reflected light from the rocky pools below flowed across the ceiling like a spatter of silver coins.

Marion and I were not required to contribute a great deal to the conversation, for the two 'Madams' at once plunged into gossiping memories of an island that neither of us knew, so I listened with one ear and looked about me, as it were, with the remainder of my senses.

The house, I thought, was of an earlier and finer period than the Great House of Paradise and to judge by the furniture and its arrangement, its curtains and ornaments, Mrs Denholm was a lady of more detailed and discriminating taste than Madame. As tea was brought in, I was aware of Madame saying: 'And your young people are not about today?' but at Mrs Denholm's reply I felt all my senses concentrate because of something in her voice.

'Isobel is down at the Bay,' she said. 'The young man at the hotel is teaching her to water-ski. Isobel is very athletic. As for David, I'm not sure where he is.'

The voice, the words and their content were, on the surface, completely normal, but I was conscious of some strain behind them, a guardedness, as if a subject had been opened which Mrs Denholm preferred not to discuss. To get away from it, I plunged as I often do, recklessly, for I loathe above all things any feeling of mental discomfort.

'What beautiful silver, Mrs Denholm! Queen Anne, isn't it?' Too late, I felt the jerk in Marion's mind at my words.

Mrs Denholm picked up the teapot and held it poised for a moment before beginning to pour from it.

'Yes. A very elegant period, I think. The tea-caddy is later, but a rather fussy design. Are you interested in silver, Mrs Alexander? My husband's family made one of the finest collections in the island. When I am properly settled and all unpacked, you must come and see it – what I still have, that is.'

The last six words were what Twice would call 'loaded'.

'I think Georgian silver is more in keeping with our houses here,' said Madame, and these twelve words were even more heavily loaded.

'Many people have that idea,' said Mrs Denholm smoothly, and turned a little in her chair as if addressing me alone. 'The interesting thing about the Denholm collection,' she said, 'although some of it is earlier than Georgian, is that each piece was commissioned from the silversmiths directly by the family. We know the history of each item. It has not been bought up piecemeal round the island as so many collections have been. . . . I believe these sandwiches are cucumber, Mrs Maclean. The others are ham, I think.'

'And when can you come over to Paradise, Beattie?' Madame enquired.

As if she had spoken aloud, I heard the mind of Marion warn

me: 'Wait for it!' We did not dare look at one another.

'Oh, some day soon, Lottie.'

'You will find many changes. Many things are gone, from Olympus to Riverhead, but Paradise is still there.'

'Yes. I had heard that Paradise was now leading the island sugar — ' There was the merest hint of a hesitation before that word of such devastating Victorian import ' — trade'.

With my hands clenched in my lap, my eyes fixed on the wall beyond Marion Maclean's head, I gave thanks with all my heart as the door of the room opened and Isobel Denholm came in.

'Oh – hello,' she said, and her voice indicated that she did not expect to see us and that she was not particularly pleased now that she *had* laid eyes on us.

I am old-fashioned. I was brought up in a tradition of behaviour for young people and their attitude to their elders which, I realize, is now out of date, but this does not mean that I approve of the new order. I have never been an ardent follower of fashion. As the girl reached out and helped herself to two sandwiches, which she wadded together double-decker fashion before going to the window, turning her back to us and starting to eat as she stared down at the river, I was aware that I was not the only person in the room with out-of-date ideas, but I found discomfort in the fact that Mrs Denholm was the most disapproving of all of us. Why then, I asked myself, doesn't she *do* something about it? She was not the sort of person to be 'put upon', as she had amply demonstrated in her exchange with Madame, and even as this thought was crossing my mind, I happened to glance in the direction of my hostess. I saw her dart a glance of cold, arrogant dislike at her grand-daughter's unconcerned back. I had a sudden impression that this strong-charactered woman was, in some strange way, the enemy of her own grandchild. The room was suddenly dimmed and there was a chill in the air.

'Damn!' said Isobel. 'Rain. I left the car windows open.' With her curious aggressive stride, she left the room and did not return.

When we were leaving a short time later, when the shower had passed, she was standing at the bottom of the dark mahogany staircase in the dim light of the panelled hall. Her short red hair was catching the light from the doorway and her white skin had a pearly look, so that she had an over-dramatized, unreal appearance, as if the hall were a stage setting and she were being picked out by a special spotlight. She fixed her eyes on me in her queer, sudden way and said: 'You are the one they call Janet, aren't you?'

'Yes,' I said. 'I am Janet Alexander.'

She continued to stare at me for a second, then turned away and, as if the spotlight had been switched off, she disappeared up into the dark cavern of the staircase.

I do not even remember the journey homewards through the jungle tunnel and down the precipitous gorge, for my mind was too full of Isobel Denholm and her grandmother.

When Madame and Marion dropped me at Guinea Corner and I went into the house, Twice was on the verandah with a jug of iced lime-juice beside him.

'Well,' he said, 'how was Mount Melody?'

'Oh, very nice.'

'I must say, I enjoy seeing you really dressed in proper clothes for once – I hadn't realized you were such an elegant glove-wearer at home where you wore them all the time.'

'You never miss the water till the well runs dry, if that is what I mean,' I said. 'Where is Dorothy?'

'Round at the Club playing tennis with Yates and some of them. And she's going back for dinner to the Murphies – she said to tell you. She's settling in very nicely, it seems. She is hardly ever in the house. . . . Aren't you going to take your hat off? You look extraordinarily witless. Did the Madams fight over the teacups?'

I took the wide-brimmed hat off and laid it with my gloves on a chair. 'Almost,' I said.

Twice laid aside his paper and rose to his feet. 'Sit down,' he said. 'I'm going to get us a tot of something stronger than lime juice. Did the sway of the Rolls on that corkscrew of a road upset you? You look uncommonly squeamish.'

I can never squeeze past Twice with anything. As he came back with the whisky, I said: 'Thank you. I feel kind of squeamed, but it wasn't only the Rolls. . . . Twice, that girl, Isobel Denholm – she's queer.'

'Oh? In what way?'

'She – she *hates* me, Twice!'

He stared at me wide-eyed for a moment, then began to smile and then to laugh. 'That is very, very queer of her indeed, isn't it?'

I realized how absurd I must have sounded and began to laugh myself, but when we had both recovered, I continued: 'No,

70

but *isn't* it a little queer just to up and hate somebody out of the blue like that, for no reason at all?'

'I suppose she *has* a reason,' said Twice reasonably, 'only you don't know what it is.'

'But how *can* she have? I've only seen her about twice in my life and I've hardly spoken to her.'

'Maybe you remind her of a nurse who smacked her when she was three. She looks a vindictive sort of type. . . . But are you sure? I don't see how she could do a big hate act over tea – especially with Madame there.'

'It wasn't anything she said or did – it was just something she *was*.'

'Was?'

'Hating.'

'Oh.' Twice swallowed a mouthful of his drink. 'Oh, well, we won't invite her *here* to tea. That's one blessing. We don't have to have her hating round Guinea Corner.'

'That's true,' I agreed with him. And at the time I believed it. That is the sort of reasonable thing that, on the face of things, one does believe, but the trouble is that life has more to it than a face.

Chapter Five

THE YEAR spun on its course. The rains, as predicted by Marion, duly came at mid-July and persisted through August into September. Shoes and all leather articles grew a fine crop of grey mould which caused Twice to wonder if it had commercial possibilities as low-grade penicillin; furniture and all polished surfaces became dull and sticky to the touch; people also became very sticky, both to touch and in temper, and I suspected all of us of growing blue fungus in our odd corners of body and brain as well. Sashie and Don closed down the Peak to all but Hugo and Miranda and a skeleton staff and took to scrounging meals around Paradise which, they said, although wet, was slightly cooler than the coast and had an inestimable benefit in that the sea sand was not blown into the soup.

As an outlet for energy, everyone tended to gather at Guinea

Corner with the excuse of 'seeing how the Play was getting on', but really to indulge in a nice, nerve-releasing quarrel of some sort. The Play, now entitled *Varlets in Paradise*, was a large, untidy bundle of paper which lived, in the main, in a heap on a table in the drawing-room.

'Got to get it finished, ye know.' Sir Ian said in an energetic, businesslike way. 'Now's the time to do it, while the rains are on an' people can't come in around criticisin' an' that. Then, in October, present the perishers with a what-d'ye-call-it an' say: "That's your part – take it or leave it!" The Cranston woman'll kick like a steer an' start alterin' everythin', but we won't allow that. Don't hold with alterin'. Tell you what, though, I've been lookin' at that helmet an' it's the kind old Whatsisname with the wart on his nose wore. Think we'll change the play from the Middle Ages to *his* time. We could have a splendid fight then – Cavaliers an' Roundheads – what d'ye think?'

'We couldn't have Sashie as the jester then,' I said, being determined not to alter the script again. It had already been set in the time of Christopher Columbus, in the 1939 war because Sir Ian had a wish to hang Mussolini from a lamp-post, and for a week during June in the time of William the Conqueror. My view of the play was that the 'Middle Ages', that vague ragbag of a period, was the only period sufficiently elastic for it, for the people of that time were as varied in their whimsies as were Sir Ian and Sandy. Given the Middle Ages, I felt Sir Ian and Sandy could have all the poisonings, dagger murders. pourings of boiling oil, drownings in butts of malmsey and bellowings for stoups of sack that their savage hearts desired.

'As a matter of fact ' I went on hastily, to get away from old 'wart-on-his-nose', 'it's coming on like anything. Just let me give you a rough outline of the story.'

'Siddown, boy, an' stop fidgetin' an' hold your tongue!' Sir Ian told Sandy, who was quietly reading a magazine in a corner, and then he sat down himself and composed himself to listen.

'Here we are! Here we are!' said Sashie in the doorway. 'We are come upon this merry morn to join in the jousting! Mark me, sirrah, with my lance *not* in rest – *quite* the reverse!'

He poked Sir Ian in the ribs with his large coloured golf umbrella and there followed him into the room Don, Marion Maclean, Dorothy, Bertie Yates, David and Isobel Denholm and Miss Maud Poynter of the Peak.

'We suspect you, Sir Ian,' Don said, 'of cooking up this play

72

behind our backs with the idea of presenting us with a *fait accompli.*'

'*That*'s the word I was lookin' for, by Jove! . . . Hey, what d'ye mean?'

'I insist,' said Sashie, 'but insist on censoring my part. Why, there's no *knowing* what Janet might expect me to say!'

'I wish there was!' I said.

'Darling, don't be rude. And we've brought you a new actress. Miss Poynter is a professional – were I ungallant, I would say old trouper!'

'And you would be quite right, Sashie,' said Miss Poynter in her beautiful resonant voice which came so unexpectedly from the thin-lipped, brightly-rouged mouth.

During the time we had spent at the Peak, I had seen very little of Miss Poynter, for much of her time had been spent behind the scenes, in the kitchen and the linen cupboards. If I had thought of her at all, I had thought of her as a fantastically ugly old woman whose grotesque make-up made her more ugly than ever. In actual fact, she was no older than fifty, but she had suffered an early deterioration which her devotion to cosmetics hastened rather than arrested. She had the unnatural pallor of the tropically-born 'white' and the fleshiness that tends to over-take the under-exercised 'verandah woman'. Under her henna-coloured hair, which was so thin that its parting was almost a line of baldness, the thick, pallid skin hung in festoons over the bags under her eyes and under her jaw-bones, and on this wobbling foundation lay the layers of rouge, powder and eye-shadow, offset by long dangling ear-rings, a tight 'Venus collar' necklace round the non-Venus-like throat and rows of bracelets on the fat-slobbered arms. Until this moment, I had never looked at Miss Poynter in any detail – being by nature an avoider of the unpleasant – and I found myself embarrassed now by her grotesque mask of a face. She was like some macabre caricature. I turned away from the sight and concentrated on the sound of her voice as she continued: 'I am old and I was a trouper once, when I was young. There is no point in losing sight of basic facts.' In spite of myself, I looked back at the ugly, made-up face. She looked like a painted-up old toad. 'Keep your feet on the ground, I say,' and she dropped into a chair and her fat feet swung clear of the floor by several inches. 'Good afternoon, Sir Ian.'

'Nice to see ye here, Maud. You ought to get about more. Ye're gettin' fat.'

'No fat in my brain though. Got more sense than some. How's your mother?'

'Fit as a fiddle. . . . Come round an' see her later. She's a bit short in the temper – can't get out with the rain, ye know.'

'Well, what *about* this play?' said Isobel Denholm in her aggressive way and what seemed to me a thousand voices made reply.

'Shut up, the lot o' you!' said Sir Ian at last. 'An' let's get on with the readin'. Come on, Missis Janet.'

This was different. I did not, now, want to read the nonsense thing; I did not want to be responsible for it or, indeed, have any part in it or of it, but there they all were and there was I and there was this wretched bundle of paper and the rain beating down against the windows as if driven by all the spite in the world.

'Well,' I began very shakily, 'my idea is to keep the plot very simple so that all the estate workers in the audience can follow it easily, so we have the Lord Dulac – that would be Sir Ian – and his wife and their grown-up son and their daughter, also grown-up. Their daughter is the Lady Clare and she has a noble boy-friend that she is going to marry, but the villain – Red Gurk, I've called him – is also in love with her, and one day, when she is out walking and picking flowers, he kidnaps her and carries her off to his castle. That would be the first act. But a wandering minstrel sees this happen – the minstrel would be Sandy — '

'By Jove, boy, the very thing! Play "Brown-skin Gal" on your guitar an' the cane-cutters'll sing like billy-ho! Go on Missis, Janet!'

'— and he comes and tells the Lord Dulac what has happened – this is Act Two now – and the hero, the noble lover – I've called him Sir Lancelot – calls Red Gurk out in single combat – that will give you your jousting bit, but Red Gurk, the coward, when he sees that Sir Lancelot is going to beat him, turns about and runs.'

'Flees,' said Sashie. 'They invariably flee – not e-a, but double-e, although I've no doubt they had the e-a sort too.'

'Shut up. But before he gets back to his castle, the minstrel boy has got Lady Clare out of her dungeon and brings her home, but the minstrel boy is really the gipsy girl that young Giles Dulac wants to marry. The second act ends with everybody having stoups of — '

'And me tipping simply *every*body with my bladder — '

'— but Red Gurk is not yet finished. He knows that everybody

74

at Castle Dulac will be carousing, so he and his varlets attack the castle and there's a terrific fight, but in the end Sir Lancelot kills Red Gurk and everything is fine.'   ..

'By Jove! Splendid!' said Sir Ian. 'Ye know what? Where'll the moon be at Christmas?'

We all stared at him, even Sashie.

'Because the house verandah looks jolly like battlements by moonlight! Think, boy, we could toss rocks over an' pour boilin' oil down an' everything!'

'Gosh, Sir Ian!'

'No oil,' said Sashie. 'No oil, either lubricant or laxative. Not even not boiling – quite the reverse.'

'Not *real* oil, you fool! Missis Janet, how many people d'we need?'

'Here's the list,' I said weakly and gave him the sheet.

'The Lord Dulac – that's me. Right. The Lady Dulac – can't expect Mother to do it.'

'Miss Poynter, of course,' said Marion firmly.

'By Jove, the very thing! Maud will bellow for stoups o' sack like billy-ho!' Miss Poynter inclined her head in acquiescence with great dignity. 'The Lady Clare — '

'She has to be small because of getting kidnapped and carried about and things,' I said. 'Dorothy.'

'The very thing. Giles, Lord Dulac's son – oh, anybody can do that – he can't have much to say. Sir Lancelot — '

'Don!' said Sashie. 'But definitely! What is known as a natural!'

'Yes, that'd do. . . . Can you ride, me boy?' Sir Ian asked Don.

'Oh, we won't have horses!' I said hastily.

'Rubbish! No point in havin' joustin' without horses! Can you stick on a horse, Don?'

'Yes, sir, if required,' said Don.

'Right. Red Gurk – another rider. Rob'll have to do it, Missis Marion.'

'You know he won't,' said Marion in her calm firm voice.

'Then who? Ha! *You*, Denholm! All the Denholms can ride!'

The sulky, dark young man had not spoken until now and I expected a scornful refusal, but instead he said: 'All right, Sir Ian. I'll do it', and I do not think I was the most surprised person in the room.

'Good. The Lord Dulac's Jester — '

'That's me, with my little bladder!' said Sashie.

'Hum. Waiting-women, varlets etc. By Jove, yes, got to have plenty o' varlets for the fightin' an' plenty o' waitin'-women for the screamin'. Mrs Murphy'll make a splendid waitin'-woman – can scream like a bloody banshee – so can Mrs Cranston. We'll make *those* two *your* waitin'-women, Maud, an' then you can keep them in order. A very difficult couple o' women, very. One's psychological an' the other's Irish an' they just don't get on, ye know. No explainin' these things. . . . Well, by Jove, this is goin' to be a *real* play. Not like that thing we had last year – wasn't a play at all. Could have happened to anybody. No sense in a play that's just like what happens every day!'

As enthusiasm gathered momentum, I was a little appalled at what I had done, and I hoped in a gormless way that some unforeseen power would arise to control the rush of events, but, of course, no such power arose. Quite the reverse. I had hoped, for instance, that Madame would take exception to horses jousting and stamping all over the Great House lawn, but she did not; and when it was suggested that the verandah should be used for battlements and the large entrance porch at the top of the front steps as a 'banqueting hall', she showed tremendous enthusiasm and said: 'And you can have all those pewter tankards from the Vine Grove sale for your stoups of sack! I *knew* they would come in useful some time!'

Sir Ian and Sandy, meanwhile, were recruiting varlets and waiting-women right, left and centre, Sir Ian making a list of the varlets and Sandy of the waiting-women, and they worked on some idea of their own that we must have equal numbers of each.

'But why?' I asked.

'Can't have a proper play unless everybody can kiss somebody at the end, dammit!' explained Sir Ian.

'Except me,' said Sashie. 'I will *not* be kissed by the Murphy! I wish to be left alone with my bladder.'

'You an' your bloody bladder!' said Sir Ian.

All of this took place at Guinea Corner and I used to feel that I was going very, very mad indeed and, one evening when Marion and Rob and Twice and I were, thankfully, having a quiet meal together, I said so.

'The cast now numbers between forty and fifty,' I told them. 'How we are going to dress them all – quite apart from staging them – I don't know.'

'The main thing is,' said Rob, 'are they all white?'

I stared at him. 'I don't know. Sir Ian could tell you. Why?'

'Only Sir Ian and Sandy have been recruiting people?'

'Oh, yes.'

'Then that's all right.'

I felt uncomfortable. 'Rob,' I said, 'I somehow don't take well to this colour-bar thing.'

'We don't discuss it as a rule,' he said. 'In theory, there is no bar. But – as long as Madame is alive, we can't have what she calls "the people" cavorting about on a social level at the Great House. She just won't have it.'

'I see,' I said and added: 'I don't actually. But is it just what my friend Martha would call a Just-Because?'

Rob smiled. 'Precisely. My position is "My employer right or wrong". My own private views don't come into it. She is an old lady, she is my boss and as long as I take her pay I'll respect her orders, spoken or tacit. . . . As for the people in this play, nearly fifty is plenty – too many. I'll have a word with Sir Ian.'

'I'd be more than grateful, Rob. . . . Marion, all these varlets. How will we dress them?'

'In American tourists' shirts,' said Twice.

'You ass!'

'Sugar bags and rope,' said Marion.

'Good Heavens! You are quite right!'

After Marion and Rob had gone and Twice and I were going to bed, I said: 'You know, Twice, this island, this place and the people in it have me in a complete dither. I started globe-trotting too late in life. I should have stayed at home in a country I know, among people that I understand.'

'The trouble is that you don't globe-trot. You keep delving below the surface – a globe-trotter doesn't. She takes a firm hold on her Baedeker and skims along from château to cathedral and sees nothing in between. . . . You are shocked by the colour-bar thing, of course?'

'Aren't *you*? It's so peculiar. Madame is *fond* of the coloured people. She treats them like a mother – she looks after them far better than any British factory employee is looked after. I just don't see how she can be like that one minute and – well – be the other way the next. It just doesn't make sense.'

'A farmer takes care of his animals – often more care than he takes of his own children – but he doesn't have them at table with him.'

'Twice, that's a horrible thing to say!'

'I think it's along true lines, though. Madame regards "the people" as a different form of life. Instead of animals, let's imagine that a race from some planet like Mars descended upon earth and in course of time they and the human race came to a peaceful arrangement to share the available earth's surface. Let's imagine them as people with one eye instead of two; six arms and four legs and so on. Would you feel like having one of them to dinner? He might have an intelligence superior to your own, powers you have never dreamed of, but I think that, socially, you would prefer your own kind. That is Madame's attitude to "the people". I think she likes them and respects them, but socially she feels no kinship with them. And it is all further complicated by guilt-feelings about slavery and oppression – these were the sins of our fathers – but if they had never been committed, if the negro had never been enslaved, I still think that you would prefer to associate with your own kind and I think the negro would prefer *his*. It is the slavery that was the sin. It gave the negro the idea that the white man, having the power to enslave him, must also have some sort of glory. He was too primitive to realize that power and glory seldom go together and he contributed, unwittingly, to the situation by embracing the sin of ambition and trying to share in the white man's power and glory by emulating him. That is where the wrong seems to me to be – in the black man trying to develop along white lines, and it originated in the white man's sin when he took the negro into slavery. Basically, I believe that Madame is right. We should not have close contact with the negro, because we are as different from him as the creatures from Mars might be from us or from him. Where Madame is wrong, in my opinion, is in trying to develop him along white lines of civilization and at the same time excluding him socially. You can't have your cake and eat it too. But Rob is taking the only attitude he *can* take. He knows that Madame is too old a tree to be twisted now, but he also sees the writing on the wall. So, by the way, does Sir Ian. It is the end of an epoch here – the white man will have to take himself off and let the negro dree his weird. From our point of view, it may be a weird weird, but at least it will be the black man's *own*. That is something that every man, black or white, is entitled to – the freedom to design his own fate.'

'Twice, why is it that I always seem to come in just at the end of every epoch? I saw the sun set on a certain way of life in the

78

north of Scotland – probably the last place in Britain where it set – and here I am, in at the death here too.'

'I am no speaker of the French language,' said Twice, 'but a Frenchman once said: "Qui n'a pas l'esprit de son âge, de son âge a tout le malheur." If you had the spirit of your time, you would be so full of this play – like everyone else around here – that you wouldn't have time to think of big colour questions and ends of epochs. . . . Go and brush your teeth and take your foolish head off to bed instead of sitting here making me talk a blue streak.'

When Twice is persuaded into giving his views on anything other than engineering matters, he always refers to himself shame-facedly afterwards as 'having talked a blue streak', but he has the ability to rationalize things for me and to prevent me from becoming submerged. In those days at Paradise there were enough high seas of feeling running to submerge a battleship and even major affairs like the colour problem were concealed and forgotten, as the deep, dark ocean currents can be, under the waves and swells of the surface storm.

From morning till night, our house was full of people, it seemed, so that I could never find a moment to call my own. I am not much of a character, I often think, as I have remarked already in this tale. I seem to be very subject to the influence of other people, so that in a single moment I could be aware of Mrs Cranston working herself up to be really nasty to Mrs Murphy; of Marion Maclean biting her tongue to stop herself flying at both of them; of Sashie obscurely laughing at me – for some unknown reason; of Bertie Yates falling in love with Dorothy Davey; of David Denholm glooming at them as if he grudged them their happiness; and of Isobel Denholm glaring at me from the other side of the room like a caged tigress. You cannot – I do not care who you are – be aware of all this sort of thing and a lot more, all at the same time and still have a soul to call your own, especially if, in the midst of it all, Sir Ian and Sandy come roaring in and shout at you: 'I'll tell you a thing! We ought to have a portcullis!'

'Yes, and a drawbridge, by Jove!'

'Don't be stupid!' I said. 'Go away!'

They went and I turned to Sashie who happened to be nearest to me. 'This whole thing is farcical!' I said.

'But, darling, how true! Only, why persist in treating it as if it were all in deadly earnest?'

'But *do* I, Sashie? Am I being soulfully earnest and Girl Guidish?'

'Yes, my sweet – even to letting them tie knots in you.'

'What d'you mean?'

'Oh, the Davey and Yates and their bread-and-butter little romance. Darling, he *won't* take her into the bush and ravish her and her sea-going parent hold you responsible. And if the Murphy *does* clout the Cranston with her shillelagh – such a phallic-sounding instrument – it cannot really be laid at your door, the clouting, I mean, not the shillelagh. You must *detach* yourself, darling, and let them all weird their own dree, if that is what I mean.'

'It's dree their weird, actually. That's what Twice says about the negroes,' I said stupidly.

'My dear, so *right*, as long as one isn't called upon to *be* here when they've dree'ed it. A very balanced person, Twice – just like one of his own tachometers or whatever you call them, or that engaging little bubble that always insists on being in the middle. So terribly *human* of it, when you remember that it is only some nothing in a skin.'

'I believe that's what *you* think everybody is!' I said. 'Just so much nothing in a skin!'

'Darling, don't go *penetrating* me – so rude!'

'You can't call that Isobel Denholm nothing in a skin! She hates me like stink. I can feel it.'

'Yes, my sweet. Isn't it simply *howwid* of her?'

'Sashie, be serious just for once. *Why* does she?'

'If you knew, what would you do?'

'I don't know. I could tell her to stop it,' I said.

'You could do that now,' he suggested and I suppose that I looked nonplussed. He reverted to his usual manner. 'My dear, I shouldn't bother – quite the reverse. Let's you and I go on being little hatees together – so cosy.'

'She had it in for you too?' I asked.

'My pet, so *un*perceptive of you! But, of course! She'd loathe my guts – if she believed I had any. . . . Don't you think this piece with the libidinous parrots on it for the Cranston's wimple – or *do* I mean the stomacher?'

Apart from the interference in the routine of my household that the play was causing, the whole tempo of Paradise had altered when the rains started and I now discovered that a year of life on a sugar plantation tends to be divided into two periods, known as 'In Crop' and 'Out of Crop'. I speak, of course, of sugar plantations on West Indian islands. I have no doubt that things are quite reverse in Peru, where they also grow sugar, as I have had a conviction from childhood that everything must be in reverse in Peru, because if you spelled it in reverse it would sound very much like Europe. But never mind that now.

The 'In Crop' period at Paradise started as soon as the staff and workers had recovered from the Christmas and New Year celebrations and were able to cut the cane and set the factory in motion, and the 'Out of Crop' period set in when the rains came or when they had cut all the cane that was available, whichever happened first. Either way, they usually came out of crop some-time in June or July and everybody got drunk for a week on raw rum from the distillery and pretended they had never heard of the factory, or cane, or sugar, or molasses, or bagasse, or any of sugar's other horrible smelly by-products, except, of course, the rum. This phase having been got through, Madame got busy estimating the profits on the crop and writing cheques in large amounts for charity; the Compound parents took their children away for a fortnight to the sea or the hills, and then, returning like lions refreshed, the women got down to a new and more intricate series of quarrels and the men descended like the Assyrian horde on the factory, to tear everything apart, clean it, oil it and make renewals where necessary in preparation for the next year's crop which would start in January.

A large part of the reason why Twice and I were in St Jago at all and living at Paradise in particular was that the Paradise Factory was installing a considerable amount of new equipment which had been purchased from Twice's firm, and he had arranged the remainder of his work in the island so that he would be available at Paradise throughout October, November and December.

In my no doubt childish way, I had looked forward to this time when Twice would be at home for every meal instead of at the other end of the island while our house was full of com-parative strangers shouting about varlets and stoups of sack, and October opened auspiciously with a decline in the theatrical visits, behind which I suspected the ladylike but determined hand and tongue of Sashie. The early days of October were marked, however, by another visit which was quite unexpected, for one afternoon a large American car pulled up at Guinea Corner and out of it stepped Mrs Denholm of Mount Melody.

81

Marion Maclean had told me that, long ago, she had returned Madame's call, so that Marion and I had thought that the formalities were over, but it was apparently now my turn, although the lapse in time was greater than I would have expected in a stickler for the formalities. I went out to meet her, brought her in and installed her in a chair in my varlet-papers-ridden drawing-room.

'I am glad to find you at home, Mrs Alexander,' she said, taking off her long white gloves. 'I have wanted for some time to see you' – she looked up from the gloves which she had smoothed on her lap – 'to thank you for all the kindness you have shown to my young people. From what I hear, they are seldom out of your house.'

I was taken aback and conscience-stricken in one fell stroke. It was shameful to be thanked by this gracious, white-haired woman for the grudging house-room and odd cups of tea I had given to her stony-eyed grand-daughter and glowering grandson and I felt embarrassed to death.

'Oh, not at all, Mrs Denholm,' I said. 'It is all this silly play we are organizing and we all have a great deal of fun out of it.'

She went on to talk of the play and of the people taking part in it and then: 'Oh, yes, Mr Candlesham at the hotel. You knew him in England, Mrs Alexander?'

'Not exactly,' I said. 'My brother served with him in the same ship for a time in the Navy, during the war, and a friend of mine, Lady Monica Daviot, has known him since her childhood, more or less. My husband and I did not meet him until we came to St Jago.'

'I see.' She was silent for a moment and appeared to come to a decision. 'You may think me very old-fashioned, Mrs Alexander, but I *do* like to know what type of people my own young people are associating with. Isobel – both of them – spend a great deal of time at the Peak Hotel. I feel much relieved at what you tell me of Mr Candlesham.'

I did not know what to say, so I said nothing. If I were interpreting correctly Sashie's innuendoes – and I thought I was – Don and Isobel were spending half of their time together in the sea and the other half in bed, but I did not feel it incumbent on me to tell Mrs Denholm this. After all, Isobel might not like *me*, particularly, but her sex life was not my affair. Besides, for all I knew, Mrs Denholm might not object in the least to Isobel's behaviour, provided her bed-companion was out of the socially correct drawer. And above all, if you are a person like me, you cannot look a dignified lady of seventy or so in the eye in your own drawing-room and say: 'As a matter of fact, Don and your grand-daughter are fornicating like fun, old dear.' Behind all this too, forbye and besides, as my friend Tom would say, I had a queer feeling that if *I* were the woman *in loco parentis* to Isobel, I would not have to be driving round in a Cadillac asking comparative strangers what she was up to. I felt sorry for and irritated by Mrs Denholm all at the same time and covered it by going to the kitchen and asking my cook to send in some tea.

The tea was brought in by Clorinda, a perky little coal-black chit of the modern school who, Marion Maclean had warned me, if not kept in check, would quickly begin to indulge in that characteristic of the ambitious but uneducated which the British Army, with its gift for naming the un-nameable, calls 'dumb insolence'. So far, I had had no trouble with Clorinda, for she had developed a dog-like attitude to Twice, to whom she referred as 'Da Boss' and at whose feet she placed his polished shoes every morning like an offering upon an altar. 'Da Boss', in return, was practically unconscious of Clorinda's existence and, in a contrary way, she seemed to find this an adorable feature in him. If, on the other hand, I did not compliment her occasionally on her well-laundered apron, she would begin to wait at table in a limp, grey rag and, when questioned on the subject, she would indicate in a hurt way that, yesterday, when she had looked so smart 'ya don' speak no wudd, Ma'am'. I was a little overcome, therefore, when this character entered with the tea-tray and, on seeing my guest, stopped with her load in mid-floor and curtsied. 'Good evening, child,' said Mrs Denholm and turned back to me.

'Good evenin', Ma'am. T'ank you, Ma'am,' said Clorinda, setting down the tray quietly and professionally for once and then, having dropped another curtsy, going quietly out of the room.

Later, when I asked Marion for an explanation of this phenomenon, she merely said: 'Don't ask *me*! The T'ank-you-Ma'am, as we call the curtsy, was out of date when I came here thirty years ago and Clorinda wasn't born then, but these old tartars like Mrs Denholm can still call it out of them as though they woke up some old instinct. I don't know how it's done.'

The Mrs Denholm who partook of tea with me, however, could not be described as an old tartar, for she was as pleasant and gracious as any guest could be, as she led the conversation round and about the island and over to Scotland.

'We have a great respect for the Scots here in the island,' she told me. 'Some of our best people in the óld days came out from Scotland, especially engineers. Many of them were penniless lads wi' lang pedigrees – is that how I say it? – but they had a way of making good.'

'My husband and I are not the pedigreed sort,' I told her, 'but we like the island.'

'I am very glad. And a long pedigree can be a doubtful blessing.' She pulled on her long gloves and rose to her feet. 'Thank you, Mrs Alexander, for a delightful visit. I hope you will come to see me at Mount Melody one day?'

'Thank you, Mrs Denholm.' If there was one place I never wished to visit again, it was Mount Melody. 'But I foolishly have never learned to drive and my husband is busy all day.' She looked at me from under raised eyebrows. 'You don't drive? How very unusual in these days! Are you nervous then?'

'Not exactly, but I am not at all mechanically-minded and I have no confidence in myself to handle mechanical – contraptions.' She did not join me in my smile over the word. 'I notice that you always drive yourself, Mrs Denholm.'

'I am something of a faddist about my car,' she said. 'I dislike anyone else to drive it or interfere with it in any way.'

As I watched the black Cadillac slide away down the driveway, it occurred to me that she was a faddist about more than her car and, wishing that Twice would come home and blow away the queer feeling that had come into the house with her, I went inside to find him standing in the hall.

'Twice! When did you come home?'

'Over an hour ago.' He grinned at me. 'Been hiding upstairs.'

'But why?'

'My car had a puncture and Rob was driving me back from the factory and from the corner down there we see this ten yards of Cadillac sitting at the door, so Rob says to me: That's funny, he says, that's the Mount Melody Cadillac. What's funny about it, I say to him, and he says to me: The Madam of Mount Melody is famous for visiting only the very great. So I snuck in the back way so that youse girls could have a nice heart-to-heart chat. . . . What did she want?'

'I don't know. . . . Have you had tea?'

'Yes, but I could do with some more.'

We went into the drawing-room. 'She seemed to be kind of checking up on the antecedents of Don Candlesham at one point,' I said.

'I would have said it was a little late for that or for asking him his intentions,' said Twice.

'I know. Twice, it was all very odd.'

'That seemed to be Rob's idea too.'

'She asked me to visit her.'

'Maybe she just likes you.'

'Queer, isn't it?'

'Now, look here,' said Twice, 'you have to make up your mind, you know. You said the girl Isobel was queer because she *didn't* like you and now you are saying that her grandmother would be queer if she *did*. What precisely do you want, my pet?'

'It's not a question of wanting anything or liking or not liking or anything. It's just that there's something queer about them there Denholms.'

'You are rapidly taking up the attitude that everybody in this island is queer except thee an' me!'

'And I'm not sure I'm not right at that!' I told him rather snappishly.

Chapter Six

THE RAINS now being over, the weather was much cooler as what was called 'winter' set in and the young people, when not at Guinea Corner discussing the play, were at the Estate Club playing tennis or badminton or billiards or down at the Peak swimming or loafing about on the beach. Little Dorothy and young Yates were as settled with one another as some middle-aged couple of twenty years married standing, and Captain Davey, when he visited us for weekends, seemed to be as pleased with the wag of the world as they were.

Dorothy had also struck up a friendship with Isobel Denholm which, I felt, was odd and unlikely, but I supposed that it was rooted in the fact that they were the only two unmarried girls in this younger set, many of whose members were the younger husbands and wives of the Paradise Compound and the local surrounding plantations. Nevertheless, Dorothy and Isobel were an ill-assorted pair. Dorothy was essentially a 'small-town' girl, with a small-town appearance, manner and social outlook, while Isobel, although very little older in years, was very much the sophisticate and woman of the world. For Dorothy, undoubtedly, Isobel had the appeal of glamour, with her strangely exotic looks, her brilliance at tennis, swimming and all sports and the fact that she was much in the company of the 'film-starrish' Don and the 'smart crowd' at the Peak. I could understand what attracted Dorothy to Isobel, but I could not see what made the sophisticated Isobel bother with Dorothy, for I had the impression that Isobel was not the type to befriend anyone out of kindness of heart. I was, indeed, inclined to wonder if Isobel was possessed at all of that quality we refer to as 'heart'.

'It's all very peculiar,' I said to Twice. 'I should have thought that Dorothy would be shocked to the core by Isobel's goings-on with Don.'

'My dear idiot,' he said, 'Dorothy has no idea of the goings-on as you call them. Dorothy thinks that Isobel and Don are having a nice romance that will finish up with a diamond on Isobel's finger just as her own romance will – only a far bigger, brighter and more glamorous diamond, of course.'

'But Twice, she *can't* not know! Why, half the time you can see Don and Isobel going to bed with their eyes in the middle of the tennis court or the dance floor! Besides, look how people talk! She's not deaf or half-witted.'

'I seem to remember you telling me once how shocked *you* were to discover that your friend Rose had a lover, and you were about twenty-five at the time, not eighteen. That sort of thing simply does not enter the heads of nicely brought-up, working-class girls from Scotland, even in this up-to-the-minute, sophistication-for-all-through-the-films world of 1950.'

'Golly, that's true!' I said. 'I got the shock of my life with Rose and I had seen Mae West on the films and had read Michael Arlen by then!'

'As for how people talk, they don't talk to Dorothy. It is something to do with innocence being its own armour. *You* probably talk more to Dorothy than anybody else and *you've* never said a word to her about what Don and Isobel get up to in private I bet!'

'One couldn't!' I protested.

'Exactly. And Dorothy won't notice it for herself. She has literally never *thought* of such a thing.'

'I suppose it's all right letting her run about with Isobel? If Captain Davey knew everything, I don't think he'd care for it.'

'I don't see that Dorothy can come to any harm. There's always a bunch of them together, not to mention the limpet-like Yates and the ubiquitous Sashie. Dorothy will be all right, especially when Yates gets around to declaring himself, and that looks very imminent now. I've never seen a bloke so pregnant with unexploded good intentions.'

'I think he's pretty dull myself,' I said.

'Now then! Don't you start anything. Dorothy is not designed to set the heather on fire either and they will make a very solid, dependable couple.'

'Like us, you mean?'

'You know, Flash, for a woman of forty, there is something rather indecent about you. You *will* say the provocative thing.'

'I didn't mean to be provocative.'

'That's the trouble. The ones who mean it seldom are. You simply don't seem to be able to help it. How it hasn't got you into trouble before now I don't know.'

'You speak as if I were in trouble now,' I said. 'Nothing so interesting. I wish I were.'

'There you go again. You remind me of the old Frenchwoman of about eighty who was asked at what age women lost their interest in sex.'

'What did she say?'

'That she wasn't old enough to know yet. . . . Apparently you will never be old enough to know what sort of remark or what sort of look gets you into trouble.'

'But I'm not *in* trouble!'

'That's merely because I have lots and lots of understanding,' he said.

He was grinning at me in a screened-eyes sort of way and I felt a little at sea. 'How did all this start?' I asked.

'With you saying that Yates was dull.'

'Well, he is, isn't he? Compared with – well, *you*, for instance?'

'Darling, it is only eleven in the morning, but would you care to take a step up to bed?'

'Don't be ridiculous!' I said.

'Then stop it! It is quite extraordinary how you can have lived so long and never have learned that there are more ways of laying a man at your feet than hitting him over the head with a rolling-pin.'

87

'What in the world do you mean?'

'Oh, forget it! In some ways you are more innocent than Dorothy and a damned sight stupider too!'

There were repeated little conversations like this when Twice seemed to come to the brink of saying something and then drawing back, as if putting off an evil day; as if postponing some pronouncement that would, in the end, have to be made or as if avoiding some truth which, he knew, would inevitably declare itself. Several times, I was on the brink of saying: 'Look here, Twice, what *is* in your mind?' but at the very brink I too would draw back because of a lurking fear of the outcome.

After these conversations, when he had gone back to the factory and I was alone in the house, I would stare out of a window across the glare of the lawn to the riot of growth in the shrubbery and think how different everything had become since we had arrived in this strange country. In my time, I had read, I think, my share of what are called 'travel books', but these books must have been written by people of much stronger character than myself, who were not affected by the countries they travelled in as I felt myself being affected by St Jago. It was only after about six months of life at Paradise that I, in my slow-witted way, began to become dimly aware that there is as much difference between the temperate and the tropical zones as there is, say, between peace and war, and that there is a commensurate difference in the impact of day-to-day life on the mind. A climate, in other words, is not only a physical thing; topography is not merely so much land-space furnished with certain features; vegetation is not merely some stuff that grows out of the ground that one either eats or does not.

I feel that it is a shameful exposure of mental inertia to admit that I reached the age of forty without becoming aware that the life of the mind is inextricably bound up with the physical surroundings, and I would try to mitigate my appearance of stupidity and excuse myself a little by saying that, until I was forty, I had never lived for more than a week or two out of Great Britain. I had been delighted at the prospect of travelling abroad when Twice became consultant for his firm, but here in St Jago I had fallen into something I had never imagined and, what was truly frightening, the mental climate was as foreign to me as were the physical terrain, the weather and the vegetation.

Staring into the tangled shrubbery, I would feel that my small mind was lost in some dark, fearsome jungle where its former weapons of reason, truth, logic and honesty were of no avail. It was like being equipped with a compass in a strange world that had no magnetic pole, or walking through a wood in which the trees, which should have been steady landmarks, marched and counter-marched about me in accordance with some strange law to which I had not the key.

From time to time, I made attempts to tell Twice and one or two other people – Marion Maclean or Sashie – how I felt, but it was too difficult to find the words for something so all-embracing and so deep. And then, with Twice these days, there was this atmosphere of reserve which was, itself, a large part of my lostness and, at the same time, prevented me from trying to put that lostness into words. Sashie, too, had his reserves, in front of which he dropped a screen woven of the stinging nettles of his bitter tongue, while, with Marion, there was always the danger of the descent into the particular and into personalities. Also, Marion had been in the island for so long that, to me she was part of it; part of the strangeness, at home and comfortable, apparently, in this riotous jungle which was to me so terrifying.

And then, in the sky above this foreign world, in the earth beneath it, crawling and slithering like a great hidden serpent among its vegetation and ever-present in the brilliance of its sun and the blackness of its rain – its possessing demon, as it were – was the colour problem, the eternal problem of black and white. In regard to it, all the people I knew lived in a state of compromise. Sir Ian had the humane attitude of the backward race that should be helped; Rob Maclean had his 'my employer right or wrong' standpoint and Twice tried to maintain an attitude of 'I'm temporary in this island – it's not my pigeon', which was hard sense, I suppose. But I have not been endowed with much hard sense, I have little gift for compromise and I found the natives gentle and callous, faithful and disloyal, generous and mean, straightforward and dishonest and such a mass of contradictions that they exasperated me to the point of frenzy. But more haunting to the spirit than my exasperation with them was my conviction that they belonged to this zone of the earth, this climate, this topography, this vegetation in a way that I never could. It was in league with them, allied to them, while I, and all the other whites, were playthings at its mercy.

I had read too – although little practical good it seemed to have done me – of the degeneration which is apt to overtake the white man in a tropical climate, but I think that, to most of us, degeneration is like murder – it is something that happens in sensational books but does not happen to oneself or the people one knows.

And so, I did what most of us do and call it 'living'. I muddled along from day to day, happily enough, except for those times when I stared out at the exotic tangle of vines and flowers in the shrubbery and wondered about it all and, on the whole, I did not have much time alone to stare at the shrubbery or to wonder. Life at Paradise was like the vegetation – crowded with events, a tangle of personalities, and situation arose out of situation as suddenly and garishly as the passion vines grew overnight from branch to branch and put out their flowers that looked like sea creatures suspended happily in the airy breeze, adding one more crazy feature to this topsy-turvy world.

A feature of the winter season on Paradise was the series of weekly dances at the Club to music provided by three or four noisy instruments under the direction of Big Maxie the head sugar-boiler, a good-natured negro of enormous size who could make more extraordinary noises with a saxophone than I have ever heard emerge from that instrument. Madame was not aware of the nature of these dances. Madame, indeed, was not aware that the 'Staff' as she called us Europeans went regularly to the Club at all. The Club, set well away from the Great House in a grove of bamboos, was 'Part of the welfare scheme for the people', Madame would tell you. 'The People' were the coloured workers, from senior office staff down to labourers. We of the Staff were not 'people' according to Madame and I have never found out in what category she thought of us.

Sir Ian and Rob Maclean had a different and, I thought, wiser attitude to the Club, regarding it as neutral, friendly ground on which all could meet socially, and even people like the Cranstons, who regarded dancing as 'non-intellectual and a waste of time', were given to understand that they must occasionally put in an appearance. Twice and I used to enjoy these dances, which had something of the atmosphere of the country barn dances in Scotland which we had both attended in our youth, and Twice who, in spite of a quick outspoken temper, has a flair for becoming popular, knew all the Estate workers by name and, in his wake, I found myself accepted and welcomed on a footing of real friendliness.

One evening, Twice and I were at the dance and it happened that we were the only European couple present that evening and things were going along very nicely until about ten o'clock when Dorothy, Bertie Yates, Isobel and Don arrived. 'Hello,' we said, 'this is fine. Come and have a drink.'

'Bertie said it was a while since he was at the Club Dance,' Dorothy told me in a solemn, good-wifely, dutiful sort of way, 'so we said we would come and Isobel and Don came too.'

'I'm very glad. It's great fun. Sashie didn't come, Don?'

'*Some*body has to look after our so-called business occasionally,' Don said. 'Mrs Alexander, will you tread a measure with me?'

'That's done it,' said Twice. 'I might as well go home and read a book. Unless – Dorothy, will *you* dance with a poor old man?'

We all had a fine time, I thought, and danced until about one in the morning, but as you will have gathered by now, I am so slow-witted that I can only do one thing at a time, and when I am dancing, I am dancing and that is that. And I put in a fair amount of dancing, when I think of it, for at one point Maxie announced that he would 'blow de Scawtch' if Twice and I would dance to it, so that I found myself caught in a lively schottische, and a little later Maxie was inspired to 'blow it de Souf American way' and I found myself giving an exhibition tango with Don.

The next morning at breakfast, Twice said: 'It was a pity about Don and that girl Denholm coming to the Club last night.'

'Why?' I said. 'I thought it was great fun.'

'The people didn't think so. There's no point in coming to a thing like that to behave like that.'

'I noticed she didn't dance much.'

'You didn't happen to notice her refuse to dance with Wallace the foreman mechanic and then take the floor with Yates?' I had not noticed this. 'The bloody little fool should never have asked her. Mind you, I don't think he knew she had turned down Wallace.'

'Oh, lord, I didn't know about that, Twice.'

'Oh, you! When a dance band begins to play and your toes begin to itch your brain turns to water! . . . And then, a week later, you'll open your great big eyes and wonder why you're in trouble!'

'Look here, Twice Alexander, what's got into you? *I* didn't high-hat anybody! I danced with Wallace and Madame's chauffeur and everybody! It's not *my* fault if Isobel Denholm was all deep-south and Mason-Dixon line! I danced all night and had a grand time!'

'You had a grand time all right! You *always* have a grand time!'

'Look here, if we're having a row,' I said, 'let's draw up a sort of charter of what it's about and then take it point by point, don't you think?'

'Oh, shut up!'

'Alexander Alexander, Overseas Consultant for Allied Plant Ltd., behaving like a second-form schoolboy! What the blooming blazes did *I* do at the ruddy dance?'

'Oh, you didn't do anything more than usual! . . . That damned Denholm girl should never have *been* there!'

'*I* didn't bring her!'

'Maybe not, but you could have helped to get her away instead of letting her stare down her nose while you kicked up your heels until one in the morning! Dammit, you're *forty* – not nineteen!'

'All right! So I'm forty! And all right, I didn't *notice* what was going on. And all right, as the senior woman present I *should* have noticed. I am sincerely sorry about all that, Twice. But don't you think that in the position of helpmeet or -mate or what have you, you, *seeing* what was going on, couldn't you have given me some sort of hint?'

'How could I?'

'Perfectly simple. The old hiss in the ear during the waltz or something – the fate of an Empire can be decided in the course of a waltz. The disposal of the Denholm should have been a flea-bite!'

'Oh, leave it!' said Twice. 'Whatever damage there was is done now and I don't imagine she'll come to the Club again. I apologize for blowing my top, too. It's – it's just that this white-negro thing is particularly revolting to me, and to see that red-haired bitch sitting there and – Oh, the hell with it!' He finished his coffee and rose. 'Time I was off, darling. I'm not mad at you really. You couldn't help it.'

He went off to the factory and left me staring at the remains of the toast in the rack and I was still staring at it when Dorothy came into the room.

'Sorry,' she said, 'Clorinda didn't wake me.'

'That's all right. They'll bring fresh coffee. Twice wanted to get out early.'

'It was nice at the Club last night, wasn't it?'

'Yes,' I said. 'Very nice. . . . Will you have breakfast on your own, Dorothy? I'll send Clorinda in. I've got a lot to do this morning.'

Everything was always 'nice' for Dorothy, I thought, as I stamped in high dudgeon up the stairs.

Twice and I have been known to have some very undignified and noisy lettings-off of steam from time to time, but neither of us is capable of remaining ill-tempered for very long at a stretch and in the course of the forenoon, we recovered. Dorothy had gone over to School Bungalow for lunch as she was doing now nearly every day and Twice and I had the midday hour to ourselves.

'Well, here's to peace in the house,' I said, over the pre-lunch beer. 'As you rightly point out, I am forty and it is time I learned not to throw things at people. I apologize for losing my temper this morning.'

'Me too,' said Twice. 'Let us consider the hatchet, the tomahawk and the claymore decently buried – for the moment, anyway,' he added with Scots caution. 'And talking of claymores and other lethal weapons, how are the varlets getting on?'

'Oh, awful,' I told him. 'They are all learning their parts now and Sir Ian and Sandy and Sashie keep putting in bits of their own and putting the rest off. Our short spell of peace, comparatively speaking, in this house is coming to an end. We'll have to start real rehearsals in November and we'll have to have them here. We can't have that crowd jousting and stampeding round the Great House, and our porch and lawn have a similar layout. . . . How did I get *into* all this, can you tell me?'

He laughed. 'I've never known how you get into anything you do.'

'Well, I'm sorry about it, darling. I never meant to turn your home into a set of coulisses or whatever they are.'

'Lord, I don't mind! Rob and I will be longer and longer hours at the factory – there's still a lot to do and this labour is so hamhanded and slow compared with home that my time estimates have all gone to hell. We're putting on an overtime shift in the middle of November, so I'm glad you'll have plenty of people coming in around the house.'

'Talking of people coming around the house,' I said, 'I can't think why these Denholms come. This is quite without reference to anything that happened last night. I can't think why they got themselves mixed up in the Varlets at all. The girl couldn't be less interested in dressing up and being a waiting-woman, and as for the bloke in the part of Red Gurk, it's pitiful. . . . Oh, I know the whole thing is silly anyway, but if people are going to play the fool they ought to do it as if they meant it, like Sashie and Sir Ian and the rest. I wish to Heaven the Denholms weren't in the thing at all.'

'How did they get in in the first place?'

'Oh, Sir Ian, of course. They happened to *be* there and you know what he is. I never thought for a moment the young man would *take* the part but he did. I wish I could see why. I suppose the girl came in because of Don being in it, but the boy I just don't understand. You can say what you like, Twice, but these Denholms are *queer*. There's something peculiar about them. They do everything as if it wasn't really what they were doing but only a secondary consideration in connection with the thing that they are really doing that nobody knows about.'

'Lucid, aren't you, my pet?'

'Oh, go on, laugh!' I said irritably. 'But they are unnatural, that's what they are. Oh, don't give me all that stuff about my sight being warped by this strange place and varlets and pet alligators and things! People are *people*, after all, and there's something queer about these Denholms.'

'Queer in what way, Flash?'

'That's what I don't know! If I knew, I wouldn't mind. . . . That girl, she's not in love with Don Candlesham, for instance. Her – her *mind* isn't engaged in any way with Don – he's secondary to her. This affaire she's having – it's – it's just animal and disgusting.'

'It's good enough for Candlesham,' Twice said.

'That sort of thing isn't good enough for anybody!' I snapped. 'But never mind that now. The boy is the same about the play and about everything he does – he's not doing the thing for *itself*. And it's in the old woman too. She comes to call, I meet her at tea at the Great House – there's always this sense of an undercurrent, something *behind* everything, like eyes peering about as if they expect a dagger to come through the arras or something awful. I tell you, there's something *wrong* with these people!'

'Don't you think, Flash, it is simply that they are so different from anyone you have ever met before? That and all Sir Ian's talk about regicides and so on?'

This was the voice of Reason. Now, as a rule, I imagine Reason as a very old man with rheumy eyes and long, ragged, dirty-grey whiskers who sits about puffing at his pipe in the chimney corner, croaking occasionally a few harsh words out of his bitter experience and spitting occasionally on the fires of youth which give him all the light and warmth he now knows. In general, he is an old man I do not care for and I seldom listen to his bleak croakings. But, in this case, the voice of reason sounded to me as sweet as a siren-song. I wanted to listen to it and I did and I was carried away on its music into the belief that these Denholms were just like everybody else and perfectly normal and that they and I and everybody were just having a nice, happy time over this nonsense of a play.

About mid-November, one afternoon, I had a sewing-party round our dining-room table, cutting holes in sugar-bags for the heads and arms of varlets to go through while Sir Ian and Sandy measured and cut lengths of rope for belts, and Sandy said: 'Here! I'll tell you a thing – if we've got thirty varlets all in the same ol' sugar-bags, how is people goin' to know which is Lord Dulac's lot an' which is Red Gurk's lot when they're all mixed up fightin'?'

'There now!' said Sir Ian, as if a fine point had been scored. 'How're they goin' to know? Tell me that, now!'

'Oh, God!' I said, and gazed round at the unhelpful faces of the Compound ladies.

'*Our* purpose,' the faces seemed to say to me, 'is to *make* a little difficulty now and again, not help *out* with any!'

Marion Maclean came into the room and I fell upon her, told her what Sandy had said and ended: 'And *now* what?'

'Mrs Cranston,' said Marion, 'take my car and go to the Club and bring all that red and blue bunting we had for the peace celebrations.'

'Yes, Mrs Maclean,' said Mrs Cranston with a triumphant look at Mrs Murphy at having been chosen for this special duty.

'We'll give Red Gurk's lot red sort of tabard things and Lord Dulac's lot blue ones. . . . Janet, come upstairs for a moment. I want to talk to you.'

In my bedroom, she sank down on my bed and said: 'Janet, the most appalling thing has happened.'

'Marion – what?'

'It's Madame. D'you know what she's done? She has sent out letters inviting practically the whole island to this entertainment as she calls it.'

'*What* entertainment?'

'The *Varlets*, you idiot!'

'Oh, *Marion*!'

95

'She has invited the *Governor* and Lady Dene-Jorrocks!' said Marion and began to laugh in a manner too hysterical for my comfort.

'Here you! Stop that!' I barked and Marion stopped and stared at me. 'What in God's name got into her?'

'It's to be a p-party for Edward,' Marion stuttered. 'On the t-twenty-third of D-December. The entertainment and a buffet supper. S-seventy-six letters she's sent out. The G-Governor has already accepted for himself and his wife and a p-party of eight. That's how I f-found out what she'd done!'

'But, Marion, what are we going to do? It's an *awful* play! It's – it's *terrible*!'

'I know and she's put Written by My Friend Mrs Alexander and everything.'

'Oh, *Marion*!' I wailed and sank down on the bed beside her. 'You'll have to help!' I said hysterically. 'You'll just *have* to! You people got me into this and — '

'Me help *you*?' squealed Marion. 'Who's going to help *me* with supper for hundreds and all the Compound women running about dressed in old curtains?'

'Get a caterer!' I said.

'*Caterer*? Where d'you think you are? Berkeley Square? This is *St Jago*, an outpost of Empire, you idiot!'

'Oh, God, I wish Twice were here!'

'Me too – Rob I mean.' She looked at her watch. 'Four o'clock.' She wrenched the door open and bellowed down the stairs. 'Sandy get on your bicycle and go to the factory and tell Dad and Mr Twice to come here at once!' She closed the door. 'There!' she said vindictively.

'What can *they* do?' I asked belatedly.

'I don't know,' she said fiercely, 'but at least they can be as miserable as *we* are!'

'Anythin' wrong?' Sir Ian asked, coming into the bedroom. Marion and I fell upon him horse and foot with our story and went on until he silenced us by bellowing: 'It is *not* a terrible play! It's a bloody good play, by Jove, an' I think Mother is quite right! No decent entertainment for people here 'cept these films all about sex an' croonin'. Dene-Jorrocks'll love it! Nice fellah, Dene-Jorrocks, but lucky we didn't have anythin' about old wart-on-his-nose, Missis Janet.'

'Is His Excellency a regicide too?' I asked bitterly, feeling some kinship with suicides, homicides and all the -cides myself at that moment, with a leaning in favour of Dulacide. 'God bless you, no! But he ain't keen on anythin' political – gets too much politics in connection with his work. Good God, no. Not a regicide! Can't have a Governor with ideas like that, dammit!'

'What's up?' said Twice and Rob arriving simultaneously and breathlessly in the doorway.

We told them and Twice sank on to a chair. 'Lord Almighty! Rob and I thought somebody had been killed!'

'Sir Ian an' me said all along we should do it prop'ly with a drawbridge an' a portcullis an' everything!' said Sandy.

'Go away!' said Marion, leering at him in an infanticidal fashion. 'And take Sir Ian with you!'

'Come, boy,' said Sir Ian with dignity. 'Let's get on with the varlets' ropes. No point in *every*body hangin' about doin' nothin'.' With their heads held high they withdrew and Marion watched the door close behind them.

'Varlets' ropes!' she said spitefully. 'I'd like to hang them all as high as Haman!'

'You know, Rob,' Twice said, 'if there's one thing I hate more than another it's a real botch of a job.'

'I agree,' said Rob.

'This is a fine time to talk about your blooming factory!' I said.

'I'm not talking about the factory,' Twice snapped. 'I'm talking about this botch of a play!'

'It *isn't* a botch!' snapped Marion. 'It could be very, very funny if it were properly handled!'

'Then we'd better get handling it,' said Rob. 'What's all this about a drawbridge?'

'Where's the script?' Twice asked.

The play, from that moment, was not only the Thing – it was practically the Only Thing.

Twice and Rob, having read the script and made notes, made a survey of the Great House verandah, porch and lawns and decided that we could have a drawbridge and portcullis on the steps and verandah, part of the lawn for jousting, and still have seating for five hundred people and standing room for the three hundred more which we expected, for the entertainment was primarily and traditionally for the Estate workers.

'If it rains, of course,' Twice said, 'that's that.'

'I've never seen rain round Christmas,' said Rob.

'Marion can't feed eight hundred!' I protested.

'Oh, the workers don't expect supper,' Rob told me. 'The

supper's only for the house-guests – they'll be around two hundred or so. Marion will cope. Complain like all bedamned, of course, but the supper'll be all right.'

I wished I could feel as confident about the play, but as we came into December I began to have some slight hope. Something – it may have been the thought of high society in the form of the Governor and his lady – engendered a new and co-operative spirit in the Cranston and the Murphy, our house hummed with massed sewing-machines, and costumes and draperies began, as Twice put it, to 'come off the belt'. With the help of Madame's old Letty, her personal maid of some fifty years' standing, I concentrated on the finicky things, such as Sashie's cap with the horns and bells and his red and yellow tunic – he insisted on providing his own nether garments as he called them – Sandy's beggar's rags and gypsy frills and Dorothy's and Maud's high, veiled head-dresses.

Excitement began to mount and excitement is infectious. Rob and Twice, having designed the portcullis and drawbridge, were having them made from wood in the carpenters' shop at the factory and the factory electricians were round at the Great House fixing chains of lights in the trees and the powerful arc lights from the factory crane to the eaves of the Great House itself, from where they would shine down on to the 'battlements'. In the parkland outside the Great House wall, in a pegged-off area, Don and David Denholm could be seen, mounted on Cadence and Nimble, two of Sir Ian's polo ponies, charging at one another with wooden lances poised, cheered on by the squad of men and women who, in theory, were weeding the nearby cane-piece. By mid-December, indeed, all work on Paradise was the merest theory and no one thought of or talked about anything except 'de Vawlets'.

I have read somewhere that, in the last analysis, even the most experienced and hard-bitten impresario of musical comedy is at a loss to know what will 'take' with the public, so I have no shame in saying that I do not know what caused the 'Vawlets' to take to such a degree with the negro staff around Paradise. In early December, a strange throb could be heard in the air which, by the middle of the month, had resolved itself into a song which could be heard from the cane-pieces, from the vegetable women on the road with their baskets on their heads, from the carpenters' shop at the factory and from the kitchens of all the houses in the Compound. . . .

'De Vawlets am comin' – rah-rah! rah-rah!'
It was sung to the tune of 'The Campbells', with a strange rhythm that gave it a jungle, tom-tom beat.

In my weekly letters home to my father and the people at Reachfar, telling them of our activities, I naturally kept them informed on the progress of the play and I thought that this conversion of a Highland marching tune to tropical terms, as it were, would be of interest to them, but when I tried to describe the negro handling of the notes and the rhythm I found myself at a loss. I became aware that I was trying to describe something for which there were no terms of reference in my own mind or my father's, and that Twice's comparison of the negro mind in relation to ours as being like a comparison between us and a new, unknown breed from Mars was something like the truth. It interested me that it should be their transformation of a tune and their attitude to 'de Vawlets' in general that should bring the difference so strongly home to me.

In my few months in St Jago, I had talked with anyone who would discuss it with me about the negro-white problem, for anyone who thinks at all, even in my limited fashion, must be haunted by it if he lives even for a few months in the melting-pot of a tropical colony. In these discussions, I found myself frustrated by the blank wall at the end of many a blind alley.

Most of the people I talked to were, naturally, white people of my own kind, for I was sensitive to the fact that I was too new to the island to approach any negro on a subject on which he, too, was hyper-sensitive, and the white people, in the main, did not impress me favourably by their attitude. The mind of man, faced by a big problem that spreads, a *terra incognita*, vast before the fear-filled, slow-moving, exploring mind, is all too ready to take flight back from the edge of *terra incognita* and hide in some safe, built-in, little blind alley of custom, prejudice or even a stone-walled determination not to accept that *terra incognita* exists or that there is any problem at all.

Of all the people I talked to on the subject, the one who seemed to me to be least afraid of *terra incognita* and who seemed to stand the best chance of finding a safe pathway through it was the one who, on the outside, seemed to be the most unlikely, namely the fugitive-from-Poona Sir Ian. Maybe it was the light from the star of kindly truth which was reflected from his own mind to cast a glimmer on the path before him that gave to the steps of his thought the clear sound of fearless confidence that the unknown could be conquered. This light by which Sir Ian walked was not caught and extinguished in any back alleys that would betray his footsteps and lead to nowhere. It shone steadily ahead and, fearlessly, Sir Ian followed it.

For the 'jousting music' for the second act of the play, I wanted a well-known tune of somewhat military character to which the horses could be made to move well and it seemed to me that the obvious choice was the familiar 'Colonel Bogey'. Maxie and his confederates of the Club Band played entirely by ear, as did Sandy with his guitar, and this, I thought, was a tune they all knew, for I had heard it sung and whistled many times around Paradise. When I suggested it to Twice, however, he said: 'Lord no! Not on any account! That's the tune the negroes use to warn each other that Sir Ian is about. Rob told me about it. We don't want any of that significant sort of thing cropping up in this affair.'

I dismissed 'Colonel Bogey' from my mind forthwith, but I had difficulty in finding a substitute and gradually all the music to be used was listed and the blank against 'Jousting Scene' remained.

'Got to get that decided,' said Sir Ian one morning when he was poking about among the 'play papers' as he called them.

'I know,' I said. 'It's difficult. We want a sort of circus tune or a cavalry trot or something.'

'I'm not much of a hand at chunes, but what about that thing that goes TUM-tum, tah-ra-ra, RAH-RAH-RAH – ye know the thing! *You* were in the Air Force – the men have their own words for it: Something, was all the band could play – *you* know the thing, dammit!'

'Colonel Bogey?' I said and Sandy began to strum out the tune on the guitar that was always with him nowadays. 'It would be perfect.'

Sir Ian turned to the boy. '*That*'s the chune, boy. Go an' practise it in the garden.' He turned back to me. 'Oh, *I* know what it means here, all right. Wasn't born yesterday. Rob an' them think I don't know about it – ain't much goes on around here that the boy an' I can't find out between us. Little beggar can understand their dialect, ye know, although he never speaks it himself. An' they talk in front of him as they wouldn't talk if you or I were there. . . . You put that chune in for the joustin' – time they learned that I know what it means. Just you arrange for me to say to the band: "Play my chune, Varlets!" when I come walkin' on to the lawn to the joustin' with old Maud an'

Sashie an' them. It'll make them laugh like billy-ho an' it'll stop them whistlin' the perishin' thing round the factory – I'm sick of it. They're cunnin', ye know – took me a week or two to catch on to that business o' that chune, for they're always singin' or whistlin' or makin' a damn' noise o' some kind.'

'It's really a kind of up-to-date version of the talking drums, isn't it?' I asked.

'In a way. But this lot here have lost the art o' the drums. They've lost everything o' their own – or rather, slavery took it away from them. That's why I get mad when fools like that Cranston woman call them thievin' an' ignorant an' that. What would *she* be like in a few years if somebody took her away from everything she knew, took her a few thousand miles in the hold o' a ship and when she got there made her work for nothin' but a little food, made her speak a new language an' never allowed her to own even a handful o' rice o' her own? I bet you she would turn into a more ignorant thief than any black woman! And she'd be a bloody sight lazier too! . . . What the white man in this island has to learn is that the negro here is mostly his own work an' if he don't like what he's made, he's got to try an' make it over to a better model if he can an' if he can't he's got to get out. I'm not much of a hand for the Bible, but there's a lot o' sense in it here an' there, like the sins o' the fathers bein' visited unto the third an' fourth generation an' that. Slavery was a sin an' I'm delighted to see it bein' visited on people like that Cranston woman an' gettin' all her mangoes stolen off her tree, for I'm sure her forefathers'd 've been slavers if they'd had the guts to sail the Atlantic. What was I talkin' about?'

By this time, as was usual when Sir Ian got 'talkin'' to me, I was not quite certain, but he remembered for himself.

'Oh, yes, the talkin' drums. You'll hear them drummin' a bit sometimes on old kerosene cans, but that's mostly in connection with some o' these queer religions they keep sendin' down from the States. Things like the Jurymen o' Jehovah an' that. The Jurymen is a very popular religion with them – plenty o' noise an' shoutin' an' judgments an' confessions o' sin an' rollin' about on the ground an' bein' washed in the blood o' the lamb – the Rio d'Oro river, ye know. Might be blood or treacle when it's in spate – bright yellow, sometimes, too. That's why the Spaniards called it Oro – gold, ye know. The Spaniards were always thinkin' about gold – had it on the brain. But goin' back to these queer religions an' the drums an' that, the people only take to them because all their own tribal things were stamped out o' them an' they feel a kind o' need for somethin' – like me feelin' like a tot o' whisky when the sun goes down. Can't help it – it's in the blood. Same with the negroes. An' how do I know that my tot o' whisky ain't a bigger sin than them jumpin' into that perishin' river an' callin' it the blood o' the Lamb? Thing is to keep everything in moderation. It's no good me drinkin' too much whisky an' it's no good them spendin' all their time rollin' about in religion an' doin' no work. Too much whisky would make me fightin' drunk an' too much drums an' religion would make *them* fightin' mad. In the things o' the mind, they're like youngsters yet, ye see. You know what it's like when some youngsters get religion – boy at school with me in Edinburgh got a touch of it an' used to go into the silence as he called it an' everything. Started wettin' his bed in the end an' had to be sent home. Shockin' business. Same with a youngster that gets to thinkin' he's devilish clever an' cunnin' – turns into a juvenile delinquent before ye know where ye are. That's why it's time the negroes knew *I* know they whistle that perishin' chune to warn each other I'm about. It's time they had a set-back an' learn that I'm still a little smarter than they are. That ain't boastin', ye know, Missis Janet, that's just facts. You an' I have more adult brains an' more sense than they have just because we were luckier. Civilization came to our race earlier than it did to the negro race an' you an' I have had a better chance. It ain't anything to our own credit. But where our people went wrong was in the enslavement business an' ye can't turn back the clock an' undo it. All we can do now is try to show the negro what we think is the right way, teach him to benefit by our own experience. . . . Ye know what a man said to me at a meetin' in the Bay the other day?'

'No. What?'

'He an' his wife got Mother's invitation to the play an' he said: I see you're still workin' the bread-an'-circus principle at Paradise. . . . Shockin' thing to think. Been considerin' it. This play ain't like that, ye know.'

'Sir Ian, I *know* it isn't!'

'Don't want that kind o' feelin' on Paradise. Damn' nearly told the perisher to stay at home. Can't do that, of course. Mother wouldn't like it. But people like Mother an' the body o' opinion at home that says the Government is givin' the Empire away ain't got their eye on the ball. It ain't the Government that's givin' the Empire away – it's the people at home, like that perisher that's visitin' the Bay, that ain't *fit* to have an empire any longer. They're not producin' an' trainin' the men to run it. . . . Given a few more like your Twice an' Rob here instead o' that perisher that said that to me about circuses, an' this island would stick to the old country for ever an' it would be a far better thing for the negro in the end. Twice round there at the factory has them eatin' out o' his hand, an' they're *learnin'* from him, that's the important thing. He don't sit on his backside an' make drawin's an' give them orders – he climbs about among the girders *with* them. That's what turns the trick at this stage. I don't mean that's what keeps the Empire – I mean that's what's needed for the development an' happiness o' the negro. One man like Twice or Rob can do more to raise their status than all the development loans an' motor cars an' anti-syphilis serums that were ever invented, but we're not *gettin'* Rob's an' Twice's sort out from home now. We're gettin' a lot o' poops that are lookin' for an easy livin' an' ye can't blame the negro for hatin' the perishin' sight o' them, although he'll take their tips when he gets the chance. *Twice* don't tip them! I heard him givin' a squad o' them a cursin' yesterday that would have done credit to old Pickerin' o' Castle Cardon an' they just said "Yes, sah" an' did the job all over again. Negroes ain't fools, ye know. They've got sense – sense to know the man to listen to an' the man that's a fool, except when he's one o' their own politicians. . . . An' that reminds me – I told Twice again yesterday that he works too hard. Been tellin' Rob Maclean the same thing for years, but they won't listen. Say what ye like, this ain't a white man's climate. They can't do the things here they can do in Scotland.'

'Oh, Twice has always been over-charged with energy,' I said. 'He's very mild here compared with at home.'

'Well, there it is. I must say, I never saw a fellah climb like that – goes about the factory like a perishin' monkey. Talkin' o' monkeys, where's that boy? Time we were goin' – must be nearly lunchtime.'

'I hear Sandy's guitar in the kitchen. Have a glass of beer. That's Twice turning in at the gate.'

'Thank ye, my dear. I'm thirsty – been talkin' too much. 'Mornin', Twice, me boy. Been chattin' to your missis.'

'Here, listen – hello, Mr Twice,' said Sandy appearing from the kitchen along with Clorinda and the beer. 'Listen, I'll tell you a thing – I've been talkin' to Cookie an' Clorinda an' I've had a great idea for the play! We should get Mr Mackie to play his bagpipes!'

'There!' said Sir Ian, like a dog with two tails. 'It takes the boy an' me to think o' things like that!'

'I've been tryin' "De Vawlets am Comin' " on my guitar, but it's not the right instrument for it.'

'There *is* no instrument for it!' I said.

'Come now, you can't be Highland an' be like that about the pipes! 'S not reasonable!' said Sir Ian.

'I *am* not reasonable,' I said with proud dignity. 'We already have the Club Band complete with Maxie's saxophone, *plus* that guitar. *No* bagpipes!'

'Aw go on, Missis Janet! Just at the beginnin' to put people in a good mood an' then for the fight! The people love the bagpipes!'

'Let them have the bloody pipes!' said Twice. 'What is one more noise among so many?'

It was arranged that Mr Mackie, one of the junior engineers, who was already a varlet, should play his pipes as an overture and then again as a rallying call when Red Gurk's band rushed the castle walls.

'But Mackie has to be on *my* side!' said Sir Ian. 'Can't have the enemy havin' the pipes an' maybe gettin' boilin' oil poured down the thingummyjigs o' them. I'll swop Denholm young Christie for Mackie – they're about the same size. . . . An' look here, what's this about Candlesham an' Denholm havin' pages next? *I* am supposed to be the Lord High Cockolorum o' this castle an' *I* ain't got any perishin' pages!'

'It's only to create a bit of a fandango for the jousting scene,' said Twice wearily. 'To give us a kind of procession of horses coming on to the lawn instead of just two. Besides, you've got your Jester.'

'Oh, I see.' Sir Ian was mollified. 'I was watchin' them round in the field yesterday – that Denholm girl can ride. Should have had *her* for Red Gurk instead of her brother. Looks more like a Gurk. Young Denholm is a weedy-lookin' runt. . . . Well, come, boy. Let's go an' have lunch a' then tell Mackie about the pipes.'

Chapter Seven

EARLY IN December, Captain Davey spent one of his weekends with us and on the Saturday evening Dorothy and Bertie Yates came home from the Bay, Dorothy wearing a small diamond on the third finger of her left hand and, as Twice said, 'actually expecting us all to register Surprise, Surprise.' We were all genuinely pleased and we all did our best to look genuinely surprised and Dorothy was very appealing in her youthful, uncomplicated happiness. On the Sunday evening, therefore, I was a little taken aback when she came into my bedroom where I was lying on the bed reading and, without preamble, said viciously: 'That awful Isobel Denholm! I'll never speak to her again or her horrible brother either!'

'Good gracious, Dorothy, what's gone wrong?' I said. 'I thought that you and Isobel were the best of friends!'

'I thought so too, but we're not! She is awful! She is wicked and – *awful*!'

'Sit down, Dorothy, and tell me all about it. What happened? Was she nasty about you and Bertie?'

'She wasn't very nice. But it wasn't that so much. She said *awful* things!'

'What sort of awful? What about?'

'I can't tell you. It was all just *awful*!' said Dorothy and began to cry.

'Now, come, Dorothy, this won't do. Nothing that that girl said is worth crying about like that. If you don't want to tell me, don't, but you are not to cry and worry about her. She doesn't mean anything to any of us, you know, and we needn't know her if we don't want to. She is rather an odd girl, I think, and — '

'She's odd, all right!' sobbed Dorothy. 'She's *awful* — ' She gave a hiccup. 'She – she goes to bed and d-does things with Don Candlesham and they're not even *engaged*!'

Hard put to it not to burst into an overwrought squeal of laughter, I merely said: 'Oh, dear.'

'And I said that Bertie and I would never think of going on like that and I thought it was awful and why didn't she get married to him if she wanted to be like that with him and she said he would never marry her because – because — '

'All right, yes, because?'

'Because he was in love with *you* and you were c-cleverer at doing things in bed than she was and it was all AWFUL!'

With a final bellow on the last word, Dorothy cast herself across my bed and sobbed her heart out and all I could find to say for a moment was – to myself – 'God, you are quite right. It *is* AWFUL.'

When my moment of private communion with myself was over, I began to laugh and said: 'Dorothy, pull yourself together! The girl is demented! You don't believe her, do you?'

'Of course not!' bellowed Dorothy. 'She's simply aw—'

'Dorothy, please don't say "awful" again or I shall scream. Now, stop crying and listen to me. You have been living here with us for months and you know Don Candlesham never comes here except with all the others about the play and Isobel is just talking a lot of rubbish. I don't know where she got the idea from or why she said such a thing, but I think maybe she is just jealous of you and Bertie and wanted to hurt you and she probably knows that you like me a little, does she?'

'Of *course* she knows I like you and love being here! Everybody knows that!'

'Well, you see, jealous people can always find a way of hurting you through your friends. And she is silly as well as being jealous, I think, if she is – carrying on with Don as you say she is — '

'She is! She said so! It was aw — '

'Maybe she thinks it is very modern and clever, but I don't. Anyhow, she is not worth crying about and worrying about and just try not to think of her any more. There's the play, of course, but we can get through that all right and after that you need have no more to do with her.'

'And there's my engagement party at the Great House tonight!' said Dorothy.

'Oh, well, never mind. Dorothy, when you are married to Bertie and living here, or anywhere else for that matter, you will often find yourself having to go to dinners and parties where there will be people you don't like,' I said, feeling like 'Auntie Janet's Hints on Etiquette' in some fourpenny weekly. 'Sensible people just go on as if nothing had happened.'

'All right,' said Dorothy sulkily, 'but nothing will stop me from thinking that she's — '

'AWFUL!' I said. 'All right, go and get dressed for goodness' sake.'

106

Madame, in giving an engagement party for Dorothy, we all realized, was not giving it because of any particular feeling for Dorothy, but because (a) she enjoyed giving parties, (b) she approved of engagements on principle and took the view that any Paradise engagement was her own achievement, and (c) – according to Marion – she wanted to 'come it' over Mrs Denholm who 'hadn't got that girl of hers off yet.'

The party, therefore, having all the earmarks of being uncomfortable and embarrassing anyway (which it was), I did not see fit to tell Twice before we went to it that Dorothy and Isobel had had a cat-clawing that afternoon, and after the party was safely over, I decided that there was no point in worrying Twice with Isobel's fantastic fabrications at all. In Sandy's terminology, I decided in my own mind that Isobel was a good-going case of 'psychology' and lost sight of the whole matter and no wonder, with 'Varlets in Paradise' mounting round my ears like some overwhelming tide.

'We're going to erect the portcullis and drawbridge tomorrow,' Twice told me the day after the party. 'After that, you'll have to call the rehearsals at the Great House. The whole thing depends on these crowd scenes of jousting and fighting and we've got to get them something like right. The only thing is to plug away at it two or three times a week right up to the night.'

'Oh, lord. I suppose it had better be Tuesdays, Thursdays and Saturdays?'

'Except for this first Thursday. Rob and I won't be here.'

'Aw, Twice!'

'Can't help it. Madame can say what she likes about this damned entertainment as she calls it, but the factory really comes first. This turbine that was held up is through after all – the ship gets into the Bay on Thursday night. We are going down the night before to see it landed and loaded on to the transporter at first light on Friday morning. Can't have these hams dropping several thousand pounds-worth of turbine into the Caribbean, play or no play.'

'Or down the Rio d'Oro gorge off the transporter,' I added. 'Oh, well, there's other Thursdays!'

On the Tuesday night, at the first rehearsal on the real site at the Great House, with Madame in a chair on the lawn where the front row of the audience would be, the players were all too fascinated with the drawbridge and the portcullis to take any interest in their parts. The drawbridge was a ramp of wood hung by ropes through pulley blocks on the roof of the house so that it could lie over the front staircase or be raised to cover the entrance to the porch on the first floor. The portcullis, similarly suspended, was a grille that could be dropped over the entrance. All very ingenious, I thought, and only my faith in Twice as an engineer sustained me in the hope that it would not all collapse and kill somebody. When everybody had seen it all going down and up and up and down several times, Twice bellowed for silence, handed a stop-watch to one of the typists from the office and said: 'Write the number of minutes here and there on that script as we go along. All right, places, everybody!'

The drawbridge was down, covering the steps, and the portcullis was also down in front of the entrance. It was dark now, but as Rob, who was controlling the lights and mechanical contrivances, threw his main switch and the floodlights came on on the roof and the pink lights behind the aluminium-painted grille of the portcullis, the effect was very striking. At the same moment, from somewhere in the shrubbery, Mackie's pipes began to play and all the carpenters and electricians who were on duty began to sing: 'De Vawlets am Comin'. I had a sudden uplifted feeling that maybe the thing was going to be all right after all.

'Ho, varlets!' came the parade-ground voice of Sir Ian from behind the grille. 'Raise the portcullis!'

Smoothly, the grille disappeared into the upper darkness, exposing the Dulac family around a table in the porch, the table furnished with Madame's silver candelabra and the Vine Valley pewter mugs, while lounging on the floor in front were Sandy with his guitar and Sashie with the inevitable bladder.

'Music, boy!' bellowed Sir Ian, and Sandy and the band under the front steps romped into the calypso 'Brown-skin Gal' and automatically the carpenters and electricians began to sing.

'Janet, it's going to work!' said Marion.

'Excellent!' said Madame.

'Oh, don't, for pity's sake!' I said superstitiously.

Still, at the end of the second act, when the jousting on the lawn had started in an astonished silence followed by a lusty laughing singing of 'Colonel Bogey' and had gone with a great swing while the carpenters and electricians shouted: 'Stick him in de gut, sah!' indiscriminately to hero and villain, I admitted to Twice that it was all more of an 'entertainment' than I had thought.

'The worst thing,' he said dampingly, 'is this confounded fight. Still, let's press on.'

For the beginning of the third act, some of the big lights were switched off, so that Red Gurk and his band could move in, unseen by the audience, from the shrubberies, and the act opened with the group round the table in the porch again. There were several hitches and re-groupings of the attackers by Twice and me, but in the end, with much swarming of invaders up pillars and much heaving over of sacks of straw and pails of water by the defenders, a most entertaining fight was achieved and Red Gurk eventually died in a dramatic attitude over the verandah balustrade. With a last bellow from Sir Ian to his varlets for stoups of sack, the drawbridge was lowered, the portcullis raised on the carousing Dulac family round its table, and with 'Music, Varlets, Ho!' and a rendering of 'De Vawlets am Comin' ' the lights went out and the performance was at an end.

'Most amusing indeed!' said Madame. 'Janet, I congratulate you. And when they are all dressed in their curtains and things it will be very pretty. . . . Ian, come here!'

'Yes, Mother?'

'Ian, did my eyes deceive me or did I see you hit Mr Denholm on the head with – with a *chamber* pot?'

''Smatterofact, Mother, they *did* in those days. Poured *everythin*' over when they were bein' attacked, ye know.'

'We will not have verisimilitude to that degree, Ian. Lady Dene-Jorrocks might not like it and Beattie Denholm would certainly find it extremely vulgar.'

'But, dammit, Mother —'

'That will do, Ian. I am perfectly certain that Janet made no allowance for such – such articles. . . . Tell them to serve the drinks on the west verandah.'

'Listen, the lot of you!' came the voice of Twice from the darkness away behind us. 'I'm down here on the garden wall. Can you hear me?'

Several voices called back to him.

'Well, that performance you gave wasn't just bad – it was abominable stinkin' awful. I couldn't hear a word, not even a squeak from all you waiting-women – I've heard more noise at a vicarage tea-party. As for the varlets and the fight, all I can say is that if the Germans had been any good we'd have lost the damn' war. The next rehearsal will be on Saturday at eight an' for Pete's sake put some guts into it!'

'Oh, dear,' I said.

'My dear Janet,' said Madame, 'you know what engineers are –

never pleased. They won't be content until they've blown us all up with their atoms. . . . Come and have a little refreshment.'

Two mornings later, Twice and I were loafing over our early morning tea when Sandy on his piebald cantered up the driveway and I said to Twice: 'I wish to put on record that I could not like this child more if he were my own, but if he is coming here with one more suggestion about varlets or bagpipes, I will probably strangle him.'

'Gummornin',' said Sandy from the landing outside our bedroom door. 'May I come in?'

'Yes,' we said guardedly. 'Good morning.'

'You not feelin' well?' he enquired.

'We're all right,' I said.

'You look sorta sick. Dad sent me.'

'Oh?' said Twice.

'He's in bed with a tempercher an' he says will you come an' see him.'

'Goodness! What's wrong?' I asked.

'Oh, nothin' much. Touch o' fever, but he's not gettin' goin' to the Bay for the turbine. My mother's got her foot down. She says if he goes to the Bay an' gets all sweated up he'll get a chill an' be real sick an' she's not goin' to have it with the play supper an' all the roast pigs an' everything, so you'll have to go by yourself, Mr Twice, an' he's askin' you to come an' see him after breakfast, please.'

'Oh, dammit!' said Twice.

'Dad said worse'n that,' Sandy told us, 'but it didn't do any good. I don't suppose you've ever seen my mother with her foot down. The two worst things that can happen here at Paradise is Madame at the Instrument and my mother with her foot down. So I have to go home now so g'bye for now.'

Twice left for the Bay in the middle of the afternoon to see the big transporter over the Rio d'Oro road before darkness fell about six in the evening, and I fitted Dorothy with her Lady Clare dress for the last time before sending her off to a dance in the Bay with Bertie Yates and the Murphies. As I sat sewing after they had left, I was thinking how utterly and simply happy were people like Dorothy and Bertie compared with the Isobels and the Dons. What was the reason? Dorothy and her Bertie had seemed to slide together in space and time and having met accept each other in the simple faith that they were going to be happy for ever more. What made the difference between a Dorothy and an Isobel? A

Bertie and a Don? Were Dorothy and Bertie less complex? Probably. Was it partly that Isobel and Don *had* too much – in the way of wealth and looks and so on? Possibly. Did people who had a lot still always want more? It seemed so. Wasn't it better then to be like Dorothy and Bertie and just take in good faith what came? Probably, but a bit cabbage-like as an existence. Wasn't it better to be a happy cabbage than a tortured orchid? But why *was* Dorothy a cabbage and Isobel an orchid? Thinking thus in a circle, I hemmed round the circle of Dorothy's dress and, selfishly, at the back of my mind, I was glad that I seemed to be neither a Dorothy nor an Isobel, but some mean between the two extremes, even if a little mentally dismayed at times.

I had had my dinner and was busy with Sandy's orange and green gypsy frills when a car pulled up outside, so I put the heap of tarlatan on the sofa and went to the door, for I had already sent the servants out to their quarters. Don came up the verandah steps.

'Hello, Don,' I said. 'Where's Sashie?'

'At the Peak,' he said. 'Why?'

'I just wondered,' I said foolishly. 'Come in. Did you see Twice?'

'He was in the bar having a drink when I left. Maclean is sick, I hear.'

'Yes. His fever is down this evening, though, but Marion thought it safer to keep him in bed. Have a drink?'

'Thanks. Whisky and water.'

I mixed the two drinks and came to sit beside my work-basket on the sofa, but Don did not sit down. He remained, drink in hand, in the middle of the floor. The room became full of a miasma of uneasiness which, I realized, was emanating from myself and, jerkily, I reached out to a nearby box for a cigarette. Don brought out his lighter and, with an effort, I held the cigarette steadily to the flame. My lips felt loose and uncontrollable. He let the lighter drop to the floor, caught my wrist and in the same moment set his glass down on a small table.

'They always told me,' he said, drawing me up and towards him until his arms were about me, 'that everything comes to him who waits, but when the good Twice walked into the Peak tonight, I was getting pretty tired of waiting.'

The time of thought is incredibly swift. I do not think I was in Don's arms for more than thirty seconds, but in that time I saw every hour of every day since I had arrived in the island unwind before the eyes of my mind and I saw again all the significant glances, heard all the two-meaninged exchanges, felt all the rising excitements that had passed between Don and myself as we looked at one another, talked and danced together. But, on the screen that flickered before my mental eyes, I was astonished and appalled to see that the woman in these scenes bore the physical semblance of myself. Horrified and amazed, I watched the be-haviour of this woman and saw her as divorced from my essential self as if, then, when she looked like that, said these things, felt these uprushes of the blood, she was not the essential I at all, but someone as different from me as if my body, while these things took place, had been occupied by a foreign spirit. And then the film was blotted out by a surging red tide that threatened to drown me as Don's face came nearer and nearer. I pushed with my hands against his chest.

'Don't,' I said.

'Darling, don't be coy!' he said with a small, triumphant laugh.

But for that note of triumph, faint as the echo of a trumpet from beyond the hills, and the superior, male use of the word 'coy', I do not know what might have happened. At that vision of myself as I had been over the last few months, my reaction had been one of shamed guilt, of disgust with myself, of a need to apologize to Don, to the thought of Twice, to all humanity for my own behaviour, but at Don's words and the note of triumph in his voice, I broke suddenly into anger. The anger was largely at myself for my responsibility in bringing this ridiculous situation about, at myself for being unaware of what I was doing, but the need to bring the situation to an end was so urgent in me that I sprang at anger as a mode of expression and sprang upon Don as a victim because this was a simpler and faster way out than the way of truth.

'Let go of me!' I snarled, wrenching myself free. 'You small-time Lothario!'

He stared at me, amazed, and, even in that moment when I was lashing myself into a fury, I granted that he had reason to be amazed. He threw himself into a chair and stared at me and a supercilious sneer began to slide on to his handsome face.

'Don't behave like a suburban housewife who has been lasciviously attacked by a vacuum-cleaner salesman!' he said.

'Why not? A suburban housewife is exactly what I am and the description of yourself could *not* be more precise!'

'What?' he shouted and sprang to his feet again.

I stood looking at him, shaking with the rage that replaced, now, all my confused shame and other emotion. We began to hurl insults at one another. I do not remember all that was said and the things that I do remember still make me blush with shame because, from beginning to end, the whole thing was spurious. While I abandoned responsibility for this situation which I had helped to bring about by screening myself behind assumed anger at Don's attempt on my wifely virtue, Don took refuge behind a sneering superciliousness and lofty scorn, and all the time I was aware that what we should both be saying was: 'I have behaved badly and so have you. This thing between us is not real – it is a trick of the light of this country – one of its sudden, meaningless bursts of furious storm – nothing more.' But I did not say anything like that and neither did Don. Like most people, I will go to considerable lengths rather than admit that I have played the fool, and Don, apparently, suffered from the same weakness.

So, having rendered my brain almost numb with this counterfeit rage, I continued to storm at him: 'What you see when you look in the glass, I don't know! How does it *feel* to consider yourself body-servant to half the sex-hungry women in the Caribbean? *Your* place is with Isobel Denholm, not here! Go back to her! And remember to tell her where you *really* stand with me – or will you go giving her a further glowing report of me as your mistress?'

Don sprang at me and gripped me by the shoulders: 'What do you mean?'

There was suddenly no longer anything spurious between us. My own defensive, lashed-up rage seeped away like water into moss and Don's defensive superciliousness seemed to break away from him, falling in splinters about the room, and it was replaced by only too genuine raw rage that quivered in his every muscle as his hands gripped my shoulders that had become rigid with sheer abject terror. His rage, I know, was not directed against myself, but blind violence always terrifies me. In a suspension of time, we were standing there, both physically and mentally help-less as we waited for the force that gripped Don to burst over both of us, when the door suddenly flew open and Sashie came dancing into the room.

'Janet, darling, I *know* it's long past bedtime, but *do* look at my new bladder! Specially imported from the States under private licence!' He seemed to dance through between Don and me – we must have involuntarily broken apart to make way for him – as water sparkles through between two rocks and he was waving on a stick the most obscene balloon I have ever seen, consisting of a green central sphere with three red, sausage-shaped protuberances, each about a foot long. 'Why, *there* you are, Don, my sweet!' he said with affected surprise, coming to rest between us. He turned his back to Don and faced me. 'Isn't it the most vulgar thing?' He flicked the sausages one by one. 'Faith, Hope, Charity!'

'You little beast!' said Don, seizing Sashie from behind and throwing him off balance so that he cannoned into me and I fell on to the sofa. 'I'd like to murder you!'

While Sashie got a grip on the end of the sofa and pulled himself upright, I sprang back to my feet, recovered my voice and completely lost all control of myself.

'Get out!' I shouted. 'Get out of here – both of you! And don't either of you show your faces in here again with all your spurious passion and your bloody affectation! Get *out*!' I could hardly believe that the raucous, fishwife shout had come from my own throat and, horrified, I listened to it die to silence, a silence that was broken after what seemed like an hour by the light, emotionless voice of Sashie.

'Janet, darling,' he said, 'couldn't I have just an eensy-teensy little drink? And you haven't said pleased to see me or anything – not at all Highland and hospitable – quite the reverse.'

I was so overtaken by shame and disgust at myself and everything and everybody that I could not bear to look at them.

'Have a drink if you want it – the tray is over there,' I said surlily and stood plucking at Sandy's tarlatan frills that lay on the sofa.

Sashie bobbed a curtsy, laid his balloon tenderly on a table and pattered over to the tray. 'Thanks *most* awfully.' He poured himself a drink and came back to stand by the long sofa, facing us. 'Been having an interesting time?' he enquired, his head cocked, birdlike, to one side.

'If you are playing nursemaid to *me*,' said Don who now seemed to be feeling much as I was, 'stop it. And it won't be in order for you to go blabbing to Alexander that I've been here tonight, either!'

'You stop clutching avidly at the skirts of intrigue!' I spat at him. 'Alexander will be hearing from me a first-hand account of what went on here tonight!'

Sashie looked down into his drink for a moment and then up at

114

us again. 'Actually,' he said, 'that won't be necessary – quite the reverse. You see, Twice sent me up here to fetch Don.'

'To *fetch* me?' Don shouted.

With a shrug, Sashie took a sip from his glass. 'Yes. It was after dinner. He came to me and said: "Sashie, would you mind running up to Guinea Corner in my car and telling Don to come back? He is probably embarrassing Janet." His very words, Don, dear, so I came and here I am.'

I sat down in a rocking chair that happened to be behind me, tilted it back to its limits and laughed hysterically until I felt quite sick. The room was full of nothing but the sound of this laughter until there came a fearful oath from Don and Sashie went spinning, off his balance, into a heap on the sofa among the orange and green tarlatan, his drink flew across the room and the glass broke against the wall in the same moment that the heavy door slammed behind Don.

'I'm sorry! Sashie, I'm sorry!' I gasped. 'The whole thing is just so – so ludicrous!' and I at last sobbed and gulped myself into some sort of control. 'Sashie, he didn't hurt you?' Sashie struggled upright on the sofa and shrugged his lissome shoulders. 'Oh, dear me, no. But I must insist on having a fresh drink.'

'I'll get them,' I said and went to the tray.

'I am conscious,' said Sashie, as I handed him his glass, 'of being a little at sea. Do I understand that the Alexander citadel has not fallen to Don?'

'You do. Sashie, what did you *expect* to find when you came in here?'

'*Not* what I found – quite the reverse. I expected to say to Don in the language of the Varlets: "Flee! All is known!" don't you know. He seemed to be quite extraordinarily angry. What happened?'

I glared balefully at him and then sat down, not looking at him. 'I don't know *what* happened,' I said, wondering why I was talking like this to Sashie at all. 'I don't know what's been happening ever since April, when I was down there at the Peak. I've never been in such a damned muddle in my life. I wish I were back in Scotland!'

'Darling, you sound exactly like the Murphy keening for her ould mother in Belfast!'

'Sashie, can't you do *any*thing other than laugh at people?'

'Not really, my sweet. I can't see anything much else to do. What would you *like* me to do? I *do* try to be helpful, but *always*!'

I drew a deep breath. 'Look, I'm prepared to admit that Don's coming here tonight must probably be partly my doing — '

Sashie laid aside his glass, put back his head and began to laugh in an abandoned way that was new in my experience of him.

'What the devil are you laughing at?' I asked.

'Darling — ' Sashie gave a hiccup. 'Darling, simply your aggrieved grandeur, your proud nobility in admitting something to be your fault that is so *entirely* your fault that even to mention your responsibility for it couldn't be more superfluous.'

'Sashie,' I appealed to him, 'do try to be serious for a moment. If what you say is true, I am very, very sorry for what I did, but from start to finish I am right out of my depth. I don't understand what has been going on and I don't understand Don and the way he jumps in and out of bed with all sorts of people. *Why* does he do it?'

'Angel, I'm no psycho-analyst, but I suppose he gets fun out of it or he wouldn't do it.'

'Has he always been like this? How long have you known him?'

'Since 1943 – until 1946, he didn't have much chance to be "like this" as you put it, in that refined way. You see, he and I met in one of the war holiday camps run by the Japanese.'

'Oh.' I felt a flush rise from my chest, up to my neck and into my face. 'I – I'm sorry, Sashie. . . . Can I get you another drink?'

He held out his glass to me with a grin. 'Darling, don't be like that about things. Don and I are not war-scarred heroes, you know. Quite the reverse. But since we were repatriated to England, Home and Beauty as they call it and came over here, Don has shown a remarkable propensity for what one can only call whoring around.'

Pouring drinks, with my back to Sashie, I said: 'Still, if I'd known about the – the prison camp thing I would not have been so beastly with him tonight,'

Sashie waited until I was standing in front of him, holding out his glass to him, before he said devastatingly: 'Darling, his prison camp experience would be *no* excuse for getting into bed with him. That would be whoredom indeed.'

'And that is an extraordinarily nasty remark, Sashie.'

'But true – like a lot of life's nastiness.'

'There's the crux,' I said. 'I don't agree that life is nasty – that's the belief that leads to the whoring and all the artificial things like

116

tonight – they are only attempts to get back at the supposed nastiness.'

'I wouldn't know, darling. I never think about it if I can help it. . . . I really must go home.'

'Another form of escapism, yours, isn't it?' I said.

'I suppose so. Why not?'

'Or why?' I said. 'I don't see the point of everybody running away all the time without stopping to look at what they're running away from. It doesn't make sense. There might be nothing there. How can you know if you don't stop and take a look?'

'Sometimes I take a look, like tonight, and I don't care frightfully for what I see, if you know what I mean. As far as life is concerned, I have a little submarine. Life is a great, big ocean, and I swim about in it, safe in my little submarine. *Proper* sailors regard the escape hatch as a way out to safety, but I am different. *My* escape hatch is the way *in* to safety. As soon as I see a big wiggly eel coming along or one of those goggle-eyed fish that *glare* at me, I pop down the little hole and slam the lid shut behind me. I do not wish to be wiggled around or glared at.'

'Why did you pop out tonight and come here after Don?' I asked.

'Because, if you must know, your Twice shook me to the core by giving me the impression that Don was making an ass of himself.'

'Why should that worry *you*, safe inside your little submarine? Don spends a large part of his time making an ass of himself.'

'You're wrong, you know. Most of the time, the ladies co-operate like anything, so Don feels splendid and not at all asslike – quite the reverse.'

'Never mind that. Why should *you* mind him being an ass just for once?' He merely stared at me, his mask quite expressionless. 'You couldn't be ordinary – even bourgeois – enough to be *fond* of him, could you?' I asked.

'And if I were?'

'It would be comprehensible and, for once, unaffected.' I rose and put my empty glass on a table. 'You'd better go home before I start in and have a scene with you too. You people feed me up, Sashie, and that's the Gawd's truth. You'll neither live life nor let the damn' thing alone and then you have the impudence to wonder what's wrong with you and blame other people like me. . . . Not you, so much, maybe. You at least have the decency to keep yourself to yourself and don't slobber yourself all about.

117

. . . By the way, what's going to be the outcome of tonight? Does Don take up an attitude of never speaking to one again and refusing to be Lancelot in the play?'

'Hardly. He's not an adolescent, you know.'

'No? He adolesces like one in lots of ways. You needn't be so snooty.'

He looked at me from slitted eyes. 'Darling, I always avoid expressing opinions if at all possible, especially personal ones, but you are one very bloody irritating woman. You seem to have forgotten again that you gave Don – not to mention all the rest of us – the idea that you would like to be adolesced with by him.'

'I am sick of this whole discussion,' I said. 'I've already said I'm sorry for what I may have given in the way of impressions. How am I supposed to behave about Don *now* in order to please you? As if he had done me a favour?'

'That at the very least.' Sashie smiled slightly and I could not resist smiling back, wondering even as I smiled why it was that I could never be ill-natured with him for long. 'Weren't you even at the least a little flattered?'

'No. I wasn't. Nobody *could* be by a thing like that.'

'On the contrary, most women are extremely flattered – and more. . . . A thing like what?'

'All that spurious claptrap – that here-we-are-alone-at-last routine! Golly, you could spit peas through it, as my friend Tom would say!'

'My *dear* Janet, how fearfully coarse you can be! How did you know it was claptrap, as you call it?'

'*Any*body would know!'

Sashie stared at me. 'Darling, in some ways you are the perfect original clot of stupidity. *Any*body would know, she says!'

'What d'you mean?'

'My dear, only about one person in a thousand in this age can recognize claptrap when he sees it or feels it – can separate the real from the false. Don't you see that that is just what is what you call *wrong* with people like Don? This is the age of the man-made gem that looks like a diamond. Man has dropped through a trap from reality into claptrap and the trap has shut with a clap behind him. The only place he can go is through another trap into more claptrap and the box he lands in is getting progressively smaller. In the end, he'll have himself scared and compressed into an eensy-teensy little space inside one of his own man-made diamonds and be peering out through the facets as if they were a lot of lenses, which will turn the world and everything in it into what he chooses and wishes to see.'

'And what then?' I asked.

'He'll have his heart's desire, he thinks. He'll be encased in claptrap, looking through claptrap at a lot more claptrap.'

'And he'll live in that state for ever and ever?'

'He hopes so.'

'And you?'

'I am utterly repelled by matters scientific' – Sashie's voice became suddenly savage – 'but I understand from people like Twice that if you compress a live thing – such as steam – it tends to become explosive. I sincerly hope that this is true and that man, having compressed himself into the last stage of claptrap, will explode and blow his bloody little self either to Kingdom Come or back to earth. I am sick of every -ism and -ology in existence! I'm sick of watching people chasing their own tails, decorated with synthetic diamonds, under a tropic sun! Suicides and homicides, the whole perishin' lot of 'em!' he ended in Sir Ian's voice. 'And now that you know what I really think, darling, I wish to go home.'

'All right, Sashie.' I rose, took his empty glass and put it on the tray. I felt shy suddenly. 'Thank you for – talking and every-thing. And – give Don my love.'

'But of course, my sweet.'

He remained seated on the sofa, looking at me out of slit-like eyes in his satyr's face and I thought that there was something else that he wanted to say to me.

'What is it, Sashie?'

In a disconcerted way, he looked down at his hands. It was unusual of Sashie, who made a hobby of being disconcerting, to be disconcerted himself. 'This,' he said, 'is quite extraordinarily embarrassing. I had hoped that if I stayed long enough you might excuse yourself to go to what the Cranston calls the toilet, or something. Darling, *would* you mind leaving the room?'

'What's wrong, Sashie? Are you ill? Can't I help?'

'No, you can't!' he said harshly.

Sashie's light voice had never, in my hearing, been coloured by any emotion, not even tonight after the moment of savagery before he exposed a little of his real mind for once. Never had I heard him slip out of his own ridiculous, artificial idiom which was so posed and precious, as were all his physical movements, that I had always been sure they were the outcome of hours of practice before a looking-glass. Now the voice was husky and strained, the familiar half-satyr's-grin half-silly-simper had gone from his down-turned face and I was amazed to see in him that look that is characteristic of the severely crippled, the graven lines of long patience through intense suffering, both physical and mental.

'Sashie?' I said, and I probably made some stupid, ineffectual movement.

He looked up at me and the familiar mask was back in place. 'What is one more confession among so many?' he asked. 'These legs are not my own. They are very snob – *quite* the best on the market – but Don disarranged their arrangements a little earlier this evening. Please go, darling, and let me be *quite* alone with my mechanical adjustments!'

I fled from the room, sat down on the bottom step of the stairs and burst into tears.

I had more or less pulled myself together by the time Sashie emerged from the drawing-room, his hideous 'bladder' in his hand.

'I can never aplogize,' he said. 'A most disgustingly naked sort of evening. . . . My dear Janet, you *haven't* been *crying*!'

'I can cry if I like!' I said, like a silly, defiant child.

'But, of *course*!' he agreed. 'Only, let us sit down and have another little tot and let you get over it, for how can I report to the good Twice that I left you sitting on the stairs in tears because you had lost your glass slipper?'

I got up and followed him back into the drawing-room. 'Sashie, please don't be funny at me,' I said. 'Maybe I'm a sloshy, muddle-headed, middle-aged, old cow but I can't help it. Sashie, *what* sort of person *are* you?'

He handed me a glass and sat down opposite me. 'Darling, what an absurdity of a question! If one knew, one wouldn't be such a person, would one? I mean, so many other kinds would be *so* much nearer to the heart's desire, don't you think? . . . On the surface, I was shot down out of an aeroplane bang into the middle of a Jap prisoner-of-war camp – the little brutes were furious with me because the engine of my machine went slap through the place where they cooked their rice – their *own* rice, nothing to do with the prisoners – they wouldn't have minded that – and burned it to ashes, but *ashes*, my dear. And but for Don Candlesham giving me drinks of water and tearing up people's shirts and things to bandage me, I wouldn't be sitting here telling you all about my gallantry in the war. And now we won't talk about it any more, and if you tell the Cranston – or indeed anyone, except perhaps your Twice – I will quite definitely put prussic acid in your Christmas pudding. I will *not* be wallowed in by the populace for motives that are basically sadistic or discussed as if I were an American pulp thriller. . . . And I shall be extremely severe with Don when I get back,' he ended.

'Why Don?'

'He knows as well as I do how easy my arrangements are to disarrange.' He held up his glass and stared into its contents. 'I think I must be getting a little drunk. I am talking too much. . . . He had no business to side-swipe me like that. . . . You know, I shouldn't be surprised if he isn't a little in love with you in a genuine way, to forget himself so. Darling, isn't it *killing*?'

'Oh, shut up! You *are* getting tight, Sashie! Don is no more in love with me than you are. What interests me, to be drunkenly truthful, is why he tried with me at all, even if I *did* look encouragingly at him without meaning to. There are masses of younger, more attractive-looking women about.'

'You are a quite fantastic mixture of the stupid and the penetrating, my sweet. It is a pity that you and I don't get together, really. With your native wit and my worldly cunning, this earth would be our oyster. In wondering why Don "tried with" you as you so rightly put it, you have gone to the heart of things. Don *tried*, my precious, because he was trying to get in on the stability.'

'Stability?'

Sashie held out a slender hand, palm down, and rocked it from side to side. 'The old thing, you know, of flying straight and level. That's what these youngsters are looking for. Compared with Don, you know, I am an old man. I was born in 1917 – you and I are about contemporary.'

'I've got the edge on you,' I told him. 'I'm 1910 vintage.'

'Really? I should have said about 1915. The fact that you are earlier only strengthens my argument. You see, if you share in the common belief that it is the wars and revolutions of this century that have upset people like Don and the Denholms, you and I ought to be considerably more upset than they are, in particular myself, if it doesn't sound too frightfully immodest and boastful. I was conceived in Moscow in the midst of a revolution – how my parents came to think of such a thing at such a time I do not know – born in France when the war was at its worst and brought up in London in the roaring Twenties and at the age of twenty-two I was pitchforked into another war. If what the psychiatrists say is to be depended upon, darling, I should be a seething mass of complexes, don't you think?'

'And aren't you?' I enquired.

'Do you know, I really *don*'t think so? I behave in a most affected and offensive manner, but to conceal a physical disability, and that is only a fairly normal and natural desire for a certain degree of privacy. . . . To continue my argument, as the sententious people say, I think all this stuff about wars and revolutions generating complexes in people is nonsense. What *is* happening is that the people's complexes are generating all the wars and revolutions but people don't want to admit that, so they escape into the claptrap of being imposed upon and made to suffer by some naughty outside agency.'

'But *why* do they go generating these complexes that generate all these wars and revolutions?'

'So like the house that Jack built, isn't it? My dear, they can't help it. They are trying to climb on to a new plane of consciousness. They are like a little boy who has got half-way up the big tree in the garden and has lost his climbing head. He can neither get back down to where he started from nor can he go on up to the place he was trying to reach. He becomes aware of the wind blowing, the tree rocking about, gets into a panic and doesn't know *what* he is trying to do. . . . The only people with any sense, really, are the ones like you and me. Here we sit in our little forked branch, comfortable and unambitious, having a pleasant drink and waiting for the *tree* to grow and carry *us* up with it.'

'Isn't that a little uninspired of us?'

'Of course! But one who is not inspired is uninspired. The important thing is, I think, to recognize one's lack of divine inspiration. The ones who get into a panic are the ones who *think* they are divinely inspired and end by getting themselves out on a limb. The truly inspired ones don't get into a panic – they go on and up and take the tree – and incidentally *us* – on and up with them. It all goes back to the fact that the common man has got above himself. Every manjack of him is now convinced that he is the son of God and in actual fact millions of him are only by-blows. They are the rank and file, the common ruck, the rabble. And the rabble has got out of hand. It has broken ranks, made a nonsense of all discipline, and until each unit of it looks inside himself and re-values himself on a realistic basis and stops clambering about and falls into line, the army can't move forward. . . . Where in the world did this conversation start, darling?'

'With Don's instability,' I said. 'And, by the way, if he was unstable before, he's probably a good deal more unstable now when I remember some of the things I said to him tonight.'

'What *did* you say, my sweet?'

'I'm rather ashamed of most of it, but he made me extremely angry, Sashie.'

'Darling! You sound just like a governess who has found something prickly in her bed! *Do* go on!'

'I called him a cheapjack bagman peddling spurious emotion and a few other odds and ends like that.'

'What a *time* you must have had! I do wish I'd got here earlier!'

'It's neither funny nor pleasant, really, Sashie.'

'My sweet, don't worry – quite the reverse. I regard it as a picking of Don off his panic-swayed branch by the seat of his over-ambitious little trousers. It will do him all the good in the world.' He rose and set his glass aside. 'I am really going this time. I can only apologize for the fact that Don and I have been something of a nuisance. . . . There is one more thing I want to say – you won't mind?'

'Of course not. What?'

'This – this nonsense won't cause a drama of any sort between you and Twice?'

'Not a chance,' I told him. 'If it did, would it worry you?'

'Oddly enough, it would. I have a great regard for Twice. I should simply hate anything to go wrong for him. And he has been worried about this business of Don and you.'

'Oh, rot! There has *been* no business of Don and me.'

'Darling, don't go *on* being stupid! That Don has been rushing you has been obvious to all of us since the day you landed at the airport.'

'Oh, don't start that again!'

'You are quite right – I won't. We won't worry about things any more at this stage. There would be no point. Just you make it all right for Twice and tell him, by the way, that I would not have stayed so late and have compromised you like this if Don hadn't made such hay of my mechanical arrangements. . . . I don't mind Twice knowing about them. If they should need oiling or anything at any time, I am sure he would come along quietly and do it discreetly with a small plain can.'

'Sashie, you really are very, very nice.'

'I like you too, darling, but forgive me for liking Twice even better. And nothing peculiar about it – quite the reverse. He is so very intelligent and so modest withal.' He picked up his obscene balloon. 'This is really the absolute end, isn't it? It was that woman from Chicago who sent them to me – *three* of them, my dear! How *does* one get into the position of being sent balloons?'

I began to laugh. 'Don't ask *me*! Life just sends me one balloon after another and I've never known why.'

'The essential thing,' Sashie said solemnly, 'is to keep one's feet on the ground and anchor the beastly things.' He flipped me on the cheek with one of the protuberances. 'Goodnight, my sweet. Don't worry about a thing. Don and I will turn up for rehearsals as usual.'

He went tripping down the steps into the car. There was a negro driver asleep at the wheel. Only then did I realize that I had never seen Sashie drive a car, swim or wear anything other than his gaily-coloured slacks and I had never realized either that I had never seen him dance. As I walked upstairs, I found myself imagining myself in the witness-box after a murder had been committed at the Peak.

'Remember that you are on oath. Where was Sasha de Marnay at the moment you heard the shot?'

'He was dancing with Miranda Beaumont.'

I felt that I would have given an answer like this on oath, in the conviction that it was true. I had thought that I had seen Sashie dancing so many times.

Chapter Eight

TWICE ARRIVED home in the middle of the following fore-noon and when I heard him shouting to Clorinda for beer, I left my sewing and ran on to the verandah.

'I'm drier than a wooden god!' he greeted me. 'Cripes, what a morning!'

'What happened? Did you get the turbine here all right?'

'Yes, but I'll never be the same again. . . . Thanks, Clorinda. Bring a bottle for the Missis and another one for me. . . . These negroes give me the willies – how half of them weren't either killed or drowned this morning I don't know. Life and limb are held very cheap in this island. I've never seen so much all hell and no notion in my life. That's better.' He finished the first bottle of beer and began to open the second. 'And how are *you*? Anything been doing?'

He was standing, legs astride, in mid-floor with the glass of beer in his hand, looking at me. There are certain moments that fix themselves in the mind, clear-cut and in every detail. His face, tanned by the sun, had the reddish dust from the gorge road sticking in the sweat in every groove, his eyes glittered brilliant blue and his teeth brilliant white as he grinned at me, and his shirt was sticking to the sweat on his chest and shoulders.

'A pretty trick you perpetrated last night,' I said.

'No trick at all, anywhere, my pet. All strictly above board and on top of the table.'

'You made me feel a bit of a fool, Twice, when Sashie came in and repeated what you had said.'

'You'd *been* a bit of a fool, hadn't you? No sense in being one if you don't feel it.'

I sat down and said: 'No. I suppose not. Logical, aren't you? I didn't *mean* to play the fool, Twice.'

'I realize that. People usually don't.'

'You don't feel you might have mentioned to me, sort of, that Don was thinking along those lines?'

'I've tried to mention it, sort of, several times along these last eight months or so, but you never seemed to take it in. . . . I did a fair amount of thinking too, last night, when I discovered that the Coyote had left the hotel as soon as I arrived.'

'So you decided to send Sashie?'

'It was that or come myself. You still don't seem to have a full grasp of the situation. If I had come myself, I'd probably have throttled him. I know he's a fair size and well put together, but he hasn't my weight and, if you don't mind my saying so, my sort of temper or, and this is vulgar, my feeling of possession.'

'Twice, I've been worrying you – making you unhappy?'

'I have been worried and a little unhappy at times, but I know you didn't intend that. If I'd thought you did, I'd have come here myself last night. As things were, I thought Sashie would get you out with more dignity and tact. I confess to getting the wind up about eleven-thirty – I began to think that Sashie must be pressing *his* attentions on you next. On the whole, last night wasn't much of an evening.' He suddenly sat down.

'Flash, could I have a sandwich or something? I feel sort of light-headed.'

'You didn't have any breakfast, of course?'

'Not much.'

'And no dinner last night? Just stay there and don't move.'

I went to the kitchen and came back. 'Coffee and sandwiches in a minute,' I told him. 'Twice Alexander, you are a bloody fool. I may be an ordinary one, but you are a really bloody one. And if I had Don Candlesham here I'd kick him in the teeth, just for good measure.'

'Poor devil, I feel sorry for him now.' Clorinda brought the sandwiches and he fell upon them. 'The smugness of being on the winning side. . . . At this time yesterday, I was wondering whether to emplane for home and leave him the field.'

'Twice, don't be ridiculous! It's disgusting to say a thing like that and it's utterly without reason! You must be off your head and having delusions or something.'

'Iphm – I and half the island! We've *all* got delusions! My treasured idiot, don't you realize that *every*body knew about Don and you?'

'But, dammit, there wasn't anything to *know*! I don't think I've ever been *alone* with Don until last night! Certainly nothing has ever – ever *happened* between us. Besides, look at all the other women he's been jumping in and out of bed with like a hopping dick! What *is* this about people thinking that *I* am involved?'

'God give me patience!' said Twice. 'Listen, the thing Don had for you stuck out all over him like a system of neon lights! It filled the patio down at the Peak like an electric charge – it filled the Club that night of the dance to bursting point! You'd get to dancing, the two of you, and I tell you it was practically unbearable. And *think* of him, his looks and so on – people couldn't believe you could resist him. Besides, they didn't *want* to believe it.'

'And *you* – what did you believe?'

'I used to sit there with my head going round. I know you fairly well, Flash, and I knew that if you were going to bed with Don while I was out at work — '

'Twice Alexander! Do you want me to slap you?'

'Slap away! I don't give a damn!'

'Oh, shut up! Let's forget the whole stupid thing! – Are you feeling better now you've eaten something?'

'I'm fine. I was just hollow. . . . And we are not going to

forget the whole thing and there's no good you blowing your top and taking a swipe at me either. You just sit down and listen to me – what I was saying was that I knew that if you and Don were having a carry-on, you wouldn't carry on with *me* at the same time. . . . Sit still and don't interrupt. . . . You just aren't *made* that way, as Rose would say. . . . I have to confess that a lot of the fun and games that took place in the Peak's Number One love-nest under a tropic moon began because a bloke had the need to reassure himself.' He grinned at me. 'All I can say is that he was invariably amply reassured.'

'It's all dreadful. You should have *told* me in plain words what an ass I was being and how people were talking and everything. It's – it's terrible! Twice, why didn't you *say* something?'

'I was scared. That's the honest truth. I began to be scared that if I said anything, woke you up as it were, you would start to think that Candlesham was preferable to me after all.'

'Twice!'

'It's the Gawd's truth. I could have burst with joy the day Marion packed up you and your sunburn and brought us out here.'

'I suppose she knew all about all this too?'

'Undoubtedly.'

'Twice, what am I going to do? I feel I can't look any of them in the face and I'm mortally ashamed of myself.'

'So well you might be,' he said smugly.

I glared at him. 'You needn't take up that holier-than-thou attitude, Twice Alexander! I don't think *your* part in all this is all that admirable. In fact, I think you've behaved disgracefully. I am disgusted that you should have thought that I could be involved with Don Candlesham. You know perfectly well that I have no time for substitutes and synthetics – why should you get to thinking that I would involve myself in a plastic love affair?' Twice began to laugh uproariously. 'What the devil is there to laugh at?'

'Plastic love affair! I wish poor Don could hear you!'

'Oh, I told him last night it was plastic.'

'Flash!' He stared at me. 'What *did* happen here last night?'

'What d'you mean? Nothing much happened. Don rolled in here full of darksome drama and plastic passion and started giving me a line of bull about how here we were alone at last and I got in a bit of temper and told him some of what I thought of him and then Sashie came in and he went away. What did you *expect* to happen?'

'Look, don't you get mad at *me* next! *I* haven't done anything. I consider that I've been extremely patient and circumspect about the whole thing. Instead of coming up here myself as I had every right to do — '

'That would only have been another dollop of plastic — '

'You be quiet! The point you won't see is that nothing was plastic except to *you* and — '

'It wasn't *any*thing to *me* – not even plastic — '

'Don't keep on saying *plastic* like that — '

'*Who*'s keeping on saying plastic?'

'Who *first* said plastic?' Twice bellowed.

'Look,' I said, 'you keep on telling me that I'm forty. I am only six weeks older than you – *you* are forty too. What are you bellowing about?'

'I'm not bellowing *about* anything – I'm just bellowing on principle, psychological principle. It is what the psychologists call release of tension and — '

'Psychology my hind leg! Sandy Maclean is quite right – there is far too much psychology around here among people who have no right to have any at all. Look at Sashie! Now, he's got some *right* to be psychological and he's about the sanest person in these parts!'

'What do you mean – *sane*?'

I then realized that Twice did not know of Sashie's disability and the telling took a little time but also induced some measure of calm in both of us.

'And that's an odd thing,' Twice said at last. 'When we first met Sashie, my instinct was to run a mile from him, but I found myself getting to like the little blighter and I couldn't think why. That's why I asked him to come up here last night. I couldn't have asked anyone else to do it. But I felt he really knew Don and – well, I *like* him, Sashie, I mean.'

'That's nice,' I said. 'He likes you too. In fact, everybody just adores everybody while I am being ground to powder to make a psychological holiday.'

'Powder your hind leg, in your own inelegant phrase. You are sticking up in the middle of this here Caribbean like a hunk of the original Reachfar rock – palaeolithic, or whatever it is.'

'It's Archaean – the earliest geological period,' I told him, 'and right now I feel like a dollop of lava erupted only this morning and not set yet. Sashie said last night that all these people like Don and Isobel Denholm are suffering from instability. No

128

wonder. The way they carry on is enough to make a pyramid feel unstable.'

'Talking of that, that young Denholm was pretty unstable down at the Peak last night. He was as tight as a tick, as a matter of fact. He's an unpleasant sort of youth.'

'What happened?'

'Oh, nothing really. Miss Poynter came and took him and the girl away.'

'Was the girl tight too?'

'Oh, no. She was all right and she can handle her brother. Flash, I feel sorry for that girl.'

I was not pleased at this. 'Why? I don't see much about her to pity. To be completely candid, as they say, I think she's a wicked, degenerate little bitch.'

'You may be right, but I still feel sorry for her. She's awfully young to be so far off the rails. Or am I merely being old-fashioned?'

'I wouldn't know. What I do know is that as far as Isobel Denholm is concerned, I am not my sister's keeper. She has no use for me and I have slightly less for her. . . . Shall we have lunch?'

'I'd like a bath first. . . . Listen, Flash, don't take up a cussed attitude about that Denholm girl. I know you feel that she dislikes you, but remember she probably thinks as everyone else does about you and Candlesham.'

'Oh, dear Heaven!'

'Exactly. The girl is probably jealous. You can hardly blame her, can you?'

'I'm finding it very hard not to blame the whole boiling lot of you,' I said. 'Twice, I suppose you believe me when I say there was nothing in it? Don and me, I mean?'

Twice rose. '*I* believe you, my pet, but thousands never will.'

'If *you* believe me, the thousands won't matter. . . . As for Isobel Denholm, I'll try to keep an open mind, but I don't imagine we'll ever be bosom friends. . . . Go and have your bath.'

After lunch, when Twice had gone back to the factory, I sat down with my sewing and tried to collect my wits, going back over every incident between Don and myself in an attempt to rationalize what had happened the night before. In the end, I had to admit that since Twice and I arrived at the Peak in April, the sun must have been blinding my mental eyes. There was no doubt about it – I had made a complete and very undignified fool of myself, but I felt in a vague, self-pitying way that I was not entirely to blame. I had a sense of having been victimized.

I was even more pleased than usual when Twice came home that afternoon, for I had had enough of my own thoughts in the dim shade of the verandah which was like a feeble fortress set at defiance to the menacing glare outside.

'Still at the sewing?' he asked.

'Iphm.' I shook out Sandy's frilly skirt. 'Nearly finished now, though.'

'You've put the hell of a lot of hard work into this thing, Flash.'

'So has everybody,' I said. 'One wouldn't mind that, if everything will be all right.'

'We can only do our best with it. After all, if it's a hopeless flop, it will be a bit humiliating but not a major tragedy.'

'That's true, I suppose.' I sighed drearily as Clorinda brought the tea-tray.

When she had gone back into the house, Twice frowned at me and said: 'Flash, you're not worrying over this absurd business of Don Candlesham?'

'One feels a little cheap and nasty and stupid,' I said as I poured the tea.

'Don't give it that much importance, my pet. It was all a flash in the pan and it'll be forgotten in a week by Don and everybody else.'

'That's where the nastiness comes in. I don't like flashes in pans and sudden lurid things and so on,' I told him. 'It makes me feel like one of these gaudy hibiscus flowers over there, flaunting myself for a little garish day but so impermanent that I might as well never have lived at all. It's very bad for one's self-esteem and morale generally.' Twice laughed and I went on: 'All right, laugh away! I know I've made a fool of myself, but I have a feeling of unfairness about it all, that it isn't entirely my fault, and I hate that feeling more than anything. These cock-eyed tropics have a lot to do with it and it is frightening to feel that one's temperament and mentality are being affected by a climate as mine seem to have been. It is like being inhabited by a foreign spirit and one gets the feeling that everyone else may be inhabited by foreign spirits too, so that the normal rules don't apply. Then there's this confounded place – this place is what Loose and Daze' – Lucy and Daisy were the joint caretakers of our home in Scotland – 'would call not feasible. And the people aren't feasible either. When I try to describe them in my letters home, I just know that

Dad and George and Tom are not going to believe me. *Nobody* would believe in Sir Ian and the things he does unless they could see him and they would hardly believe in him even then. He is as unbelievable as that big cabbage I grew in the garden and cut it and we ate it and then the stem upped and grew another *two* great big cabbages. Who in any sensible, feasible country would believe a thing like that?'

'You don't have to bawl at *me* in indignation as if it were *my* fault!' Twice protested. 'It was *you* who got George to send you the seeds and planted the ruddy cabbages!'

'Well, I only wanted to find out if they'd grow!'

'Well, now you know they would! And how! . . . Actually, that's what Sir Ian is – he is about the eighth blooming of an imported cabbage on the parent stem – no wonder he's sort of hydra-headed and not feasible when you think of it, from the point of view of an Ordinary cabbage-observer at home.'

'The truth of the matter is that out here in St Jago I am out of my place and on Paradise I am out of my time,' I said. 'I am not used to a place where it is always high summer and I belong to the twentieth century, not to feudal times. *You* are all right. You've got the factory – a modern industrial plant, a thing that your brain and hands are used to, a part of your own real world. I've got nothing like that. I am right out of my context – even the food I have to order from the shops is different, the very way I do my hair is different to get it off the back of my neck because of the heat. . . . You mustn't get mad at me for losing my bearings at times.'

'Lord, I'm not mad at you! . . . You're not homesick though?'

'Gracious, no! I've never been homesick in my life. Reachfar is always there in the background. So is Crookmill. But I am not a poor exile weeping for my native glen — '

'Or "Granny's Heilan' Hame"?'

'Yah! None of that slush! . . . But, mind you, I don't trust this island?'

'What do you mean by trust?' Twice asked.

'It's a silly word and not what I mean at all. What I mean is awfully difficult to *put* into words. But at home, at Reachfar, a certain kind of cloud means wind to follow and when the wind goes into the east it gets cold. Here, it's quite different.'

Twice stared at me. 'You are *not* as stupid as that sounds! Of *course*, it's different here!'

'It's *too* different here. Here, for all I know, that cloud over there on the horizon might mean that the hens will lay blue eggs tomorrow and if the wind goes to the east Clorinda might develop a trunk like an elephant and start jumping like a kangaroo. *Any*thing can happen here. I just don't trust it.'

'You've got a touch of the sun,' Twice scoffed.

'Oh, no, I haven't! But I'll tell you a thing, as Sandy would say, and it's as true as my name's Janet Alexander. *All* the white people who have been here for any length of time have a touch of this island and there's no telling what they'll do next. I tell you, I don't trust a manjack of them!'

In the middle of the following forenoon, I was sewing on the verandah again when the Rolls drove up and Sir Ian stumped up the steps and sat himself down opposite me in a vaguely threatening way.

'Good mornin',' he said.

'Good morning. Where's Sandy?'

'Missis Marion's got her foot down. Says he's runnin' about loose too much, so he's in his room doin' maths. Just spite, really, because o' the suckin' pigs for the play supper bein' too big, but that's not what I came about. . . . Here, what about these young Denholms?'

I stared at him. 'Well, *what* about them?'

'I've just been down to the Bay – went down to see about a consignment o' rum. Hot down on the wharves so I went up to the Peak for a beer – was talkin' to Maud. Fine woman, old Maud, in spite o' her looks – got guts an' sense. Maud's worried about these young Denholms.'

'What are they to do with Miss Poynter?' I asked.

'They're her *relations*, dammit!'

'Relations? I didn't know that.'

'What? Don't be stoopid! Beattie Denholm was Beattie Poynter. She an' Maud are cousins. An' Maud says these youngsters are headin' for trouble an' was askin' me what to do about it, so I thought I'd see what *you* thought.'

'Why me?' I said. 'Surely if Mrs Denholm is Miss Poynter's cousin, the sensible thing would be to go to Mrs Denholm and tell here — '

'Don't be stoopid!' he bellowed at me. 'The Poynters o' the Peak an' the Poynters o' Blueclear haven't spoken to one another since old Gulliver's time!'

'Who was old Gulliver?' I asked from a purely academic point of view.

132

'Their great-grandfather.'

'Whose?'

'Beattie's an' Maud's, of course! He left the Peak to Maud's grandfather an' Blueclear to Beattie's grandfather, so they had a row an' never spoke again. Wouldn't even go to each other's funeral. I don't suppose Beattie will go to Maud's funeral either. . . . Maud'd go to Beattie's, though – Maud's got sense.'

'She'll probably get a chance to demonstrate it,' I said. 'Miss Poynter is a good bit younger than Mrs Denholm.'

'Can't depend on a thing like that, especially with the Poynters. Never know what they'll do. But that's not what we're talkin' about. Thing we're talkin' about is this young fellah drinkin' too much an' creatin' a scandal round the Peak an' somebody has to stop him.'

'Mrs Denholm is the obvious person,' I said.

'Now listen,' Sir Ian told me severely, 'there is not a bit o' good you goin' on like that. Nobody can do anything with Beattie Denholm – not even Mother. *You* just don't seem to under*stand*!' He frowned at me as if I were an idiot who could not take in the most elementary fact no matter how lucidly it was explained to me. He then began to speak with a pause after each word. 'Beattie – Denholm – does – not – believe – that – there – can – be – anything – wrong – with – any – Poynter – o' – Blueclear – or – any – Denholm – of – Mount – Melody!' And then he went to the other extreme, rushing the words out as if they were all joined together. 'Beattie-believes-they-are-all-perfect-an'-can-do-what-they-like-where-they-like-as-long-as-they-don't-annoy-HER-or-cross-HER-in-any-way!'

'Then she's demented,' I said and calmly folded up my sewing as if I were folding up Mrs Denholm too.

'*Certainly* she's demented!' he shouted, stopping me in mid-fold. 'Beattie has always been demented! So have all the Blueclear Poynters – that's why they're like that about funerals an' not speakin' to their brothers! Good God, *every*body knows Beattie's dotty!'

'*I* didn't,' I told him.

'Then *you're* dotty too!' he said impatiently. 'Oh, I don't mean that Beattie needs a strait-jacket or a padded cell an' she doesn't think she's Napoleon or that, but she damn' nearly thinks she's a kind of empress. Very interestin' talk I had with Maud this mornin'. . . . Got any cold beer in your ice-box?'

As I went to call Clorinda to bring some beer, it was borne in on my slow intelligence that I was not really required by Sir Ian to do anything about the Denholms or, indeed, about anything. What I was required to do was listen. Marion had deprived him of his companion Sandy; she had apparently indicated that she was too busy with sucking pigs to listen to him herself and these facts left me next in line, as it were, as Sir Ian's audience until lunchtime. When Clorinda came with the beer, therefore, I laid aside my sewing, filled the glasses, lit a cigarette and prepared to give him my full attention. 'That's better,' he said appreciatively. 'Fiddlin' about with that damned sewin'. . . . A very interestin' woman, Maud, woman o' the world, been on the stage an' everythin' an' she's very upset about these youngsters goin' on like this. She feels responsible.'

'But why?'

'Well, dammit – oh, of course, you wouldn't know. Didn't know myself till this mornin'. . . . It seems that when Maud was young an' on the stage she went to Philadelphia, actin' in some play, an' one night she an' some o' her friends – chorus girls, ye know – went out to supper with some fellahs an' dammit if one o' them wasn't young Toby Denholm – Beattie's son, ye know. It seems that by this time Beattie was the social queen o' Philadelphia – an uncle o' hers was a banker up there an' left Beattie everything – didn't know that till this mornin' either – an' young Toby was always under her thumb. Same thing before they left here – Mother'll tell you that. Anyway, Maud got workin' on Toby an' told him he should stand on his own feet an' never mind Beattie an' her bullyin' an' the upshot of it was that Toby goes off an' marries one o' these chorus girls!'

'No!' I said with genuine gossipy delight. 'Golly! What *did* Ma Denholm say?'

'That's just the point. Accordin' to Maud, Beattie played the devil – she *would*, too – but by this time the chorus girl was pregnant an' give Toby his due, he stuck to his guns. These youngsters – they're twins, by the way – were born, but of course Beattie had all the money. In the end, Toby took to the bottle an' the chorus girl cleared out, leavin' the youngsters an' everything.'

'Poor little devils!' I said.

'Toby got a divorce, Maud says, but he never came to anythin'. Drank himself to death, she says, about five years ago. Shockin' business. An' of course the youngsters have been under Beattie's thumb ever since.'

'Does Miss Poynter know where the mother is now?'

134

'What mother?'

'The chorus girl.'

'Certainly Maud knows! Ain't that just what I'm tellin' you?'

'Then *where* is she?'

'Dead,' said Sir Ian and glared at me. 'That's just the whole *point*! She's dead an' these youngsters are orphans that have got nobody but old Beattie an' Beattie's dotty an' somebody should *do* somethin'!'

'Now, look here, Sir Ian,' I said firmly, 'it's no use you sitting there and saying Mrs Denholm is dotty like that. There are laws about that sort of thing. People are either certifiably mad or else they must be reckoned sane and that's that. The question is, is Mrs Denholm certifiable or not?'

'Don't be stoopid! Beattie's far too damned cunnin' to go gettin' herself certified! But that don't mean she ain't dotty. Oh, I know *you* think that half of us here in this island are dotty, but that's only because we're a little *different* from you an' Twice an' you ain't used to us yet an' then these other characters like Sashie an' that fellah Beaumont down at the Peak comin' in to cater for these tourists are complicatin' things an' muddlin' you still more. It's only an *impression* o' dottiness you get about us because we're all strange to you. Don't blame you. I get a dotty feelin' myself sometimes when I go down there to the Peak. But Beattie's quite a different thing. There's a streak o' real lunacy in these Blueclear Poynters. One o' Beattie's brothers used to dance about stark naked through the night at the full moon – danced into the river an' drowned himself in the end, poor fellah. Thought he could dance on the water, ye know. Now, when a fellah gets to thinkin' like that, that's real lunacy.' He stared at me and I stared back at him. 'Why don't ye *say* somethin'?' he barked.

'Has Mrs Denholm taken to dancing stark naked on the Rio d'Oro?' I enquired brightly.

He sighed patiently. 'Didn't I tell you that Beattie is too damned cunnin' to do anythin' she could be shut up for?' he asked. 'No.' His voice became grave. 'But she's up to somethin' just as dotty although she can't be certified for it.'

'What?'

'She's tryin' to buy back Blueclear an' the Peak an' she's been in touch with our lawyers about Riverhead as well.'

'But what for? What does she want with all that land?'

'So she can die an' leave it all to David Poynter-Denholm an' then he'll be the biggest land-owner in St Jago.'

'I don't believe it!' I said.

'Maud swears it's the truth – the girl Isobel told her. An' it's true enough about Riverhead – saw the letter meself. She refers to it as part o' the ancestral lands o' the Denholms. Beattie's dotty, all right – no question about it. I'm sorry for these youngsters, Missis Janet.'

'So am I, Sir Ian, but at the same time I haven't much patience with them. To be honest, I don't like either of them. The girl is an ill-behaved little brat in my opinion and the boy is just plain unpleasant and if they are as miserable with their grandmother as the girl seemed to indicate to Miss Poynter, why don't they clear out? Plenty of youngsters are on their own at that age – they're around twenty – I was on my own at twenty-one and so was Twice.'

Sir Ian shook his head slowly from side to side. 'It's a far cry from you an' Twice to these youngsters.'

'In what way?'

'Your fathers didn't die o' drink, your mothers weren't chorus girls an' your grandmothers weren't Blueclear Poynters. Don't be stoopid! Compared with you an' Twice, these youngsters ain't had a dog's chance!' He set down his beer-glass and rose to his feet to stand looking down at me. 'I don't like to see youngsters in trouble,' he said. 'Now, you've got an eye for noticin' what's goin' on – don't tell me you haven't! If you see anythin' that makes you think of a way I can help them, you let me know. See what I mean? The youngsters are Denholms, after all, an' the Denholms have been our neighbours for centuries an' old Toby wouldn't have liked his grandson makin' an ass of himself. . . . Twice ain't back yet? Must be nearly lunchtime. Don't know what's wrong with everybody around here – all workin' as if there wasn't another day tomorrow. All too busy to take an interest in anythin' that's goin' on. Oh, well, ye'd better get back to your sewin'. See you at the rehearsal tonight.' He strode down the steps. 'Campbell! Wake up, ye lazy rascal! Bring the car over!'

As the Rolls slid down the driveway, Twice came along to the gateway and stopped to let the big car pass through, and while he had his glass of beer and his lunch I reported Sir Ian's conversation to him.

'I don't much like the bit about Mrs Denholm's brother who thought he could dance on the water,' Twice said thoughtfully when I had finished. 'It makes me feel you were right after all.'

'I? When? What about?'

'All the times you have said there was something queer about the Denholms. I ought to have known you were right – you have an infallible instinct for that sort of thing, a touch of your grandmother's Sight, almost.' He frowned. 'I've never really had any contact with that old Denholm woman except for that first day they landed and we all had lunch at the Peak. I didn't much take to her, but that was only because I thought she was a snobbish, arrogant old cow - it didn't occur to me that there was anything more than that, but now you tell me of brothers who thought they could dance on the river, that's different. I wouldn't be at all surprised if that old dame thought she could dance on you, me and all St Jago if she took the notion.'

'Look here, Twice,' I said, 'let's you and I keep our feet on the ground, shall we? An awful lot of what goes on and what gets said here in this island is really a trick of the light – it tends to make everything sort of lurid.'

'You have to remember that the climate tends to make people behave in a way that's sort of lurid too,' Twice argued. 'Not that there's anything one can do about it that I can see. I don't see how we can stop old Madam Mount Melody trying to buy back the ancestral acres or her grandson from getting mortal tight at the Peak or her grand-daughter from sleeping with half the island if that's what they want to do.'

'No, but it *is* a pity about the young people, as Sir Ian says.'

It was all very unsettling and unsatisfactory and, when lunch was over and Twice went back to work and the sultry heat of the afternoon intensified, I sat on the verandah with my sewing, conscious of what I can only call a blight of doom over me and the garden and everything. This made me call to my aid that rheumy-eyed old man, Reason, but he is of little avail in these tropical islands which try the flesh to the degree that the minds tends to become submerged and poor old Reason has no breathing space.

Pamphlets in travel agencies have pretty pictures of palm trees and blue seas and prate of tropical paradises. I have never been to Tahiti or Honolulu which are famous in this connection, but it will take a great deal to convince me that they are serpentless paradises any more than are the islands of the Caribbean. It is true that, quite often, the sun shines all day, but it can be hot enough to burn you. It is also true that the sun sinks into the ocean about six-thirty in the evening, but at that time the mosquitoes come out and may eat you alive. It is also true that when the sun is up you can go bathing in the cool, limpid sea, but every time I did that the sand-flies were waiting for me as I crossed the beach, apparently not having had a meal for weeks. I think it is a hard fact that has to be accepted that there is no Heaven here on earth. And the heat, mosquitoes and sandflies were the least of the hell at Paradise, St Jago, for the people I knew seemed to be inspired by the devil himself to render all unreal to me and blow Reason away, his long grey whiskers flapping like tatters in the frolic wind.

Twice and I, that evening, had just had our baths and were ready to go round to the Great House for the rehearsal when Sashie and Don arrived at Guinea Corner. All day, I had been busily ignoring the thought of meeting Don again after the scene between us and had hoped that our common embarrassment would be submerged in the crowd and fuss of the rehearsal. It was Sashie, apparently, who had other ideas and he cavorted into our house in his most devilish mood before I had time to run for cover.

'Fol-de-rol and fol-de-riddle!' he carolled, tapping Twice on the head with his dreadful balloon. 'A pox upon thy hairy pate that takes all the bounce out of my bauble!'

'Holy cow!' Twice said. 'Where did you get that obscene-looking thing?'

'From America, my dear! Gadzooks and by my cod-piece, what a country!' He flipped the sausage-like protuberances one by one. 'One for the master and one for the dame and one for the little boy that lives down the lane! A totally universal bauble. Isn't it extraordinary? . . . Twice, darling, *could* you make me a little thingummy of some sort for blowing it up? At the moment I am dependent on the vegetable boy's bicycle pump – *so* undignified.'

'Ass,' said Twice.

Sashie looked round at us all, his head on one side, and sighed. 'Don, dear, I have now brought you to the water – do, *do* take your eensy-teensy little drink of humble thing and have done with it. . . . I cannot carry this conversation single-handed indefinitely.'

'Take no notice of *him*,' Don said solemnly. 'The thing is, I ought to apologize about the other night, but I don't quite know how — ' He paused.

' — actually,' Twice finished for him and grinned.

'You could hit him if you liked, Twice, dear,' Sashie offered.

'You shut up!' said Don. 'Actually, I got in a bit of a muddle one way and another and, well, there it is. I'm sorry.'

'And he won't do it ever, ever again', said Sashie.

'And I won't do it ever, ever. . . . Will you SHUT UP?' Don shouted.

'Listen,' Twice said, 'are you two two people or only one?'

'Twice, darling, you are the most intelligent thing! We are only one – *he* is the body and the uglier lusts and I am the brain!'

'You are the — '

'Don! *Not* before the lady – quite the reverse. I'll report you to Sir Ian!'

I began to laugh because it was impossible to do anything else with any conviction and Twice was already grinning. In their absurd world, it seemed in that moment, this extraordinary friendship of theirs was the only reality and I felt that Twice was sharing my thought when he said: 'You two must have been as much trouble to the Japs as Hiroshima.'

'We did our best in our subtle way,' said Sashie. '*Actually*, if I may coin a word, we *always* do our best – we merely make a little error of judgment here and there. . . . And now that everything is settled, Twice, darling, may I come in your motoring car to the varleting and jousting that your wife may ride with her paramour, you old cuckold, you?'

'Sashie!' said Don. 'Honest to God — '

'Stand forth, knave!' said Sashie, flipped Don on the face with the balloon and skipped out to the car.

'I really *am* very sorry about everything,' Don said as we drove along.

'Forget it, Don,' I told him. 'I gather that I am not entirely without blame. I am very sorry. I didn't realize how badly I was behaving. I'm pretty dumb, you know.'

'It wasn't particularly noticeable the other night. You were quite voluble.'

'I am, about some things.'

'Apparently I hit the jackpot.'

'Oh, well, let it be a lesson to you and don't harbour any hard feelings.'

'Oh, nothing like that,' he assured me airily. 'But all badinage aside, I frankly find you a most attractive party actually and don't understand the whole set-up in the least.'

'*What* set-up?' I asked with a rush of irritation.

'This marriage between Twice and you. I mean, you *are* still in love with him?'

'Yes. I am.'

'Extraordinary!'

'What's extraordinary about it?'

He slowed the car to a foot pace as we approached the gates of the Great House. 'It just *is*,' he said. 'It's simply extraordinary for a woman of your age to be still in love with the man she's married to. I suppose it's true that you're forty? Most women of forty would be quite interested in a little flutter.'

I was now growing very angry. 'Then I am unlike most women of forty! And I'll tell you something else, Don. I find this conversation rather disgusting. I find *you* rather disgusting, to be completely frank. I am always disgusted by spiritual squalor and mental untidiness and you and your kind in this island are far too full of both. . . . Can this jalopy go any faster?'

'What is meant by mental untidiness and sp— '

'I mean just what I say. Your mind makes me think of a bedroom with soiled wallpaper, a dirty floor, hair-brushes with hair in them, the bed rumpled and the slops unemptied. You want to clean it out, get the painters in and then impose some sort of discipline on yourself and stick to it.'

'Do you really mean that? Or are you just being a bitch for some obscure reason?'

'I *have* no obscure reasons. If I sound like a bitch, it is because I *am* a bitch by your standards, just as your philosophy is a squalid mess by my standards. I think your mind needs licking into shape and washing down with disinfectant.'

'I ought to be furious with you, but I'm not because I believe you really mean it,' he said patronisingly.

'Of course I mean it! And for Pete's sake, put your foot on that accelerator – they'll all be waiting for us!'

'Let them wait!' he said and stopped the car altogether under a tree in the driveway.

I opened the door on my side and swung my foot to the gravel. 'This is exactly what I mean, Don,' I said, 'about you and all the people like you. You are unreliable, undependable, have no discipline and no coherence and you don't matter one damn! I'll *walk* the rest of the way!'

'Pick your bloody foot up!' he said, starting the car again. 'I'll *drive* you to the pettifogging play?'

I slammed the door and the car moved at speed up the drive. 'And stop glowering like a spoilt child!' I told him. 'If you weren't so physically overgrown on your mental age I'd turn you up and smack your behind!'

'Shut up!'

'I won't shut up! I'd like to take you and those two Denholms and several other people around here and crack all your heads together and bash some sense into you. The whole boiling lot of you are a disgrace to the human race!'

He pulled the car up with a jerk in a shower of gravel at the Great House side door. 'Gerrout!' he growled.

'What happened?' Twice asked as he and Sashie came over. 'We thought you were right behind us!'

'Darlings!' said Sashie. 'You *haven't* been quarrelling again?'

'It's still the same quarrel!' I snapped. 'And just you hold your tongue, Sashie de Marnay! It doesn't do any good you flipping around being lightsome with that bloody balloon. Everybody around here is far too busy being lightsome and frolicsome and — '

'Now, then, Flash,' Twice broke in, 'no good letting the old temper get — '

'You be quiet about my temper, Twice Alexander! Me and my temper are about the only two real, honest-to-God things that are left around here among all the varletry and nonsense that's going on and I'll get in a temper if I darn well please!' I slewed round on the car seat and glared at Don. 'And you just once more turn up bits of me and my private life and pick them over as if they were rubbish on a junk-stall and I'll slap your pretty face for you! I have never been mixed up with so much rank, indecent, obscene lack of dignity in my life before and I'm not going to have it! If you want to live like a pig, fornicating around, stay among your own sort and wallow away – don't come clarting around *me* with your rotten stinking psychological messes and muddles!'

'By Jove!' said the voice of Sir Ian, 'I ought to take Missis Janet with me to the next Parish Council meetin'! Somethin' like that is just what the perishers need. But what's it all about, hey? Tell me that!'

'*I'll* tell you what it's about!' I said. 'It's about me being sick and tired of a whole lot of people tearing round in circles not knowing where they're going – that's what it's about!'

'Flash, behave yourself!' said Twice.

'I *am* behaving myself! But *some*body's got to say something; *some*body's got to – got to — '

'Put their foot down?' Sandy suggested with a twang from his guitar.

'That's it!' I said and turned back to Don. 'That's it! I've put my foot down – both my feet – and let's have no more of this damned nonsense!' I got out of the car and shook myself. 'Where's my script? Let's get on with this confounded rehearsal!'

Sir Ian stuck his head into the car. 'I don't know what happened, but Missis Janet is quite right! There's far too much nonsense goin' on! Time we had a bit of discipline around here!' He withdrew his head and with a furious roar Don drove his car away to park it in the garage yard. 'Denholm!' bellowed Sir Ian. 'Denholm! Has anybody seen that perisher? Is he sober? Oh, there you are, Denholm! Now, listen to me! Don't go haulin' at that pony's head tonight as if it was a mule you were ridin'!'

The rehearsal began and it is probably superfluous to mention that it could not have gone worse had the devil and all his minions been present in person to do their worst to it. We all went home with tempers considerably worse than they had been when we came out.

Chapter Nine

THREE EVENINGS a week thereafter, the rehearsals went on apace and Twice began to admit in strict privacy that the performance was beginning to take something like shape and coherence. Somehow, the costumes were all completed and handed out to their wearers to take home for final adjustments. The curtains and draperies for the 'banqueting hall' in the Great House porch were hung, the effect admired by all, and when Edward Dulac arrived from England he had to enter his ancestral home by the garden entrance through the library. But I am getting ahead of events, for Edward did not arrive until the twenty-first of December and it was at the first dress rehearsal a week before his arrival that the blow fell. When the Mount Melody car arrived, out of it did *not* step, as we expected, Red Gurk and one of his pages. Out of it did step a negro driver with a note addressed to me which said: 'Dear Mrs Alexander, My brother and I are sorry that we cannot take part in the play after all. Our costumes are in the car. Yours, Isobel Denholm.'

To say that bedlam broke loose would be an understatement,

but eventually the noise, which was like the Roman citizenry clamouring for Caesar's will combined with a Glasgow football crowd's roar for the death of the referee, with overnotes from young Mackie who happened to be tuning his pipes at the time, resolved itself into the voice of Sir Ian bellowing:

'I *told* you this would happen when you picked that little runt for Red Gurk! Regicides – the whole bloody lot of 'em! Well, what are you goin' to do? Don't just *stand* there hangin' about, God dammit!'

'Ian, what is going on here?' enquired Madame arriving on the scene.

We told her.

'Really! Quite extraordinary and *most* inconsiderate! I shall speak to Beattie personally about this – on the Instrument. . . . In the meantime, what shall we do? Rob, you can ride. It is a mere question of learning to poke about with that long pole thing – a little practice with that and you'll do nicely.'

'Who'll do the lights and pulleys?' Rob asked.

'The electricians and I will manage between us,' Twice said.

One of the varlets was then deputed to double the part of the page and I agreed to expand the costume of David Denholm to cover the larger body of Rob.

'And I,' said Madame, 'will deal in due course with Mount Melody. . . . Very well, let us begin.'

But we could not begin straight away because the beggar-troubadour-gypsy-girl Sandy was lying below the banqueting table, clutching his guitar to his bosom in a fit of hysterical giggles that had all the appearance of being fatal.

'And *what* is so uproariously funny?' enquired the capped and belled Sashie, flipping him with his bladder.

'You w-wait,' sobbed Sandy, 'till you hear the estate workers laughin' when Sir Ian clonks Dad on the head with that p-pee-pot!'

It was understood by all of us that the chamber pots wielded in the fight by Sir Ian and Sandy, although quite unrehearsed in accordance with Madame's orders, would undoubtedly take the stage on the night itself, but we now had more on our minds than this and, having pulled Sandy together, we went on with the rehearsal. On the whole, we were pleased with the costumes and properties in general, but Rob Maclean as Red Gurk was the hero of the evening. A practised polo-player, he could handle the spirited Cadence in a way that David Denholm had never thought of, and Don as Sir Lancelot, also a good horseman, had a foe

143

well worthy of his steel. Rob, too, proved to be a doughty stormer of battlements, probably because the factory ladders concealed in the thick creepers round the verandah pillars were more familiar to his feet than to those of David Denholm, so that, after he had been slain on the battlements and had come alive again, Sir Ian spoke with the voice of all when he said: 'Said at the start Rob could do it, didn't I? Goin' makin' that runt Denholm Red Gurk! In proper mediaeval times they didn't *have* regicides – *they* only came in with old Wart-on-his-nose!' And then he took off his helmet and mopped his forehead.

'I must say it's a riot now,' Twice said to me when we were going to bed. 'The costumes are terrific – I give you full marks.'

'I don't like this Denholm thing,' I said. 'I wonder what's happened?'

'Don and Isobel have quarrelled, do you think?' Twice suggested.

'You'd think Don would have *said* something.'

'But *would* he? After that tearing-up you gave him? I mean, is he likely to choose *your* bosom to bewail his lost love on?'

'As a matter of fact,' I said, 'Don has come out of that tearing-up remarkably well. He and I had a long session in a corner of the library after the rehearsal tonight. We are the best of friends on a nice, clear, new basis.'

'So that's where you were!' Twice cocked an eyebrow at me. 'I hope the Cranston is aware of the basis being clean and nice and especially new, for she remarked that you and Don were missing and indicated that that was more or less as usual and to be expected.'

'The hell with the Cranston!' I said.

'I couldn't agree more. Along what lines did you and Don kiss and be friends?'

'Well, he said I had to go right back to first base and realize that everybody wasn't as lucky as I was in the way they'd been brought up and in the person they married and everything, and so that when he asked me if I was still in love with you and said it was extraordinary on the way to the rehearsal that night, he really *meant* just that and wasn't sneering or being funny or anything.'

'Had you accused him of being funny and sneering, then?'

'Of course! And a lot more besides. I told him he had a mind like an unmade bed and several other things – that's why we were quarrelling when you and Sir Ian came to the car door.'

'I've always *said* that temper of yours was far too quick on the trigger,' Twice said. 'And how you —'

'You're in no position to say anything to anybody about tempers, Twice Alexander!'

'Now, look.' Twice swung his feet into bed. 'You may have the energy for another free-for-all right now, but *I'm* tired. I am delighted that you and Don have settled things – life should be much less wearing for everybody.'

'Life will always be wearing in this island,' I said gloomily, getting into my own bed and picking up my book. 'It *does* things to people – the island, I mean.'

'There's no sense in blaming the island because you played the fool!'

'I'd never have got in that muddle with Don in Scotland!' I flared, raising myself on my elbow and glaring at him.

'With anything as handsome as Don you'd get in a muddle anywhere, especially if he was paying court to someone you didn't like, like Isobel Denholm!'

'Twice Alexander!'

'Lie down and be quiet! You accuse Don of mental untidiness and not looking facts in the face and all the things you've said about him – you are as full of that in your own way as he is in his. You don't like Isobel, you disapproved of Don's affair with her and by sheer instinct you moved in to muck it up. And that's the truth. And don't you go blaming it on St Jago!'

For a moment, we glared at one another across the space between the beds and then I had one of these moments of truth which only Twice can bring upon me and by lowering my eyes from his I admitted that what he said was true. 'But I am delighted you have settled your differences,' he continued then. 'Tell me more.'

'There's nothing to tell, really,' I said. 'It's just that his whole approach is different and, I think, much more healthy. I'll tell you a thing, as Sandy says, and also, as Sandy says, you won't hardly believe this but it's true. I honestly think that until the time of that row between him and me, Don Candlesham did not believe that any relationship was possible between a man and a woman except a sexual one. I mean, he could honestly see no reason for my refusing to go to bed with him except prudishness or something artificial like that. I am explaining this badly. What I mean is, he could not see that because of *you* I didn't want to. As he saw it, you weren't there, he and I could have fun and what the hell? He was convinced I was going against my natural impulses in refusing him. I mean – his point of view was completely animal and pagan, if you like. He didn't believe in the existence of a relationship like ours – he still regards it as a curiosity, as if a fairy-tale he had read somewhere had turned out to be true. Isn't it queer?'

'Not really, when you think of it. He came out of school, into the war, into prison-camp and then out here, and the people who come to the Peak, God knows, are full of pretty pagan ideas. Then there's his own fatal fascination and the tropical climate —'

'I am glad you admit the climate may enter into things!' I said. 'That's largely what started that scene between Don and me that finished at the Great House. What with the heat, mosquitoes and varlets, I felt the whole thing was getting completely away and beyond me and the only thing to do was get in a blind rage and put my foot down as Sandy calls it. Do *you* never feel you are going crazy?'

'No, but I've got some fine sound normal machinery to hang on to all day as you've pointed out more than once. I'm not bedevilled with varlets and Dons and Denholms from morning till night as you are. As a matter of fact, it's just as well these Denholms have pulled out but one *can't* help wondering why. If they are as much under old Madam's thumb as people make out, you'd think the social code would have stopped them doing a last-minute drop like this.'

'Unless the old Madam *made* them drop out?' I suggested.

'But why? Apart from the few of the *hoi-polloi* like you and me and the Murphy, the rest of the players are quite respectable and the audience will be the cream of island society.'

'Oh, Heaven knows! It's like all the other inexplicable queernesses of this place.'

'Oh, well, no doubt Madame will know the reason why before she's finished. What I will say is that that girl Denholm is not particularly gifted as a letter-writer. That note she sent is just about as poor and ungracious an effort as I've ever seen.'

'She's probably never written a note before. America is the land of the telephone.'

'Then she should have stuck to her medium and 'phoned Rob at the office. Madame would have been less infuriated.'

The next day being Sunday, the Macleans, Twice and I were bidden to lunch at the Great House and, naturally enough, the talk was largely of the Denholms.

'Not a word of sense out of Beattie when I spoke to her on the Instrument,' said Madame. 'David is a very nervous boy, she says, and was finding the entertainment upsetting. They may be going back to the States, she said. It was all very unsatisfactory, as the Instrument always is. I felt that Beattie was putting me off with flimsy excuses. Impudence! Nerves! In my day, people didn't *have* nerves and I don't believe they have them now. Pure affectation, that's all it is, and lack of exercise. Why doesn't he drink a glass of rum and go out and ride twenty miles like his grandfather? *I* don't remember any of the Denholms having nerves. Do you, Ian?'

'Certainly not, Mother. But we're well shot of the little perisher. Rob's a far better Gurk. Always said so, right from the beginnin'. Denholm was too small to be a Gurk to start with.'

'Fine body of men the Gurks,' said Twice. 'Cross between a Turk and a Gurkha, you know, Rob.'

'Jolly good, by Jove!' Sir Ian applauded. 'If you were to cross a Turk and a Gurkha you'd get a damn' fine fightin' man. Some queer customs o' their own, of course, but nothin' any queerer than these perishin' Denholms can do. This business is all Beattie's fault, I shouldn't wonder. Look here, what happened to young Toby – her son, this runt's father, ye know?'

I stared at him. Only a few days ago, he himself had sat on the verandah at Guinea Corner and had told me the story of Toby Denholm's marriage to the chorus girl, and as I stared his sharp glance flickered across to mine and I looked down at my plate. I dared to glance up the table to Twice where he sat beside Madame, and Twice looked steadily at me for a second before also lowering his eyes. Madame chose to ignore the question and it was Marion who answered: 'We don't know.'

'Ye don't know? What d'ye mean, ye don't know? I thought you three women went callin' at Mount Melody?'

'So we did,' said Marion patiently, 'but Mrs Denholm didn't mention her son.'

'Didn't mention him? Then why the devil didn't you *ask*? What's the point o' callin' on people if you don't find anything *out*? That's what callin's *for*, dammit!' He champed a piece of toast angrily. 'Ye know what I think?'

'No, sir,' said Sandy, the rest of us being a little afraid to speak and there being a pause.

'It's my opinion this not playin' in the play with these Denholms ain't nerves at all. It's just a good-goin' fit o' the pique!'

147

'About what, Ian?' Madame enquired.

'God knows. Women'll take the pique about anythin' an' that little runt Denholm's no better than a woman. The blood's run out – happens to all these perishin' regicides. It's that thing that that Hitler fellah said the Royal Air Force had before they showed him different – what's the word, boy?'

'Decadence, sir?' said Sandy, in his role of Official Remembrancer.

'*That's* it! *That's* what's wrong with Denholm. Not nerves. Just decadence an' a fit o' the pique.'

When Twice and I were driving back to Guinea Corner, he chuckled and said: 'Far be it from me to make puns, but Sir Ian's dictum applies to the girl Denholm too – only in her case it's Doncadence and a fit of the P-e-a-k!'

'By Jove, sir, jolly good!' I said.

'But that old character Sir Ian is as wily as a fox. I wonder what he was after at the table when he went off about young Denholm's father?'

'I wish I knew,' I said.

'He was looking for information of some kind. He goes on like that at meetings among the coloured people, blimping and blasting away and drawing various bows at various ventures and sooner or later he jumps some negro into coming out with something that he knows and is trying to hide. . . . I think he was out to find if Madame or Marion had got a line on any gossip about old Madam Mount Melody.'

'But why is he so interested? What are the Denholms to *him*, after all?'

'He's a born interferer in other people's affairs to start with – Rob will tell you that. And he is very fond of young people and has very strong views about them. That's why he does all this juvenile court and juvenile delinquent work. . . . Old Miss Poynter really started something when she told him about the Denholms. Of course, that's probably why she picked on him to tell.'

When we arrived back at the house, Twice went to work at his drawing-board and I, in theory, went to lie on my bed and read. I lay on my bed, but I did not read.

When I had first met the Dulac family, I had shared in the common belief that Sir Ian was a good-natured old fool who was dominated, like everyone else on Paradise and a good number outside it, by Madame. I had long since come to the knowledge that this belief was a mistaken one, and ever since Sir Ian had come to me with his story of the young Denholms there had been an uncomfortable question in my mind which I had been pushing aside and ignoring. Why *me*? He loved a good gossip, but there were many people with better qualifications to share his island gossip than I had. If he wanted to help the young Denholms, why *me* as an ally? There were a dozen people better qualified to render help than I was. Unwillingly, I faced the thing that was causing the discomfort. The link between me and the Denholms was Don Candlesham. According to Sir Ian, Isobel had been 'talkin' to Maud Poynter a bit'. It was more than probable that Isobel had talked to Maud Poynter along the same lines as she had talked to Dorothy and that Maud Poynter had repeated the said 'talk' to Sir Ian. I shuddered. It was a hideous thought, but the more I examined it, the more it held water. Was I imagining things, or was it a fact that when Sir Ian said that the Denholms had 'a fit o' the pique' his eyes had fixed themselves on *me*? I shuddered again, then gave myself an angry shake, lit a cigarette and sat in my bed in an orgiastic cloud of inner cursing against Don Candlesham, the Denholms and varlets in general.

It was a typical 'amateur theatrical' situation, I told myself – two of the players withdrawing in a huff at the crucial moment – and I was far too old for this sort of thing and not the type for it anyway. Why had I ever become involved in this play at all? That line of thought being worn to shreds by over-use, I took refuge in a further reviling of the people concerned, but none of it did me any good, of course. The fact remained that I had made a fool of myself by not noticing seriously the antics of Don which, apparently, had been entertaining half the island for months, and this ridiculous situation was the result of my own stupidity and serve me right. Doncadence and a fit of the Peak.

I squashed my cigarette out in a fury, lay back and had myself a nice woolly wallow in self-pity, telling myself how here I was writing this play for everybody and minding my own business and how *this* was all I got for it. I am not, however, a very accomplished self-pitier on the whole, having no firm ground on which to take my stand for it, for I am strongly conscious, all the time, of my own good fortune. You cannot feel fortunate and pity yourself with any conviction at the same time, so I very soon gave up the pretence and concentrated my attention on the Denholms and Don.

It was all very well, I thought, for people to talk about regicides and decadence and make silly puns about the Denholms, but none of them had had, as I had had, that evening with Sashie of finding out just how wrong a person can be about other people and their motives and what actuates them and everything. Look at Twice and me, I told myself, when we arrived at the Peak and christened Sashie 'Sashie Pansy' – a fine thing, I told myself, to have done to a nice person like Sashie, now that one really *knew* about him. Now, I said to myself, you put yourself in the place of that girl Denholm. What do you *know* about her except that she is of a wealthy family and quite good-looking and has a queerish twin brother and a grandmother that looks as if she had been hewn out of granite and has lunacy in her family? What right have *you* got, I asked myself, to be peevish because she was annoyed at you through thinking that you were larking about with her boy-friend? Twice, even, thought you were larking about with him. *You* wouldn't act in *her* play if you and she were each other, I told myself, and I am here to tell you that by the time I had got all my pronouns disentangled and things sorted out in my mind, I was feeling quite friendly towards Isobel Denholm.

Having got myself all filled up with sweetness and light about Isobel, I found that I had not quite finished with the subject and the next day I found myself setting about myself on the subject of her grandmother. I was quite stern with myself about the grandmother. Since you came to this island, I told myself, your judgment, which has never been anything very remarkable, has obviously gone to the devil. The place has gone to your head and knocked you off balance so that you cannot see straight any more. You imagine things that aren't there, I told myself, just as you don't see things that *are* there, like Don. That day you went to Mount Melody with Madame and Marion, you just jumped to the conclusion that Mrs Denholm had a funny-peculiar attitude to her own grandchildren. The day that Mrs Denholm came here, you just decided to go on thinking her funny-peculiar out of sheer cussedness. What is wrong with you, I told myself, is too much imagination, too little sense and too much cussedness. Your imagination has got working on all Sir Ian's tales of regicides and half-mad island people and you are so cussed that probably you will soon be a half-dotty islander yourself, keeping pet alligators. Mrs Denholm is probably a very sensible woman who has decided that you and Don Candlesham and the rest of the varlets are not fit company for her grandchildren and can you blame her? Maybe she has found out about Don's goings-on with Isobel, and you having told her that Don was practically a bosom friend of your brother Jock and your friend Monica she probably thinks by now that you are a procuress and serve you right. No wonder, if that is what she thinks, she made Isobel write you a rude letter about the varlets! Listen, myself asked myself, who said *she* made Isobel write the letter? Nobody said anything, myself told myself, about who made who write the letter, but, all the same, it was a very queer, unnatural sort of letter. There was more behind that letter than meets the eye. There you go – queer, unnatural, more than meets the eye! I tell you, this island has gone to your head and before you know where you are you'll be beating an old kerosene can and going baptizing yourself in the Rio d'Oro!

By this time, I did not know which of myselves was talking to myself and I was in a first-class muddle, so I decided that the reasonable, rational thing to do was not to think about the Denholms any more and hope that none of them would ever cross my path again. In any case, that was what *they* seemed to want too, so everybody should be happy. I then decided I was very happy, found myself wondering what it would be like to live all alone, just the three of you, in grandeur at Mount Melody, and not knowing anybody, and then, for it was now nearly tea-time, I became completely exasperated with myself and with my own thoughts so I went out and began to weed the garden.

The garden proved an excellent antidote to the Denholms. Owing, perhaps, to my Highland peasant birth and upbringing, I am an inveterate grubber-about in the earth, although there is undoubtedly what my friend Martha would call a lotta hooey talked about gardening. In fact, gardening is a natural hooey-subject like child-rearing, leh-rve and psychology. There is a lot of gardening hooey about how it brings a look of serenity and peace to the face of the gardener, due to intimate contact with nature and growing things. If nature and growing things could bring serenity and peace to a face, the Guinea Corner garden should have made a long-necked Botticelli angel out of me, but all I can say is that it did nothing of the sort. Quite the reverse. It was, you see, a tropical garden. The tropics — grrr! As I have already attempted to drive home, there is something about the tropics, when you are new to them, that makes things not be what they seem and this applies, in particular, to things in gardens. I pulled a bundle of untidy-looking dry straw out of a tree one day and threw it on the rubbish heap and it turned out to be a very choosey sort of orchid that thrives best on that particular tree. How was I to know it was only having its dormant season? Another time, I turned up a pretty shell with my trowel, picked it up to take into the house to keep to show to Twice and it stuck out a big claw like a young lobster and nearly bit my finger off. But I am not the type to be defeated by a little bit of ground. Oh, no. Not me. By this time I am telling about, I had decided that the way to treat the Guinea Corner garden was to lash it into subjection. None of this rot about handling the sweet things of nature with love and tenderness. No. Haul up by the root everything I disliked the look of was my motto, and if some of them turn out to be Gloriosa Superba lilies, as is their wont, God wot, take a firm stand and say: 'I hate the very *sight* of Gloriosa Superba lilies!'

Wearing a pair of dirty shorts and an old shirt and sweating at every pore, I was tearing out by the root a jungly, viney thing with a lot of long, tangled tendrils, when a car came through the gate behind me. Thinking it was Twice, and having got to the point of struggle with this thing when its Laocoön tendrils were all wound about me, I took no notice of the car, muttered an imprecation and gave an almighty heave, with which the spiteful plant gave up the struggle without warning and I fell backwards into the drive-way with the green mass all on top of me and its fibrous roots shaking earth all over my sweaty face. I then became aware, as they say in the ghost stories, of a presence and, peering coyly out from my green bower, I saw above me Mrs Denholm of Mount Melody in all the panoply of wide hat, long gloves and immaculate white linen.

'Good afternoon, Mrs Alexander,' she said. 'Dear me, you *do* look hot!'

Looking up into her chiselled, superior face, all that stuff I had thought about being reasonable and rational about Denholms left me. I decided that I did not like this old woman, that I never *had* liked this old woman and that nobody would be more surprised than I would be if I ever came to like her in the future.

'Good afternoon, Mrs Denholm,' I said. 'I *am* hot. I have been gardening, as you see. . . . Do come in.'

I went ahead of her and led the way into the drawing-room. I ought to mention here that when I am angry, the back of my hands and the back of my neck tend to itch and I had this feeling now, but in a most pronounced form that I had never experienced before in a long career of frequently being extremely angry. I now itched all over, from my finger-tips to my shoulders, from my forehead down over chest and back and from the hips to the ankles. It was a maddening itch. I could hardly keep still.

'Please sit down,' I said to Mrs Denholm. 'And will you excuse me while I clean up a little?'

She remained standing in the middle of the floor. 'I do not intend to stay,' she said. 'I understand from Madame Dulac that my grand-daughter wrote you a letter of some sort.'

'Yes,' I said, trying to resist the impulse to scratch every inch of myself at once. 'She did.'

'I wish to see it,' she commanded.

Some itching nerve inside my head seemed to snap. 'Mrs Denholm, what do you mean?'

'Exactly what I say. I wish to see that letter. Is that clear?'

'Perfectly clear.'

'Have you destroyed it?'

'No. I still have it.'

'Then where is it?'

'With the rest of my private correspondence, Mrs Denholm.'

She stared at me as if she could not believe what she had heard.

'Do I understand you to imply that you do not wish to show me that letter?'

'You understand me perfectly, Mrs Denholm.'

'But *Mrs* Alexander — ' She might as well have used the phrase 'my good woman', for that was how she made my name sound. ' — Isobel is my grand-daughter! I insist that you show me her letter!'

'The letter is not Isobel's, Mrs Denholm. It is mine, and you have no right of any kind to see it.'

This, I admit freely, was pure cussedness on my part, but I come of a cussed race that has an innate dislike of being bullied and I was now itching to such a degree that I felt as if I were on fire. If Mrs Denholm wants a fight, I thought, she has picked a fine day for it and I would enjoy taking out this fit of itch in a real down-to-earth, hair-tearing free-for-all. Mrs Denholm, however, was not the hair-tearing sort. She sat down on the edge of a chair and looked at my earthy, sweaty figure with marked distaste.

'Mrs Alexander, I consider that your attitude is most unreasonable. I have noticed that my grand-daughter has become utterly out-of-hand since we came to Mount Melody and I think it is entirely due to the influence of you and the other so-called friends she has made here. Your attitude today confirms me in this opinion. I do not in the least understand why Isobel should enter into correspondence with you, nor why you should refuse me information as to what she wrote about. I understand from Madame Dulac that she told you that she and David will not be taking part in this – this entertainment?'

'That is quite correct, Mrs Denholm.'

'*Mrs* Alexander, to what degree are you in Isobel's confidence?'

'In the degree that I am in Isobel's confidence, Mrs Denholm. Just that and no more.'

'I do *not* understand your attitude, Mrs Alexander.'

She rose and drew herself up to her full height. I am fairly tall too. My hair is not white yet, but I had a fair amount of mud on my face to help out with the warlike appearance. We stared at one another.

'And I do *not* understand yours, Mrs Denholm.'

'I suppose that I must trust that you will be as discreet with other people as you have been with me.'

'That is for you to decide, Mrs Denholm. Good afternoon.'

She swept out, the Cadillac drove away and I began to rub my itching legs. I now discovered that they, my arms and my chest were bright red all over and streaked with long, raised, purplish weals. The more I rubbed, the more maddening the itch became and I was almost sobbing with pain and fury when Twice came in.

'Good God!' he said, staring at me. 'What now? What have you done to your face?'

'Please, sah,' said the yard boy who was standing behind him with a bottle in his hand, 'de Missis have pull' up de t'ing in de gahden dat me get de bottle fe Mistah Cranston's lab-tory fe kill!'

'What *thing*? *What* bottle?' Twice shouted.

'De cow-itch big weed t'ing in de gahden, sah!'

'Oh, lord! What do we do *now*, Caleb? Look at her!'

'I go to de lab-tory an' get bottle fe de Missis, sah?'

'No! *She* doesn't need weed-killer! . . . Go to the clinic and ask Nurse for something! Run!'

'Yes, sah!'

Cable ran away, I jumped about and scratched and Twice stared at me. 'I'm not sure it isn't weed-killer that you *do* need! So help me, I've never seen a forty-year-old woman that can get into more trouble!'

'This is no time to go on about my age, Twice Alexander!' I said and burst into tears, of course.

'Oh, sit down for Pete's sake! I'll get some ice. That can't make it worse and it might help it!'

The Estate doctor in person came rushing round in response to Caleb's no-doubt wildly garbled message and gave me an injection which had an immediate effect of relief.

'Mrs Alexander,' he said then, 'you are having an extraordinarily uneasy acclimatization to St Jago. I've never known a woman who has been bitten and stung by a greater variety of the island fauna and flora.'

'Just what I've been telling her,' Twice said in a smug voice which made me long to throw something at him. 'She will *not* stop looking into wasps' nests and things.'

'It didn't *look* like a wasps' nest,' I argued. 'And this thing today didn't look like a stinging plant either! And I *didn't* poke into the sand-flies that night – that moonlight beach picnic was *your* idea. And the time I cut myself on the cane root could have happened to anybody — '

'— who happened to be running across a newly-cut cane piece where she had no business to be!' Twice rejoined.

'Oh, shut up! Give the doctor a drink!'

'No, thank you. I'm due at the Club. But I'll take your boy with me and send back a bottle of lotion with him. Smear it all over the weals. You should be all right in the morning.'

The lotion, when it arrived, was of a purplish colour and it was miraculously helpful and soothing but extraordinarily messy and when Sir Ian walked into the drawing-room I was sitting on a sofa, which was spread with bath-towels, in a bathing dress with my face, neck, arms and legs smeared to a powdery pale lilac tint.

'Good God!' he said. 'You got a fit o' the blues?'

Twice explained what had happened and then they both laughed like maniacs until I said sourly: 'I want a great big whisky. I shouldn't be surprised if I go on having great big whiskies all night until I *really* get a fit of the blues and start shooting pink elephants off the walls like old Pickering or whoever he was.'

'Come now,' said Sir Ian, 'you missed the point o' the story about Pickerin'. It was a *real* alligator, not an imaginary elephant. Dammit, old Pickerin' never had the blues! Drank a bit, certainly, but never got out o' hand. . . . No, it was Monty Carnegie that had the imaginary elephant – not that he really had the blues either – never imagined anythin' except this elephant. Used to take it up the river every Sunday mornin' for a bath. Horizon, the Carnegies' place, ye know, was on the coast, but Monty's elephant didn't like salt water. . . . But speakin' about Monty an' that, that's what I came about. Your blues put it out o' my head. Beattie Denholm was here this afternoon, wasn't she?'

'Yes.'

'I *thought* it was her car I saw goin' past the office when I was in at that confounded meetin'. Beattie's gettin' too old to be drivin' that American organ herself. But for the meetin', I'd have been round here earlier an' caught her an' asked her what the devil she meant, her grand-daughter sendin' you that letter.'

'That's what *she* came to ask *me*,' I told him.

'What d'ye mean?'

'She came in here and demanded that I show her Isobel's letter.'

'What for?'

'So that she could see what was in it.'

'Why?'

'How do I know?'

'And what did she say when she saw it?' Twice asked.

'She didn't see it.'

'You mean you wouldn't show it to her?' I nodded. 'Why not?'

'I was itching and she made me mad, coming in here and saying: I wish to see that letter, as if I were some black slave or something. The woman's demented. She can't go walking into people's houses and laying down the law like that, so just for pure cussedness I wouldn't let her see it and then she swept out in high dudgeon.'

'Oh, lord!' said Twice.

'An' a damn' good thing too!' Sir Ian said. 'Beattie's always been a bit high in the hand, ye know. That's why she an' Mother never hit it off. Mother can be a bit high-handed too, of course, but she's more *reasonable* than Beattie. . . . But what did she want to see the letter for? Tell me that!'

'How do I know?' I asked. 'She wanted to know how far I was in her grand-daughter's confidence, as she put it.'

'An' what'd ye say?'

'I told her I was in it just as far as I was in it.'

'In it as far as ye were in it,' Sir Ian repeated and stared at the ceiling to work it out. 'Why didn't ye tell her just to mind her own business and be done with it?'

'When I was young, my grandmother wouldn't *let* me say Mind your own business and now I *can't* say it.'

'Grandmothers! Some o' these bloomin' women live far too perishin' long!'

As far as Mrs Denholm was concerned, I agreed with him and after he had gone I said so to Twice.

'It's not a bit of good your saying that I can't keep out of trouble,' I told him. 'It simply is not reasonable for that woman to walk in here and take it as her right that I should show her Isobel's letter. Dammit, even if I hadn't been itching at the time, she would still have made me mad. . . . One thing is certain. She is afraid that there's something in that letter that she doesn't want known. She made a dirty crack about Isobel getting out of hand since she made friends with me and the people here. I wonder if she has found out about Isobel's carry-on with Don and is holding us responsible?'

'That doesn't make sense,' Twice said. 'Isobel would have met Don that day at the airport anyway, even if we had never been born. The Denholms *lived* at the Peak for their first spell. To hold *us* in any way responsible would be just plain crazy.'

'Twice, I'm not sure that old woman *isn't* crazy.'

'Oh, come now, Flash! Let's not be over-influenced by Sir Ian and his stories. Even if she *had* a dotty brother. She's a little eccentric, I'll give you that, but that's a long way from being crazy.'

'That's what people said about Hitler when he first started eating carpets and look how *he* ended up! I tell you, there was a light in the old dame's eyes when she left here this afternoon that wasn't of this world!'

'It's a pity you hadn't a glass handy to see the light in your own eye when I came in. . . . I thought it was just the effect of the cow-itch, but now I know that it was just sheer rage.'

'Oh, pour another drink and let's talk about Scotland and heather instead of mad people and plants that set a person on fire! This island is enough to drive anybody crazy!'

157

Chapter Ten

THE NEXT day, while I worked about the house and made something of a show of ignoring and scorning the garden, I had myself another think about the Denholms and I decided that I was very, very sorry for Isobel and David, and especially for Isobel, and that if I had a grandmother who drove herself about in a Cadillac asking to see the letters I had written to people, I too would probably jump into bed with Don Candlesham or anyone else who would be even moderately nice to me. Next time I saw Isobel, I promised myself, I would do my best to be nice to her and be very loving and forgiving to her about her having said all those things about me to Dorothy and probably Miss Poynter as well. In my mind, I became very, very well-disposed to Isobel indeed and thought of all sorts of clever ways of making real friends with her and letting bygones be bygones and all sorts of nice things to say to her when next we met. I do not, of course, have to draw a diagram to demonstrate that all this nice feeling was born of my belief that she and I would never cross paths again, so that when, about three days before the performance of *Varlets in Paradise*, the car that she and her brother shared drove in to Guinea Corner, all this nice feeling melted like snow in the Sahara. I simply got the old, familiar prickly feeling at the back of my neck and thought that here she was and here I was, all alone, and now what? Whatever it was going to be, it was going to be embarrassing. In fact, it was going to be what Dorothy would call AWFUL.

Isobel jumped out of the car. She was wearing jade-green linen slacks and a white shirt with big jade-green spots all over it and she strode on to the verandah like Boadicea in an unusually warlike frame of mind and said: 'I have come to apologize.' She then romped into it. 'I apologize,' she said, 'for all those things I said to Dorothy Davey – I haven't said them to another living soul – about you and Don having an affair. When I said them, I thought they were true and besides I'd had a couple of drinks at the time. Don says even if they were true I shouldn't have said them. I didn't know about that. I haven't been brought up his way. Anyways, I know now they weren't true and I am sorry I said them and I'll tell you something else just for free. I was a darned fool to say them anyways, for they didn't do a cuss of good to anybody, least of all me.'

I suddenly felt that this girl had a kind of humorous courage and courageous humour, that I had never known her at all until now and that I liked very much this little of her that I had this minute come to know.

'Now you've got that off your chest,' I said, 'why don't you sit down?'

'What for?'

'We could have tea or a drink or something.'

She sat down and said: 'Why?'

'I don't know. I haven't got anything better to do. Have you?'

'No-o. I wasn't going anywheres.'

I called Clorinda to bring the tray of drinks, for I did not feel, somehow, that tea was adequate for my needs, and when the tray came I said: 'Well, what will it be?'

'Is that a bottle of Coke? I'll have that, thanks.'

'Are you on the waggon?'

'Not entirely.'

I poured myself a noggin of whisky and added water to it.

'It was generous of you, Isobel, to come here and apologize like that. And I don't blame you for thinking the things you did about Don and me – a lot of people older than you thought the same things and it can't be helped and it doesn't matter anyway. . . . You shouldn't have cried off the play because of all this, though. That was stupid and has only made an unnecessary fuss between Madame Dulac and your grandmother and everybody.'

'Listen, Mrs Alexander — ' she began.

'Why don't you just say Janet like everybody else?'

'Okay, Janet. . . . Listen, I didn't write you that letter about not acting in the play because of that thing about Don and you. As for fusses as you call them between Grandma and this Mrs Dulac, I don't give a damn. Grandma is always fightin' with *some*body and it might as well be Mrs Dulac.'

I let this interesting sidelight on 'Grandma' pass and stuck to the point. 'Then why *did* you write me that letter, Isobel?'

She stared into my face and suddenly all the hard, brash self-assurance left her, falling away like gaudy leaves from a young tree in an autumn wind, until she seemed as childish and defence-less as Dorothy Davey and considerably less sure of herself. I found myself thinking absurdly that this young Isobel Denholm would not be even able, like young Dorothy, to describe some-

159

thing as 'awful', for she had no mental yardstick to differentiate the awful from the un-awful. She was no more than a lost, bewildered child behind the façade of a self-assured, beautiful young woman.

'I *had* to write it. It's because of my brother. My brother's *sick!*'

The young voice had risen to a note of childish, grievous protest on the last word.

'Isobel, I am very sorry. Your – your Grandma told Madame Dulac that he suffered from his nerves. I am — '

' — Grandma and nerves!' she burst out.

'Isobel!' I said. 'That is no word for you to use!'

She clenched her hands between her knees and stared at me. 'Words! Words! I'm sick of words! Nerves!' She drew a harsh, grinding breath. 'My brother's turning into a *drunk*, a slavering, drooling *drunk*, you hear?' She put her head down on her knees and began to sob. 'And Grandma won't take any notice. She – she says he has to learn to control himself and behave himself. She – she's going to *kill* him, j-just the same way she killed my father!'

She was now crying uncontrollably and, watching her, I thought it kinder to let her cry. She was not in any way hysterical, but crying out of some dreadful need for relief and some terrible bitterness of grief.

Twice, home from the factory, ran up the steps and found us there – me sitting smoking and, opposite me, huddled in the canvas chair, the shaking, sobbing girl.

'Have a drink and sit down, Twice,' I said. 'Isobel is in trouble and she may want you to help her.'

Isobel raised a swollen face for a moment. 'Nobody can help us,' she said. 'Grandma won't let them.'

Twice and I glanced at one another and she put her head down again.

'We are the Denholms of Mount Melody – nobody can help *us*. We're big shots. Especially David. He is the last man of his name *He's* a *hell* of a big shot!'

She began to sob again and I said to Twice in as calm and reasonable a voice as I could muster: 'David is sick, Twice, and Isobel is very worried about him. She came to see me and we were talking and I asked about David and, well, you know how it is when you are worried – she just got into a sort of state, but she'll be all right in a minute.'

160

'I think we should all have a dram,' Twice said. 'Oh, you've got one already? Well, Isobel and I then. What would you like, Isobel? A little whisky?'

'Aw r-right.' She mopped her face, took the glass and said in an astonished voice: 'Say, you folks are being *nice* to me!'

'It's an act we have for visitors,' Twice told her. 'We're terrible when we're on our own.'

She smiled faintly and began to sip her drink. 'I – I just don't know what to say,' she said next. 'I just don't know what happened to make me bawl like that. Listen, you won't tell anybody about these things I said?'

'Certainly not,' I promised.

'Isobel,' Twice asked, 'have you and David any family besides your grandmother?'

'I don't think so. Father died. Our mother walked out on Grandma when we were babies. And she was quite right!' she said fiercely as if we had attempted to criticize her mother's action. 'I would walk out too if it wasn't for David.'

She stared out into the new-fallen dark as if communing with herself.

'Does David want to stay?' I asked tentatively.

'It's funny about David.' She did not look at us, but continued to stare out at the dark beyond the verandah screen. 'I'm not very good at explaining. Grandma *likes* him, see? At least, she makes David *think* she likes him. . . . I don't know why I'm telling you folks all this – that old Miss Poynter was asking me things the other night when David got drunk down at the Peak there, but I didn't tell her anything much. She's another of them, you see.'

'Another of what?' Twice asked.

'These crazy people like Grandma that live around this crazy place. I mean, maybe that Miss Poynter's all right, but knowin' Grandma I just don't *trust* any of these folks. Maybe you think it's funny me tellin' you all this, but I gotta tell *some*body and you folks don't belong among all this crazy bunch. Grandma's *queer*, you see.'

'Queer in what way?' Twice asked.

'Well, it's sorta as if she had what they call a power complex. I been trying to read about these things, but I don't get on much with it, because I never went to school or anything. It was all governesses an' I never learned anything. Grandma don't believe in schools for girls. Grandma don't really believe in *girls*, come to that, because they can't carry on the name, see? But she believes in boys an' that's why she likes David, only she don't really *like* him, not for him*self*, the way *I* like him. Grandma likes him because of Mount Melody an' Blueclear – that's another thing she has. She wants to buy back Blueclear from these folks that don't want to sell it to her because it's the place where she was born an' then David will be a real big-shot land-owner, see?'

'And did David go to school?' Twice asked.

His voice was no more than expressionlessly polite, but Isobel responded to his calm with calm.

'Oh, sure! David had to have what Grandma calls an education befitting a gentleman, so he went to school an' then to college an' then he wanted to be an architect. David is very smart, y' know,' she ended proudly.

'Good!' said Twice. 'Architecture is a fine profession.'

'That's what *you* think! When Grandma found out about it, she took David outa college an' brought us down here. An' now David's started drinkin'!'

'You mean, your Grandma doesn't want him to be an architect?' I asked.

'What do you think? Who ever heard of a Denholm of Mount Melody bein' an architect? Are *you* crazy?'

'I don't know,' I said slowly. 'But surely if the boy wants a profession it isn't reasonable — '

'*Now* you're talkin'! Grandma *ain't* reasonable, but what can you do about it? What can *I* do? What can *any*body do?'

'But what about David himself?' Twice asked. 'Surely if he *wants* to have his profession he can make his way somehow — '

'Listen, Mr Twice, I ain't clever at explainin' these things. David's *weak* an' Grandma plays on it. She's got David now so he don't know where he's at. She keeps talkin' to him about the property an' what a big shot he is and as long as he's listening to her an' *with* her, he believes it an' then he goes down to the Bay an' around among folks an' he sees he's just a little shot that wants to be an architect an' then he starts drinkin' an' gettin' in trouble. . . . I tell you, he was all *right* as long as he was at college an' doin' what he wanted to do – never drank too much or anything an' spent his vacations ridin' around looking at houses an' churches an' things an' now he's like this! Maybe you don't know about drunks, but *I* know about them – the real kind – like my father. They hide the stuff an' then they hide themselves an' *soak* themselves in it until they're *crazy*, you hear?' Her voice began to rise hysterically. 'An' then they fight with people an' with imaginary snakes an' devils an' things an' they get sicker all the time until they die! My brother's gettin' like that – God knows what he's doin' right now, but he was ravin' last night, ravin' like a madman — '

She buried her face in her arms and began to cry as if her heart were breaking.

'Isobel!' Twice said sternly. 'Does your Grandma know about this?'

'Grandma!' She looked up, her eyes blazing in her wet face. 'Of course she knows! She says all the Denholms drink and David is a naughty boy to drink so much but he'll soon learn sense!'

'But, Isobel, your Grandma must know about your father. Can't she see — '

'Grandma finished with my father after he married my mother. Grandma didn't *want* him to marry my mother, see? And when somebody does something Grandma don't want, she don't care *what* happens to them. She don't care what happens to David *now* as long as he don't do what she don't want him to do an' go an' be an architect!'

'But that is sheer madness!' I exploded.

'You're tellin' *me*! But just you try an' tell Grandma!'

'Let's keep Grandma out of this,' Twice said. 'I'm starting to take a dislike to her. Isobel, how old are you and David?'

'Twenty. Why?'

'Have you any money?'

'Money? Don't make me laugh!'

'What do you mean?'

'What do I mean? How stoopid can you get? Would I be sittin' here watchin' my brother takin' to drink if I had any money? *Grandma* – Mrs Denholm of Mount Melody – is the money, ya dope! Grandma owns everything and everybody! She owned my father until he died of drink, she owns David, she owns *me* and these pants I'm wearing and that car out there! Go look at the licence disc if you don't believe me! . . . Do you know I've never paid a cent for an ice-cream soda in my life? We *charge* them, to Grandma's account! We can spend anything we like, through *Grandma's* accounts. We can have a wonderful time! We can — '

'Stop that! What happens when you are ill?'

'*Grandma* decides whether we're ill or not. If she decides we are, with something decent like the measles, we get the best

163

doctors in the States. If she decides we're not, we die, like my father! Like *David*!'

She collapsed into another storm of tears and we waited, in the hot still darkness, for her to become calm and at last she looked up at us, hiccuped a big sob and picked up her drink again.

'Isobel,' Twice said gently, 'if you had some money, could you and your brother get on a plane and clear out?'

'Not if Grandma knew.'

'I'm not talking about Grandma. . . . What I am asking is whether you could lay hands on your passports, these kind of formalities, and persuade your brother to come away?'

'Without Grandma?'

'Oh, that-word-you-said Grandma!' I said. 'Isobel, Twice is asking if, if you got a chance to go on your own, with David, can you do it?'

'What?' She sprang to her feet like a tigress springing. 'If I had the money, sure I could do it! Even if I have to murder the old bitch!'

'Isobel!'

She sank limply back into her chair. 'If I had the money I could do it,' she said ruefully. 'But what's the good of that? I ain't got the money an' I ain't got no way of gettin' it.'

'If you *had* the money,' Twice persisted, 'would David be willing to go?'

'Willing? Are you crazy? Listen, three months ago David an' I sold that darn car out there – got the cheque for it an' everything. Oh, we were a right pair of smarties! Then it came to givin' the car to the guy an' he asks us about the insurance an' the licence an' everything. Then they tell us we have to get Grandma's signature! Grandma's signature!'

'What did you do?'

'What'd *you* have done? You'd've had to do just what we did. We gave the cheque back to the guy an' went to the Peak an' got drunk. Then David had another idea, but we haven't started on this one yet an' now I've had this fight with Don an' he says he never wants to see me again, I don't suppose we ever will start it, but Grandma pays our bills at the Peak for meals an' boat-hire an' that. We thought maybe I could fix it with Don so we don't *have* the drinks an' stuff, but he sends in the bills just the same an' gives us the money. . . . If we could get the plane fare, we'd *go* all right. You bet we would!'

'Have you got friends up in the States?' I asked.

164

'Some – not many. Grandma don't know about them, of course. David's got a raft of friends, with college an' that – *he'd* be all right. An' so would I – I beat it two or three times before an' did all right, but I always had to come back on account of David. Then Grandma got this idea of bringin' him down here.

'When he wrote an' told me about how he was havin' to leave college an' come down here, I just *had* to come, see? Grandma don't want me here. It's *David* wants me – we're twins, see?' Her eyes filled with tears again and she began to cry once more in that hopeless, heartbroken way. 'I just don't know what to do. This island is sorta like a prison. I wanted us to make a run for it before we left the States, but David said that Grandma would get used to the idea of him bein' an architect or somethin' an' send him back to college later on, maybe, when she saw his mind was made up, but David is kinda silly about Grandma. She – she's *nice* to him, see? An' at the same time she tells him he'll never be any good as an architect an' just to run along down to the Bay an' have a good time an', well, that's what happens. It's – Grandma wants her own *way*, you see. An' David kinda sees that and yet he kinda doesn't either. She's smart, you know. She don't like the way I talk – she says I'm common like my mother an' no better than a shopgirl, but she don't say things like that to me in front of David because she knows David *likes* me deep down an' he wouldn't like her sayin' these things about me. She can do just *any*thing so she gets her own way.' She mopped her face again and drew a long sobbing breath. 'Look, I gotta go home. It's been kind of you folks to listen to me an' maybe you don't go much on me talkin' about my Grandma like this but what the hell.'

'Listen,' Twice said, 'if we got you and David some money would you be willing to go up to the States? When you got up there, you'd have to fend for yourselves, you know.'

'Where'd you get the money? *Grandma* ain't goin' to give — '

'I'm sick of the very word Grandma! We wouldn't be asking her for the money.'

'You mean – you'd *lend* it to us?'

'Something like that.'

'Gee! We'd sure go! An' listen, I'd pay you back sometime – honest I would!'

'I believe you,' Twice told her. 'But never mind that part of it now. You go back to David and get him sober and then *both* of you come and see us.'

165

'Gee, thanks! Thanks! Listen — ' she looked from one of us to the other with hunted eyes – 'This is on the level? You wouldn't go an' tell Grandma — ?'

'Anything we have to tell Grandma will be better left unsaid,' Twice told her. 'If what you have told us tonight is the truth, neither of us will be speaking to Grandma.'

'It's *true* all right, Mr Twice, so help me, it is!'

'We believe you, Isobel,' I said. 'You go home and see what you can do with your brother and then come and see us again. Tell him you've got friends now.'

'Gee, but you're nice. Listen, I'm *awful* sorry about these things I said — '

'Oh, forget all that and off you go and don't worry any more.'

'Gee, thanks again. Thanks for everything!'

She ran down the steps and the expensive convertible, licensed in the name of Mrs Denholm of Mount Melody, roared down the driveway and out of the gate.

Twice has been known to refer to our life together as the 'Communual Sponge' because of our habit of discussing everything unusual that happens to us over drams of whisky and water until we have reduced it to our own terms and have absorbed it so that it is no longer unusual or strange. 'Isn't there,' he said now, 'some stuff you can buy from the chemist for soaking sponges in when they get all their pores and holes blocked up? I feel we could do with a half-hundredweight or so of it right now. The old CS is positively at constipation point — '

' — and a little slimy and starting to stink,' I agreed. 'Apart from getting the money to stake these kids to a journey to the States, have we got enough loose change to make a smart getaway from this island before Madam Mount Melody catches up with us? You realize we've spent the evening sowing sedition?'

'We have, rather, haven't we? Ye know what, as Sandy says, let's have a tot and take it up to the bathroom with us while I have my bath.' He began to pour two drinks. 'Listen, how did the whole thing start anyway?'

'Don't keep on asking *me* where things started! Since you brought me to these cock-eyed tropics, I've never known whether I'm on my you-know-what or my elbow. It was like those confounded varlets. She came in here and said something and then I said something and then she began to cry and then you came in and here we are, probably in peril of our lives although you refuse to recognize it. . . . God, who's that?'

166

The darkness was now as thick as black cotton-wool and the powerful headlights of the car that turned into the gateway raked along the dimly-lit verandah. I sprang up.

'It's that old Valkyrie in the Cadillac! I'm not here!'

'Sit *down*, you tone-deaf vandal! Cadillac! It's the *Rolls*!'

It was, too, and Sir Ian sprang out of the tonneau and stopped dead. 'They're gone, dammit!' We looked at him silently. 'Those young Denholms were here!' he told us accusingly. 'Don't tell me they weren't!'

'Nobody's saying a word, sir,' said Twice. 'Have a drink.'

'Hah! Yes, just a tot, my boy. Campbell saw that Wurlitzer Organ of a car of theirs an' had the sense to mention it. What'd they want, hey? What'd they got to say for themselves? Tell me that!'

'It was only Isobel who came, Sir Ian,' I said.

'Well, *she* wrote that letter, didn't she? Question if her brother *can* write. Well, come now, what'd she say?'

I felt like the accused at a court-martial with my buttons and badges of rank about to be ripped off at any moment when Twice said: 'She came to explain to Janet about her brother, sir. The boy is really very sick indeed.'

'Oh? Sorry to hear that, dammit. If the boy's sick, what's Beattie doin' bleatin' about nerves an' insultin' Missis Janet an' leadin' to a lot o' trouble? What's the matter with the boy?'

'Well — ' Twice looked at me and I at him.

'God dammit! What's wrong with ye both? *Mother* ain't here. All people o' the world. You're as bad as old Maud, beatin' about the bush! What's wrong with him? Been in some whore-house in the Bay an' got a dose?'

'No, sir, nothing like that,' Twice said. 'The fact is the boy's drinking far too much.'

'Drinkin'? Googorralmighty, we *know* that! And what d'ye expect? *All* the Denholms have been drunks since the time o' old Wart-on-his-nose! What's Beattie carryin' on about? She's used to drink. Seen old Toby at a gymkhana so drunk we had to lift him on to his horse – great savage brute called Lilliput, he was – but he could still out-ride everybody. I thought from what old Maud was saying' — '

'The boy isn't just getting drunk occasionally, Sir Ian,' I said. 'He is not just a heavy drinker. He is apparently turning into a real alcoholic.'

167

'Alco — ? Ye mean the kind that doesn't drink just *drink* but bay rum an' methylated an' that, all in secret?'

'That's right.'

'God bless my soul! That's bad. Old Toby wouldn't've liked *that*! What's Beattie doin' about it?'

'That's just the point, sir,' Twice said. 'The girl says that it's largely Mrs Denholm's fault that the boy is taking to drink and she isn't doing anything about it. She takes the view, apparently, that the boy should learn to control himself.'

'But that's just plain *stoopid*!' bellowed Sir Ian. 'Dammit, the boy only drinks the bay rum an' stuff because he *can't* control himself! But what's Beattie doin' to send him on the bottle?'

We went on to tell Sir Ian all we knew of the situation and Twice ended with: 'So if you could arrange for the Estate office to put a little money at my disposal, sir, until I can get extra funds out from Scotland — '

'Funds from Scotland, be damned! Good God, man, the Denholms have been neighbours o' Paradise for a couple o' centuries. As soon as that girl can get the boy on his feet, you let me know. An' after we've got them away, by God,' he added with relish, 'I'll go up to Mount Melody an' see Beattie! Shouldn't be surprised if I take *Mother* with me! What Beattie Denholm needs is a good, severe talkin'-to.' He ruminated for a moment, then held out his glass. 'Just you give me another tot, my boy, and then I'll go home to dinner. They can cure 'em, ye know, if they're not too far gone. Had a fellow in Palestine – fine boy, Englishman – *he* got on the bottle. Used to loose off with his revolver at purple snakes on the wall that weren't there an' everything. Put him in a place in London, his people did, an' he got all right. Married an' had a family an' everything – then broke his neck out huntin'. Wasn't drunk at the time, though. Perfectly good, decent accident that could happen to anybody. . . . Don't like this business o' Beattie, though. What was that thing the girl said? Power somethin'?'

'Power complex, sir,' Twice said. 'I didn't like that touch either. Look how she was with Janet about that letter — '

'Bad business. I remember her brother Jack – told Missis Janet about him the other day. Used to get dancin' about stark naked at the full moon, imagined he was some kind o' god or somethin'. Same idea – power complex. Don't like that. Don't like it at all. Only thing to do is get these youngsters away.' He frowned fiercely from one of us to the other. 'I know I've told you queer yarns about the Pickerin's an' Monty Carnegie an' them an' the things they used to get up to, but that's all different from this thing in the Blueclear Poynters. Gettin' down to bedrock, this ain't a white man's country – livin' here puts a strain on white men mentally as well as in their bodies. Pickerin' an' Carnegie with their alligators an' elephants were kind of blowin' off steam. That's all. Perfectly harmless an' as sane as you or me, but this Poynter bunch are different. To start with, the Poynters were all hellish tight-fisted an' it costs money to go home to England for a wife, so they kept on marryin' inside the island. Great mistake, that. When I was nineteen I was hittin' it up with one o' the Carnegie girls an' the Guvnor got hold o' me an' said: "Look here, me lad, your passage to England is booked for Friday next. You're not bringin' a Carnegie or any other damned island-white on to Paradise. You go an' do your whorin' in a white man's country!" No beatin' about the bush with the Guvnor. I was damn' sick about it at the time, but he was right. Edie Carnegie married a Gillespie an' both their youngsters are deaf an' dumb. . . . Same thing with these Poynters o' Blueclear – only with them it's the mind. . . . Don't like this thing about Beattie at all. . . . What about this girl? She all right?'

'Well, she was in a fairish state when she was here,' Twice said, 'but that's not surprising.'

'She's been hittin' it up with that fellah Candlesham – over-sexed likely – that's another thing you get with this inbreedin'.'

I had a vague desire to defend Isobel. 'I think myself,' I said, 'that the poor girl was so lost and miserable she hardly knows what she's been doing. And Don is good-looking and can be very nice.'

'Last time I heard *you* talkin' to him you didn't seem to be thinkin' along these lines,' he said shrewdly. 'Anyway, pity a young girl carryin' on like that. Not the thing at all. That's just bad upbringin' an' Beattie Denholm's responsible. Girl should be at a good school. Can't even write a decent letter. Too young for hangin' round bars an' hittin' it up round the Bay. She's a fine-lookin' young woman an' can handle a horse, too – a real Denholm. . . . Beattie'd never give them any money, you say? Queer, the way people get. Mother'd've been inclined to this power complex nonsense if the Guvnor had let her, but he was different from Toby Denholm – stricter, ye know. I'm not sayin' the Guvnor couldn't take a drink – he could, an' hold it too, by Jove! But a great disciplinarian – could hold the drink an' Mother as well. "Lottie", he'd say, "go an' do your tattin' an' don't interfere!" . . . She still hates to be called Lottie, ye know that? . . . Great mistake old Toby made leavin' all the money with Beattie like that and then her gettin' another lot from this banker uncle in Philadelphia. Never know what these women will do if you give them their head an' a lot o' money. Look at Queen Victoria!'

'Look at old Wart-on-his-nose!' I said, striking a blow for my sex.

Sir Ian rose majestically and put down his empty glass. '*Cromwell*,' he corrected me sternly, 'was different. *He* was a jumped-up, self-made upstart that had no idea o' how to behave himself. That's different from people o' *family*, like Queen Victoria an' Mother an' the Denholms – dammit, the Denholms are one o' the best old families in the island – they're *regicides*! . . . I'm off home to dinner. See you in the mornin', my boy.'

He marched down the steps to the Rolls, leaving Twice and myself in a very muddled frame of mind and yet with a feeling that quite a lot was right with the world.

Chapter Eleven

DURING THE next three days, Paradise changed from a sleepy valley among its surrounding hills to a seething volcano crater of activity. Cars and lorries flew up and down the roadways between the fields of tall sugar-cane in clouds of white dust, carrying every available table, chair, bench, plate and glass to the Great House, where Marion Maclean and I, in the middle of the huge dining-room, directed the unloading and placing while Rob and Twice, in the garden, directed the placing of the seating on the lawn. Even the bleachers from the Club cricket field had been commandeered.

All this work was much hampered, of course, by the enthusiastic helpers, notably Sir Ian and Sandy, Mrs Cranston and Mrs Murphy, and by the time evening fell each day, and the rehearsals came along, tempers were balanced on a knife-edge. The final rehearsal, on the evening of the twenty-second, went badly enough to please even the most carping of producers, who, as a breed I am assured, do not care for a too-smooth final rehearsal.

My own nerves began to quiver like over-taut wires at four in the afternoon when a negro woman called at Guinea Corner and handed in a letter which had, written on the face of the envelope, the words: 'Please pay bearer two shillings if safely delivered.' I gave the woman half-a-crown and ripped open the envelope. 'Dear Janet,' said Isobel's scrawling hand, 'I am sorry I have not been down again but can't leave. David has a lot of stuff hidden around the house and as this is only his third bad spell I don't know all his places yet and can't find it but he keeps on getting it. He is very smart at hiding it. I am sorry to ask you to pay this vegetable woman but you know how things are. Love, Isobel.'

The simply-expressed statement of her heart-breaking problem, together with her courage in facing it, tore at me, but, most of all, I was touched and made to cry by the fond pride in the: 'He is very smart at hiding it.' The letter had the effect on me of making all the excitement and high feeling about the play seem very puerile, and Madame's pride and joy in her good-looking, promising grandson who had arrived the day before only seemed to stress in my mind the plight of the tragic, perverted young lives that were fighting for survival, all alone, at Mount Melody.

When Twice and I arrived at the Great House for the rehearsal, Twice went straight away up to the roof to the electrical controls and the pulleys and I went up over the ramp of the drawbridge into the 'banqueting hall' in the front porch.

'If you had looked where you were going it would never have happened!' cried Mrs Cranston, her shaking hands holding her train in which there was a large rent.

'You shouldn't have been trailing it about on the gravel!' snapped Mrs Milner. 'You'd think you were a duchess or something!'

'It can be m-mended!' sobbed the tearful Mrs Peters, who was my wardrobe assistant.

'In the name o' Gawd!' screamed Mrs Murphy on a rising and shrill crescendo: 'It's meself that wishes Ah was with me dear mother in Belfast!' whereupon she went into a rousing fit of Irish hysterics.

Sandy, in his beggar's rags, gazed upon the scene thoughtfully with his blue-eyed stare and plucked a few sad twanging notes from his guitar while Sashie held his belled and be-ribboned obscene balloon up before him and moaned: 'Ah, me, the pressure o' the times upon me bauble!'

'Amateurs are the very devil!' trumpeted Miss Poynter, like a bassoon stressing a theme.

'What the *hell* is goin' on here?' Sir Ian bawled, striding upon the scene in all the panoply of helmet, sword, cloak and kilt. '*Mistress* Murphy, is it in drink taken that ye are?'

Mrs Murphy who, like all the ladies – even Mrs Cranston – adored Sir Ian, came out of her hysterics as if by magic and everyone calmed down and took their places while I, shaking in every nerve, went through the curtains into the drawing-room and took up my position as prompter.

The seating now being in place, all the Estate personnel within walking distance had been encouraged to come to this final rehearsal, and when we were all ready Twice addressed them from the roof: 'Madame Dulac, Mr Edward, ladies and gentlemen of the audience, we are asking you to remember tomorrow night that it is *Paradise* that is giving this play and we want you all to help. You know all the songs that will be played and we want you to sing them. In the second act, we want you to cheer for Mr Maclean or Mr Candlesham, but at the end of the act when Mars Sandy will sing a song that you all know, let him be heard and then join in the chorus. In the third act, during the big fight, we want you to cheer for Mr Maclean's or Mr Candlesham's side again. What we want during the fights especially is plenty of *noise!*'

To the negroes, noise and enjoyment were synonymous, they were blood brothers that went always hand in hand; there could not be one without the other, as they proceeded to demonstrate from the benches at the back and the bleachers at the sides with shouts of: 'Yes, sah! We gonna sing, sah! Me for Busha Maclean! Naw! Him de bad man! Me for Missa Cand'sham!' The noise was deafening.

'Quiet!' roared Sir Ian.

The noise died away and: 'Yes, sah, Sah Ian!' came the squeaky voice of Old Ezekiel the groom, replying for all.

'All right!' Twice's voice shouted from the roof. 'We're ready to start!'

The house and garden were plunged into total darkness for a moment, the portcullis lowered, and then the smaller verandah lights came on to a glow in the porch as young Mackie's pipes began to play in the 'orchestra pit' under the front steps. The Estate workers in the audience began to sing, creating their own strange negro harmonies as they went along, and when their singing and the pipes had hummed away across the dark valley,

172

Sir Ian's voice of the parade-ground with its: 'Ho, Varlets! Raise the portcullis!' rang out.

From the point of view of Twice and myself as producers, there were enough hitches to render us suicidal had it not been for the feeling generated by the audience. By the grossest accident, the whole play was entirely to its taste. Sir Ian, as 'The Lord Dulac', was precisely an exaggerated form in 'pretty clothes' of the 'Sah Ian' that they all knew, who rode about the cane-fields and strode around the factory and bellowed at them in a feudal way that was good-natured in the main. Sashie, as the Jester, was simply the 'Queeah clevah genckleman fe de Peak' dressed in clothes that were more peculiar and gay than ever, capering deliciously and using his 'bladder' with a broad, primitive licence that they could completely appreciate. And there was 'Mars Sandy wif him guitar' as they often saw him, and Maxie the Sugar-boiler's saxophone booming from below the steps the calypso songs with the one-two-off-beat rhythm that was the very pulse of their blood. And most wonderful of all, in this play of all plays, even 'Nim'le an' Ca'ence, de ponies, dem have pretty clo'es too!' for the negro loves 'pretty clothes'.

By the time the rehearsal was over and the last shout from the audience of: 'See Red Gu'k by de pillah dere, sah!' and 'Kill 'im daid, sah!' had died away, I felt as if I had spent the entire night in a very noisy underground train. My head ached, my ears buzzed and my tongue was cleaving to the roof of my mouth with a thirst induced by sheer nervous tension, when Twice descended from the roof and came to me in my corner of the dark drawing-room.

'Where are the switches in here?' he asked.

I went to a corner and switched on a standard lamp. 'Golly!' I said. 'I'm exhausted!'

'I know. But, Flash, it's going to do!'

'Oh, darling, do you think so?'

'I really do. We won't put them through it tomorrow. Leave them alone now and slap them into the real performance at night.'

'Whatever you think' I said wearily. 'If the Cranston loses her head in the third act again tomorrow, she loses it.'

Sashie and Sandy came through the curtains from the porch into the room. 'Eh, lackaday and gramercy!' said Sashie. 'If I haven't gone and bust me jumper!'

'It's only the seam,' I said.

'Oh, yes, I'll soon run it up when I get home. Twice, darling, are you simply furious with us?'

'It was all pretty ropey,' Twice told him, 'but I suppose you did your best.'

'Never mind, Mr Twice,' said Sandy comfortingly,'I'll tell you a thing. The pee-pots will just make all the difference. You wait an' see. Sir Ian an' me found four more in the cellar yesterday. One o' them's got the Flags o' All Nations painted on it – it came from the Carnegie sale, Sir Ian says – the man that had the elephant that didn't like salt water.' We leered at him in a baleful way. 'Mebbe,' he continued, 'what you are all needin' is a drink. You look sorta poorly. They're in the library, Sir Ian said.' He plucked a note or two from his guitar and strolled away, his tarlatan gypsy frills swinging, but looked back over his shoulder to say: 'Ye know what? I'm goin' to learn to play the pipes. This guitar is a sissy, dago sorta instrument.'

'I do not think,' said Sashie, 'that I can be long for this world unless I depart from this island.'

In the far depths of my soul, I agreed with him.

The quiet day that Twice and I had planned for ourselves as a forerunner to the performance could not set in until after lunchtime, for the morning had to be given to Marion and her supper preparations. Every oven on the Estate was full of roasting chickens, turkeys, beef and sucking pigs, and every refrigerator was a quivering, sick-making mass of jelly, ice-cream and trifle. On the Compound, Mrs Cranston and Mrs Milner had an openair scene about the largest roasting-tin on the Estate, which had been borrowed from the Club kitchen, which caused Mrs Peters to forget the mince pies in her oven so that they all burned, Mrs Peters thus being reduced to tears, and Mrs Murphy was so busy watching the scene from her window that she slipped with a large basin full of potato salad and it all fell into her sewing-machine. When this happened, she rushed out into the road, stopped a lorry that was going past with a last-minute load of chairs and said to the driver: 'Tell the ingineers at the factory that me machine is full o' mah-yon-eese an' me pore heart poines for Oireland!' and the negro driver went to the factory and reported to Twice: 'Murphy Missis on her knees an' her head it go befo'-hand' which caused Twice, Rob and Mr Murphy to tear along to the Compound with the factory fire-engine. I asked Twice afterwards why they took the fire-engine and he said: 'It was Murphy's idea. He said she never knelt except in cases of fire.'

At lunch-time, I had a cheering note from Isobel which told me that she thought she had found David's main cache of liquor and that she hoped things would soon be better now and the note ended with: 'And I am sure the show will be just dandy and I wish I could be there' which, in my overwrought state, only made me cry. After lunch, Twice and I took a firm hold on the books which we supposed ourselves to be reading at the moment and retired upstairs to our beds, but we could not have been there for half-an-h ir when Sir Ian and Sandy burst in.

'Here, ye know what, Mr Twice? Dad says can you come round to the Great House? Sir Ian an' me's been up at Riverhead an' ye know what? All the people's comin' down from the mountain for the play!'

'What mountain? What people?'

'The *hills* up there. Good God!' Sir Ian shouted. 'Hundreds o' them up there, on their winter grounds, growin' yam an' sweet potato an' that. They come down in the crop season for cuttin' an' loadin' an' that, but their villages are in the mountain thirty miles away.'

'And they're coming down? How?'

'They've hired every truck in the Bay, man! And there'll be eighty to a truck o' them!'

'Great Heavens!' Twice started to lace his shoes. 'What's Rob going to do?'

'He's takin' off the gate o' Poor Man's Pasture an' lettin' down part o' the fence – that field outside the garden wall, ye know. We're goin' to mark it off in parkin' lots an' they'll have to use their trucks as grand-stands.'

'Holy suffering cow! That was to be the car-park for the guests!'

'That's just it! We have to take the signs down and bring the guests in by the north drive an' park them in that field by the mule pen. All except Dene-Jorrocks, that is. *His* car'll have to come right in and round to the house garage now. Hope he gets here before the crowd from the mountain or the poor devil won't get in at all!'

Twice looked up hopelessly. 'The people on the trucks in that field won't be able to hear a word!'

'Rob's sendin' a car to the Bay for a croonin' thing.'

'A crooning thing?'

'A loud-speaker system, Mr Twice,' Sandy elucidated. 'Mr Mackie's gone for it.'

'Wired from *where*?' Twice shouted. 'The Great House lines can't take any more!'

'They're bringin' a cable direct from the fact'ry.'

Twice sprang up. 'I'll see you at the Great House when the balloon goes up,' he said to me and ran down the stairs. I sat up in my bed and glared at my star actors. 'Why don't you two go somewhere where you *can't* make any more trouble?' I asked.

'That's a fine thing! Where'd you be with your ruddy play if it wasn't for the boy an' me as an intelligence corps? Tell me that!'

'*My* ruddy play? So help me — '

'What you're needin', Missis Janet,' said Sandy, 'is a cup o' tea. I'll tell Clorinda.

I swung my feet off my bed on to the floor and into my sandals.

'That's a good idea, Sandy. Tell Clorinda tea for three of us, in the drawing-room.'

Followed by Sir Ian, I went downstairs, conscious that probably the greatest help I could render to Twice and Rob at this stage was to keep Sandy and Sir Ian at Guinea Corner for as long as possible and well out of their way.

'I wish it was tomorrow,' I said. 'I'm at the stage where I don't care if this thing is a colossal flop or not. The whole things is mad anyway.'

'Oh, come now, Missis Janet! No good bein' like that. You have some tea an' get to feelin' better. It's a jolly good play, by Jove – that's *why* they're all comin' down from the mountain. What's mad about it?'

'Everything! The play itself, the people in it – everything!'

'Oh, rot, my dear. You've just got a touch o' the jim-jams.'

'Nothing of the sort!' I snapped. 'Don't try to tell *me* it's normal for a man like you to be jumping about in a helmet and a kilt and for Rob Maclean to be cavorting about on a horse pretending to be a mediaeval knight! . . . And there are these poor youngsters up at Mount Melody!'

'So *that's* what's worryin' you!' he pounced as the tea came in, borne by Clorinda and followed by Sandy.

'Missis Janet, can I have my tea in the kitchen? I'm goin' to do a practice of some of my tunes for Cookie an' Clorinda an' Caleb.'

'All right,' I said ungraciously. 'As long as I don't have to have your tunes in here. I can't stand it.'

'You don't want to go worryin' about those Denholm people,' Sir Ian said as I poured tea. 'There's nothin' to it. When the boy's on his feet we'll get him an' the girl off to the States an' that'll be that.'

'I can't *help* worrying!' I told him peevishly. 'I've never been mixed up with so many queer people in my life!'

'You were brought up in Ross, dammit. You should be used to 'em!'

'How d'you mean?'

'Ross can't be so different from the rest of the Highlands an' my old uncle near Pitlochry – Mother's brother, ye know – is far queerer'n anythin' you'll meet out here.'

'How d'you mean?' I said again.

'Wears a kilt an' writes to *The Times* about Home Rule for Scotland.'

'There's nothing particularly queer about that,' I said.

'But he *believes* in them – the kilt an' Home Rule, I mean!'

'Well, why not?'

'Good God! We spent one half o' history learnin' that trousers were more decent as well as bein' warmer an' the other half gettin' a share o' the wealth o' England an' this old fool wants to go an' undo everythin'! If that ain't bein' queer, what is? Tell me that!'

I was utterly at a loss to answer him at all and suddenly I did not care and he seized a large piece of cake and champed at it angrily while I sat staring straight before me at the harsh light beyond the windows. I became almost unaware that he was in the room at all and I do not remember his going away.

I have no clear memory of the events, if any, of that afternoon, but I remember clearly how I felt. I am not in any way a nervous or imaginative person – quite the reverse, as Sashie would say – but I was aware of a horrible uneasiness, like the feeling in the air when the birds give themselves up to a restless twittering before a thunderstorm. Outside, the sun was brilliant, but the air was dead still and, in spite of that, there were little flickers here and there among the narrow leaves of the bamboos in the big clump at the corner of the garden, as if some secret, malicious spirit were abroad, lurking, deliberately causing that little shuddering flicker of leaf to exacerbate the nerves.

As the afternoon wore on, and Sir Ian and Sandy had gone away, the feeling of uneasiness intensified and I sat alone in the corner of the dim drawing-room, strangely afraid to go upstairs to my bedroom, longing for human company, yet too proud in an absurd way to go to the kitchen and exchange a word with my servants. Sitting very still, I faced the fact that I felt haunted and that I was full of fear of something unknown. In any difficulty of any kind, it has always been my habit to go back for comfort, in my mind, to Reachfar and to my family and, automatically, now, I found myself thinking of my grandmother, one of the most fearless women I have ever known.

Although she died long ago, the legend of her still persists in our district of Ross and many of the country people will tell you that she had The Sight, as they call it. I was remembering now an occasion in my childhood when, for weeks preceding a local tragedy, she was so ill-tempered that it was almost impossible for the rest of us of the family to live beside her. I remembered how she seemed angry with everyone and with herself as well – as if her anger were being generated in defiance of some evil influence that she could not identify and therefore could not combat. That is how I felt that afternoon at Guinea Corner – as if, in a fit of blind rage, I could hurl the ornaments through the windows, smash the furniture, tear the walls down – as if, at all costs, I must make some demonstration against this unknown, unidentifiable but inimical force.

Twice arrived home about six o'clock, just as the rapid dark was falling, ran into the hall and saw me sitting in the corner of the drawing-room. He snapped on the lights.

'Darling, you're not even changed!' he said in an accusing, overwrought voice as he came towards me, but then he stopped short. 'Flash, what's the matter?'

I longed to try to describe to him what I had been feeling, but I could not find the words and I felt, too, that this hour or two before the play began was not the time to create further anxiety. I stood up, trying to conceal my excessive gladness at seeing him. 'Nothing, my pet. Why? I was just going up to change – we'll go up together. We – we've got *two* bathrooms, after all.'

'Sit down. I'm going to get us a drink.' He went into the hall, called Clorinda and came back. 'What's been happening? Anybody been here?'

'No. Only Sir Ian and Sandy – they had some tea and then went off.'

Clorinda brought the tray of drinks and he poured a stiff tot of whisky and handed it to me.

'Great God! Your fingers are freezing! Flash, *tell* me if you feel ill for pity's sake! God damn and blast this bloody play! . . . Flash, what *is* it?'

'Darling, please don't be worried,' I told him, my voice

uneven in spite of my best efforts. 'I think I've just got a touch of the jitters – I'll be all right after this drink.' I swallowed a nauseating mouthful from my glass. 'Sit down. We needn't be round there before seven.'

'Jitters my foot! You've never had jitters in your life! You *feel* all right?'

'Twice, please don't go on and on!'

'I've never seen you like this before.'

'You've never seen me on a theatrical first night before, and take a good look, for if I can help it you'll never see me on such a night again. . . . Light a cigarette for me, darling.'

Twice has an unremarkable but dependable sort of face. His eyes are very blue and his teeth perfect and of a clear, glittering white, but apart from those features his face has, for me, no handsomeness, but only this firm dependability. The queer uneasiness seemed to seep out of the atmosphere as I looked at him and the tense, strained feeling of some knowledge trapped inside me died away.

'One can hardly be blamed for feeling a little jumpy,' I said. 'This is the queerest Christmas I have ever been mixed up in. Let's go up and have our baths.'

While we bathed and changed, I was aware that Twice still tended to look askance at me, but as I became more and more inwardly normal, he became less and less anxious and by the time we drove round to the Great House, the strange feeling of the afternoon in my memory seemed unreal, in the sense that a dream seems unreal, with the unreality of something that was actual, but on a different plane of consciousness.

Shortly after Twice and I had reached the Great House drawing-room, the three cars with the Governor's party rolled in to the library entrance where the guests were being taken capably in hand by Madame and Edward. By some miracle, an atmosphere of dignified calm, suitable to the venerable old house, prevailed. I went down to the dining-room to see how Marion was and found her with everything in apple-pie order, the gubernatorial table decorated to the last rosebud and her massed refrigerators, full of jellies, lined up in a martial row in the pantry. She was dispensing drinks to Rob and one or two others and handed glasses to Twice and myself with a: 'Have a tot. We're all going to feel terrible tomorrow, anyway.'

After this drink and an injection of Marion's unshakeable normality, I went back to my own place in the drawing-room, feeling much better, and laid out the greasepaint and powder and Sandy's gypsy dress on their table, thankful that he was the only one with a change of clothing to make. Before I had finished, the lorries from 'the mountain' had begun to come in and what Sir Ian had said was no exaggeration. There must have been eighty cheering, singing men and women in each one and the cabs of the lorries were decorated over all with sprays of bougainvillaea and hibiscus and great branches of scarlet poinsettia. As the people from the more nearby villages began to arrive on foot, the players began to arrive in the drawing-room from the back door and the business of final touches of their make-up began. I noticed that all the skins I touched were unusually cold and that not even Mrs Murphy was disposed to talk a great deal. As the hands of the big grandfather clock in the corner slipped round towards eight, a queerly blood-stirring hum was coming from outside and Twice came down from the roof and said to me: 'Slip out through the window on to the verandah with me and have a look. It's worth seeing.'

Four windows opened from the drawing-room on to the front verandah and we drew back the curtains from one of them and stepped out over the low sill. Being nearly eight o'clock, it was completely dark outside and the scene was illumined only by the lights which shone out from the ground-floor rooms of the house and by the coloured bulbs that were strung from tree to tree. Seen from above, as we saw it, the big garden lawn was an extraordinary sight. From the lorries, full of people, parked in the field beyond the wall, all over the lawn to the front rows of armchairs, empty as yet, by the roped-off 'jousting' area, the place was one great stadium, packed with a solid mass of people. Half-stupefied, I stared at it while the tense, expectant hum rose about us.

'Twice, it's – it's awful! What have we gone and done?'

I could feel his arm quivering under my hand and his voice shook too. 'The trouble is we've still got to do it,' he said. 'Are you all right? Really all right?'

'Of course I am! Don't be foolish, darling – it was only a touch of the jitters, just like *you*'ve got now!' I pressed his tense forearm.

'Oh, I've always been subject to the jumps – you know that. But it isn't like *you* to get in a state.'

As he spoke, Madame's invited guests began to come round the house from the library door and take their seats in the front chairs and we watched in silence as the space filled up except for four seats in the centre of the front row.

'We'd better get inside, Twice!' I whispered.

'Just a minute,' he whispered back, 'I want to see old Madame handle this.'

At that moment, Edward Dulac and Lady Dene-Jorrocks came round the house on to the lawn and took their seats. The rest of the audience was chattering and laughing and calling to one another across the serried rows, and little snatches of song were rising from the bleachers and the parked lorries. Madame, on the arm of His Excellency, came round the corner of the house. Very small, in her long, black evening dress and velvet stole, beside the tall man, she came to the foot of the 'drawbridge', turned to face the assembly, stopped and, even from behind and above as we were, we could feel the force of her determined eye. Dead silence fell. Shamblingly and untidily, but to the last man, the members of the audience rose to their feet and stayed standing while the representative of His Majesty took his seat.

'Say what you like,' Twice breathed, 'you have to hand it to that old woman. . . . Come on. Time we manned the guns.' We climbed back inside and drew the curtains behind us.

The 'Dulac family', Sashie and Sandy were in a tight group, ready to go through the curtains into the porch 'banqueting hall'.

'I'm going up above,' Twice told them quietly. 'Everything is fine outside. Don't worry. You can't miss.' He turned to me. 'All the lights will go off as soon as I get up there and your red pilot will come on. . . . Right, Sir Ian, out you go.'

I held back the curtains. The players went through to their places behind the portcullis. The big grandfather clock struck eight, all the lights went out and the little red bulb in the corner of the drawing-room glowed into life. There was a suspended pause of almost unbearable silence, then the porch lights and the flood-lights came on outside and Mackie's pipes tore the silence to shreds. The singing outside immediately rose in tremendous volume and died away and as it died I heard Sir Ian make a little clearing sound in his throat and then came the parade-ground command: 'Ho, Varlets!' It was at that moment that I made the two-fold discovery that I was a prompter without a script and that I could be sick at the drop of a hat.

By the end of the first act, though, I knew that I was not going to be required as a prompter, the feeling of nausea had left me and I was bitterly sorry that I was not out in front instead of all alone in the vast dark drawing-room, for everybody seemed to be having a wonderful time, but I had a superstitious feeling that for me to make a move that we had not planned would be to tempt our luck. When the second act and the 'jousting' were over, the excitement outside was so tremendous that we curtailed the interval in order to stop the noise, but the period of comparative peace thus gained was short, for as soon as the quick negro eyes glimpsed the first of Red Gurk's skulking varlets in the shrubbery, bedlam broke loose.

'Dem comin', Sah Ian, sah! Pull up yo' bridge, sah!' came a warning shout from a lorry away at the back.

From then on, all was in the nature of a family night out.

'Up de wes'-mos' pillah, Busha Maclean, sah! Ain't nobody dere, sah!' came an advising voice from the bleachers.

'T'row it on him haid, Mars Sandy! . . . Lawd! See him t'row it on him fadder's haid!'

'T'row 'im ovah, sah!'

'Lick 'im dahn, sah!'

'Stick 'im in de gut, sah!'

At last, I could bear my Cinderella position no longer and pulled the curtains apart in time to see Red Gurk, having given the audience a good run for its money, allow himself to be pushed half-over the verandah balustrade so that he could be stabbed by Sir Lancelot in full view of one and all while Sir Ian stood at the ready to 'clonk' him, for good measure, with the chamberpot bedizened with the Flags of All Nations.

In a sort of stupor of triumph at our success, and relief that it was all over, and dazed at the same time by the waves of noise from outside, I felt myself suddenly thrown aside, wrapped and half-strangled in curtain, by a man in the sugar-bag costume of a varlet who sprang in through the window. He ran on down the centre of the long room, almost invisible in the darkness, and in the same moment Sandy and Sashie plunged in through the red curtains over the door.

'Keep quiet!' I heard Sashie's hissing whisper, but he was just too late.

'Hi, you!' I had shouted at the varlet. 'Where are you — '

At the sound of my voice, the sacking-clothed figure spun round and the dim red light caught the face of David Denholm. But it was not the face I knew. It was the contorted, working face of a madman and the glow of the red light in the eyes while the waves of sound from outside reverberated round the room gave him the aura of a devil called up from some raging inferno. Beyond this, I had time for no other impression. A blatter of shots cracked in quick succession, Sashie's big balloon crumpled into a wizened rag as he fell against me and we both fell to the floor.

'Candlesham belongs to *my sister*!' I heard a voice scream above the din as I lay panting on the floor under the weight of Sashie, and the figure then ran out through the back door.

'Missis Janet?' said Sandy on a terrified, questioning note. My mind suddenly became crystal clear and I struggled up to a sitting position. 'All right, Sandy, boy. He's gone. Run out to the porch and bow with the others. The people mustn't know about this. Run *out*, you hear? Go *on*!'

Sandy disappeared between the curtains.

'A murrain on that Denholm for a scurvy knave!' said Sashie, whose head was in my lap. 'He's *bust* me bauble!'

His eyes closed, the head rolled to one side and I saw the blood seeping and widening in a black stain on the shoulder of the yellow tunic.

'Sashie!'

He did not open his eyes, but he spoke. 'Let's keep quite still, shall we? It's nothing much. Someone will come soon.'

'Oh, Sashie!'

'For God's sake, don't get in a state, my sweet. It's all right.'

Twice, having raised the portcullis and left it so to bring the applause to an end, had come down from the roof and he ran into the room from the far end. Even in the dim red light I could see the glitter of triumph in his eyes and smile. He stopped short with a jerk.

'Oh, Twice! It's Sashie! He's *shot*!'

'What?'

'But not fatally,' said Sashie.

Sandy did not go down over the drawbridge with the other players to join the audience but came back through the curtains.

'Missis Janet? I bowed like you said — '

'The very bloke we need!' said Twice. 'Go and ask Doctor to come up here. Don't talk to anyone else. Just bring Doctor.'

Sandy ran away.

'Twice, darling,' said Sashie, 'you know my secret of the legs. I am a fairylike creature, as you know. Could you and Janet put me on a sofa? Please? Just to avoid publicity?'

'Say no more, chum,' said Twice and picked the light body up and laid it on a sofa. 'All right?'

'Splendid, thanks.'

With the razor-sharp knife he always carries, Twice then began to cut away the blood-stained tunic from Sashie's shoulder. Sandy came back with the doctor and, inevitably, Sir Ian.

'God dammit! What happened? How *is* the poor fellah? Where *is* that perisher?'

'Thou pox-ridden old varlet!' said the patient. 'Fetch me a stoup o' sack!'

'Go an' bring some whisky up here, boy!' said Sir Ian. 'An' bring your father with you – don't talk to anybody else! . . . God bless my soul! The murderin' young brute! You're *sure* it was Denholm, Missis Janet?'

'That very one – a plague on all his houses!' said Sashie.

'You keep quiet,' said the doctor.

'Can't keep *him* quiet!' barked Sir Ian. 'Don't be stoopid! God dammit, I never heard o' a thing like this – goin' shootin' people in their own houses! Old Toby'd never've done a thing like that! What got into the fellah? Where is he *now*? Tell me that!'

At the doctor's request, Rob fetched his bag from his car and then Rob and Twice went away and I continued to sit in a gormless way on the floor where they left me, sipping at the glass of whisky and water that somebody had put into my hand and conscious of nothing but a relieved feeling that now the worst was really over. Even now, with the blood-stained shreds of Sashie's tunic lying on the floor beside me, and the doctor and Sir Ian round the sofa, I could hardly believe what had happened, and yet, at the same time, I was aware of my foreknowledge that something of this sort *would* happen.

'Missis Janet, are you all right?' Sandy asked. 'Can I *do* anything?'

'Sandy, I'm fine, but I'd love a cigarette.'

Sandy found a box, some matches and an ashtray.

'Would you stay with me, Sandy? I'm sort of scary all on my own. Do you know where Twice and your father went?'

'Don't you be scared, Missis Janet,' Sandy told me. 'You'll be all right now, an' Dad an' Mr Twice an' Mr Don are lookin' for Mr Denholm, you see. Missis Janet, was he crazy?'

'I think so, Sandy.'

'I saw him comin' over the end of the verandah. He didn't have a Red Gurk red thing on. Then I saw the gun in his hand and he looked sorta funny an' the only person I could make hear was Mr Sashie because he wasn't really in the fightin', you see.'

184

'You did very well, Sandy, and you are not to worry about it. And I'm sure your father and the others will find him.'

'Will they send him to prison?'

'I don't think so. He is crazy because he's sick, you see. And Mr Sashie isn't badly hurt. . . . Here, listen, I'm hungry.'

'Listen, I'll tell you a thing – Cookie's keepin' me an' Sir Ian a whole raft o' turkey legs. Would you like a turkey leg?'

'Sandy, I'd *love* it!' I lied with emphasis. 'Would you go and get some turkey legs and some sandwiches?'

'I'll be right back!' he said and strode away, his tarlatan frills swinging gaily.

When I had been eight years old, I remembered – although shooting affrays were not a feature of my childhood life at Reachfar – any disturbing thing that happened always felt less disturbing if I could have something to eat. There is nothing like the stomach for keeping the mind and the nervous system in their proper places.

'You've been very lucky,' said the doctor to Sashie at last, as he stood up and straightened his back.

'Doctor, dear, I was born that way,' said Sashie.

'Where were you when the shots were fired?'

'Right here,' I said from my place on the floor. 'Only standing up. We both were. Sashie was in front of me.'

'The bullet must be somewhere in that mahogany panelling,' the doctor said.

'Mother'll be as mad as cat's lights about that!' Sir Ian said. 'Not that it'll matter. She's goin' to be fairly damn' mad just in a general way, by Jove, an' I don't blame her. Never heard o' such a confounded carry-on in my life. It's worse'n old Pickerin's fire. After all, Pickerin's brother was shootin' at an *alligator*, not just shootin' for shootin's own sake! . . . But where did the perisher *go*? Tell me that! . . . Have a tot, Doctor. You deserve it. We all deserve — '

'Ian!' said Madame in the wide doorway. 'What, may I enquire, do you imagine you are doing? Are you aware that we are entertaining His Excellency?'

'Comin', Mother, comin'!'

It was too late. Madame had seen Sashie lying on the sofa, the bandages about the neck and the slung arm.

'Young man!' she said in an accusing voice. 'What happened?'

'I apologize, Madame,' said Sashie, 'for not getting up. I took

185

the storming of the battlements a little over-seriously and twisted the old arm, don't you know.'

'Iphm. I knew that that disgusting balloon could only lead to trouble. And Ian, after His Excellency has gone, I wish to speak to you on another matter. You have publicly disgraced me. Are you aware that Lady Dene-Jorrocks is under the impression that a member of this family actually purchased that – that Article with the flags on it, deliberately and by intent, out of personal taste, at a *shop*?'

'No, Mother!' protested Sir Ian.

'She was extremely civil and tactful. She says that in *her* family they had one with chrysanthemums in purple, but the stigma on the family taste remains none-the-less. . . . Young man, have you had suitable nourishment?'

Sashie raised his glass with his good arm. 'Thank you, yes, Madame.'

'You will stay here tonight to be near Doctor. And make Maud deduct a night's lodging from your bill – the Poynters' were always a little too sharp on a bargain. . . . Sandy, what are you doing in the drawing-room with that disgusting mess of bones?'

'Please, Madame, it's Sir Ian an' me's turkey legs.'

'Turkey legs!' She glared round at us. 'But at least you are all sober. Janet, you and Twice will come downstairs. His Excellency wishes to meet you.'

'Yes, Madame.' If Twice failed to appear, I thought, I would cross that bridge when I came to it.

'Ian, you will come *now*.'

'Yes, Mother.'

In her decisive way, she held out her fat little arm, crooked at the elbow, and Sir Ian perforce had to take it and they moved away together out of the room and along the verandah, Madame's firm little heels tapping out the message of her annoyance at this hitch in her party.

I had risen from my place on the floor when Madame came in and I now began to go round the big room, switching on lamp after lamp, for the darkness outside was like muffling black velvet and I felt that there could never be too much light. The Great House drawing-room extended through the whole depth of the house, with a door at one end opening on to the porch which had formed our banqueting hall and a door at the other on to a wide verandah. On either side of each of these doors were four large windows and it seemed to me that all these apertures, their

186

curtains now drawn back for air and coolness, admitted far too much of the blackness of the night.

'You feeling all right, Mrs Alexander?' the doctor asked from his chair beside Sashie's sofa. 'You must have got the devil's own fright.'

'Oh, I'm not a very nervous type,' I said, making my way round Sandy on the floor with his plate of turkey legs to the table that held my drink and the cigarette-box. 'Besides, it all happened so quickly — '

I stopped speaking as Twice, Rob and Don came through the back door of the room, followed by Sir Ian who had now shaken Madame off downstairs.

'All right!' he bellowed. 'Where *is* the perisher?'

'We lost him, sir,' Rob said. 'He had too much of a start and had that car of his parked under the bamboos down by the south gate. Took off in it like a bat out of hell — '

'Oh, damn an' blast it!'

'We found this, though.' Don laid the revolver on the table. 'It's empty — '

'But my dear Don, of *course* it's empty!' Sashie said. 'He stood there with his finger on the tit and pumped everything at us, but *every*thing!'

I stood by the small table, staring at them all. The light in the room was suddenly far too clear, the shadows in the corners far too deep, the edges of the windows sharply-cut lines framing black rectangles, the jaws, hairlines and eyebrows of the faces exaggeratedly marked. Something hot and cloudy formed in my chest making my breathing difficult; rose to my throat, constricting it to bursting point; rose further into my head, began to swell there, and the light in the room turned to a glaring, harsh yellow. Lines of furniture and people became blacker and even more sharply defined momentarily before the thing in my head exploded with a loud bang in a shower of evil yellow spots that seemed to drift laterally across a plane, as if a handful of coins had been spattered violently across a white table. 'They should have caught him!' I heard a high-pitched voice saying, far away, as if on the other side of a hill. 'They should have caught him!'

Then I heard the voice of the doctor. 'All right, everybody – she's coming round. . . . Swallow this, Mrs Alexander.'

I swallowed obediently and opened my eyes. 'This is a fine carry-on,' I said and sat up on the sofa which was opposite to the one that held Sashie. 'I'm terribly sorry, everybody.'

'Take that bloody gun out of here!' Sir Ian shouted and I could feel his need to let off steam in some way. 'Googorralmighty! If I had that drunken perisher here I'd throttle him!' He swallowed an angry mouthful of whisky, slammed his glass down on a table and said gently to me: 'You feelin' better, Missis Janet?'

'I'm perfectly all right, Sir Ian. I'm very sorry. I've never passed out like that in my life before.' Twice was staring at me with eyes unbearably worried. 'I'm all right, darling, honestly.'

'I don't like it,' he said in a puzzled way and looked up at the doctor. 'I've seen her in an accident in Scotland when a petrol tank blew up and there was nothing like this — '

'This was quite natural,' the doctor said. 'She had a bad shock.' Then he grinned at us. 'Maybe *now* you've reached the crisis of your acclimatization, Mrs Alexander. No. Don't move about. Just stay where you are.'

'Sandy, please give me a turkey leg,' I said.

With a smile of relief the little fellow proffered his large dish to me and then to the others, ending with a big man whom I recognized as the Island Commissioner of Police who helped himself to a large leg.

'Thanks, son.'

Sandy looked up at him. 'Ye know what, sir? I'll tell you a thing — '

'What, son?'

'Even if it does make a scandal about people shootin' people on Paradise, it's time somebody put their foot down. You should put that man Denholm in your prison!'

'Don't you worry, son,' said Mr Cardew. 'We'll fix him up all right. Can you spare another turkey leg? Thanks. . . . That was a splendid show you put on tonight.'

'Twice, have you really turned the police out?' I asked in a whisper.

It was Sir Ian, not in any whisper, who replied: 'We've got to *get* the perisher, dammit! He's dangerous! We'll keep it all as quiet an' decent as we can, but if Beattie won't come into line an' get him off up to the States for treatment, I'm goin' to ask Sashie an' you to prefer a charge against him.'

'Oh, I *say*!' said Sashie.

'Don't be stoopid, boy!' Sir Ian bawled. 'We can't have the fellah tearin' round loosin' off with a revolver every time it comes up his back! Dammit, it was only because he is a rotten shot that he didn't kill the *both* o' ye!'

'Iphm. It won't do, you know,' said Mr Cardew. 'It won't do at all.'

The unnatural light and the sharply-etched lines persisted in the room and it seemed to me that moment by moment everything became more unreal. The people became caricatures of themselves, in particular Mr Cardew who, before he came to the island, had been a superintendent in the London Metropolitan force. The mark of that great body was on him always, but tonight, instead of his well-tailored dinner clothes and black tie, I could see upon him the blue uniform and the helmet of the big man on the beat, while at any moment I expected his broad face to take on that mildly questioning look while his calm, kindly voice said: 'Now, what *is* going on here?'

One side of me longed to go home, to go back alone with Twice to Guinea Corner, shut the door and leave all this on the outside of it, but the inbred training not to make a 'fuss' or a 'scene' or to concede that matters have passed beyond the pale of the normal is a potent thing. I sat on, on my sofa, feeling, physically, completely well and hungrily eating sandwiches while I tried to ignore the fact that my mind was divided on to two planes, one the normal plane which was participating in what was going on around me, the other a plane of waiting and of knowledge at which I was afraid to look. The other side of me knew that, in any case, to go home to Guinea Corner and shut the door was useless, for it would not take me away from this thing that was impending, and I had a queer feeling that if I could only summon the courage to examine that dark second plane in my mind I would find there the knowledge of the thing that was to come, but the normal plane of the mind resents such feelings and automatically rejects them. I blinked, told myself that the light in the room was perfectly normal and concentrated on the conversation around me.

The party downstairs began to break up. Madame brought the Governor and his lady, at their request, up to see us in the drawing-room and, as soon as they had gone downstairs and had driven away, the rest of the guests began to leave. By about one in the morning, everyone had gone and the party in the drawing-room was reduced to Madame, Sir Ian, Edward, the Macleans, Mr Cardew, Don and Sashie, the doctor, Twice and myself. It was only now that Madame, Edward and Marion were apprised of what had actually happened, and Madame's furious idignation only made everything more unreal for me and added an element

189

of the ludicrous when she said: 'And I shall *certainly* not rely on the Instrument to talk to Beattie Denholm about this! I shall go, *personally*, to Mount Melody!'

Mr Cardew, at this, also felt, I think, that things were getting out of hand, for he rose to his feet and said: 'Time I went and you good people went to bed. Sorry your show was spoiled like this, but we'll get him.' He turned to Madame. 'Don't bother to go up to Mount Melody yet, Madame Dulac – there's nobody there but the servants. Seems Mrs Denholm and the girl drove out last night too.'

'What in Heaven's name is Beattie Denholm playin' at?' Sir Ian asked loudly. 'Tryin' to hide him?'

'Goodness knows, sir,' said Mr Cardew. 'But they can't get far, not unless they swim for it. I'm leaving a couple of corporals downstairs. Ring me at my house if you hear anything or if anything happens. Good night, all.'

As soon as he had gone, I rose to my feet and held out my hand to wish Madame good night.

'*Siddown!*' Sir Ian bellowed at me. 'None o' the rest o' you is movin' one damn out o' here tonight!' He strode out to the verandah, shouted: 'Letty!' and came back to say: 'Plenty o' bedrooms, all ready. Twice, take Missis Janet along there – first on your left. . . . Letty, find a nightgown an' things for Missis Janet an' Missis Marion. . . . Go *on*, *Rob* – no arguin'! The whole boilin' of ye will stay here with the police an' the doctor until I hear they've got hold o' that perishin' fellah Denholm!'

At this stage, I would have gone anywhere to get away from the drawing-room, with its lurid light and all the people with the exaggerated faces, and when the doctor, in the big bedroom with the four-poster bed, said: 'Mrs Alexander, this is only a very mild sedative, will you take it?' I took the glass from his hand and swallowed the draught without question. I would have swallowed a pint of poison in order to be rid of him, to be free of the last of the voices and impressions that were battering at and crowding my consciousness.

Chapter Twelve

I SLEPT LIKE the dead and knew nothing more until the bright morning, when I opened my eyes and stared up at the brocaded canopy of the big bed and then looked at Twice who was fully dressed, sitting in a chair by the bedside, with a book in his hands.

'Hello,' he said. 'Happy Christmas Eve! How do you feel?'

'Sort of artificial,' I said. 'What time is it? Has anything been happening?'

'Nearly seven. Cardew's been on the 'phone. The search for the two Mount Melody cars is island-wide now.'

'But, Twice, it's ridiculous!' I protested. 'It's that old mad woman, of course. She must be trying to hide him. She must be really mad!'

'It doesn't bear thinking about. . . . Flash, are you really and truly all right?'

'Physically, yes, darling. Stop worrying. . . . Oh, I know I made a fool of myself last night, but honestly it *was* a little much that bloke popping off with that gun and Sashie and the blood and everything.'

'I know that, but still — '

'What?' I asked impatiently as I got out of bed.

'Oh, nothing.'

'*You* look rotten,' I told him. 'Didn't you sleep?'

'Not much. Couldn't. With you chatting all night.'

'Chatting? Me?'

'Who else?'

'In my sleep? What about?'

'A lot of tripe. It must have been that stuff Doc gave you.'

'You should have wakened me. What was I saying?'

'Oh, a lot of stuff about water on the ceiling.'

'Water?'

'Iphm.'

'Water on the brain is more like it. I'm sorry, darling. I shouldn't have taken that stupid stuff. I didn't really need it at all. I used to talk and even walk in my sleep as a kid and I suppose last night set me off.'

I had had my bath and had dressed by the time Sir Ian strode into the room, immaculate in white drill riding breeches and black, highly-polished boots.

'Mornin', my dear. Sleep well?'

'Yes, thank you. . . . Twice tells me there's no news. Sir Ian, where *can* these people be?'

'Bah! Mount Melody! These damn' native policemen got no sense an' Cardew don't know the tricks o' these old Islanders like Beattie. Cardew thinks she's a decent, reasonable, London crook. Nothin' o' the sort! Beattie's at Mount Melody – so's the boy. Told Cardew so. They're going up there to make a proper search this mornin'.'

'But they went up last night!' said Twice. 'And what about those two big cars?'

'In the bush somewhere, boy! Could hide a battleship up there if you wanted, especially at night. . . . Sorry about that carry-on last night, Missis Janet, an' Sashie gettin' winged an' everythin', but I can't help laughin'. It's just like the old days an' Mother's so perishin' mad there's no holdin' her. Been ringin' up Mount Melody all mornin' an' gettin' no answer. She's always been so damned cock-a-hoop because we've had no carry-ons on Paradise in *her* time – she wouldn't *have* it, she said. Well, dammit, she's got it now whether she wants it or not an' serve her damn' right, in a way. . . . Feel like a little breakfast? It'll be ready in about half-an-hour.'

Sashie now came into the room in a white shirt that was much too big for him, his good arm in a sleeve that hung down well beyond his finger-tips, his burst balloon on its stick tucked into the sling on his injured arm and drooping limply over his shoulder.

'A sorry jester, forsooth,' he said. 'Janet, darling, can you pin me in any way into this outsize garment that Sandy stole for me?'

'Where's Sandy now?' Sir Ian asked. 'Not still sleepin'?'

'No,' said Sashie with some bitterness. 'He awoke at crack of dawn, came into my room, told me several things, gave a spirited rendering of several calypsos on his guitar, had a bath with *all* the sitz and spitz things working at once, then ate three turkey legs and two stale sandwiches and went out.'

'Take his guitar with him?'

'Yes, thank God!'

'That's fine. He'll be down in the servants' quarters. That's why Missis Marion can't find a perishin' soul to serve breakfast. I'd better go an' get him. Don't want any more fuss around here. Dammit, it's Christmas Eve when you think of it.'

He strode out of the room and away along the verandah while Sashie adjusted his sling with finicking fingers. 'May Columbus

192

be forgiven for not knowing what he did when he discovered this island,' he said and drifted towards the door.

'Sashie!' I said, and he stopped, looking round at me under cocked eyebrows. 'Sashie, it's stupid and inadequate to say I am sorry about how you got hurt last night, but I have to say it. It was my fault and I am very sorry.'

'Darling, don't be so down-in-the-mouth – quite the reverse! Besides, all your reasoning is so utterly wrong, but completely. Nothing is *ever* all one person's fault, you know. There are always *millions* of factors involved, simply millions! So humiliating to the ego, but so true. I can't be a hero, having been shot entirely by mistake, and you *really* can't act the heroine of a drama of passion, for the poor fellow was tight, so say no more. I'm going to look for a cup of coffee.'

He drifted out and away along the verandah as lightly as a leaf in a summer breeze and, with a sense of being lost in some wilderness of negation, I turned to Twice and as soon as I began to speak I heard my voice crack and begin to rise.

'There you are! There it is! Sir Ian, according to himself, can't help laughing because his mother has had a scene at Paradise and *that* one accuses me of trying to create a drama! The hurricane is over and the bananas are growing again on Pleasant Hill! It's a fortnight since the fire and the jungle is growing over the place where the village used to be! It's all being covered up! Another two inches and Sashie would have been killed last night, but nobody thinks of that! This is less than twelve hours later and it's already a joke! I tell you, they're all crazy!'

'Flash!' Twice said sternly. 'Pull yourself together! What the hell is the matter with you?'

I stared at him. 'I don't know!' I said. 'I don't know!' and I began to cry.

Having got me out of the chaos of hysteria. Twice set himself to comfort me.

'All right, Flash. It's all right. Now, look, we've got to stay here until they catch up with Denholm and then we'll go back to Guinea Corner and be by ourselves. They're bound to get him soon. Try to hold on until breakfast is over and we can get away. You've had a bad fright and you were over-tired before that and — '

'Listen, Twice,' I said, sitting down and forcing my voice into a semblance of calm, cold reason, 'please don't talk to me as if I were an idiot child. None of you seem to realize that David

Denholm probably thinks he killed Sashie or me or both last night – the last he saw of us we were in a heap on the floor. He's not a joke – he's a dangerous lunatic!'

'But the police are doing their best, Flash! And besides, he hasn't got his gun any longer.'

'Guns are ten a penny in this island! I think we are the only household I know that hasn't a revolver, if not two or three!'

'But – what can *we* do anyway?'

I rose and looked down at Twice while he frowned up at me from his seat on the bed. I did not know what we should do. I did not know what I felt about anything. I could not find words to describe the premonition of disaster that was brooding over me.

'I don't know,' I said. 'I suppose there is nothing we can do except what Cardew tells us. It's just that I feel – I feel — '

'*What*, Flash?'

'Oh, there's a jungle *menace* in it all! It's as if – as if the powers of darkness had got control! And I have a feeling of guilt – Denholm was after *me* because of Don — '

'Flash, Denholm was in a drunken frenzy! You were only an incident, a temporary focus for his fury. You have no responsibility for what happened to Sashie!' Twice jerked to his feet and I realized that he too was suffering from something of my own feeling of caged frustration. 'If anybody has any responsibility,' he said, 'it goes back to that bloody old Madam Mount Melody!' He spun round away from me and stared out of the window into the brilliant garden beyond the verandah. '*That's* the real power of darkness, if you like!'

'Twice, I'm sorry for making an ass of myself,' I said to his back. 'It's all this violence – I don't seem to be able to absorb it and turn it into a joke as the rest of them can.'

He turned round. 'I know. You and I don't belong among this sort of thing. . . . Look here, I suppose we'd better join this breakfast party.'

'I know. I hope to Heaven they won't be funny.'

'It's going to be what Tom would call mac-aber. They are bound to be funny, as you call it, because they're afraid to be anything else. And Madame and Sir Ian don't mean to be, but they've been here for so long that they are set in their reactions. . . . Funny how the negroes always yell with laughter when somebody gets hurt. It must be something in the climate.'

'Well, I'm not a negro,' I said, 'and the climate hasn't got that much hold on me.'

We left our bedroom and went along the verandah. The big breakfast party was slow in gathering and in the process it took on in a macabre way something of the character of a dinner-party, for we gravitated towards the drawing-room to which Marion brought a large tray of glasses and several jugs of iced orange-juice, so that we all embarked on an out-of-time cocktail session, while we waited for Madame, Sir Ian and Sandy to arrive. Madame was the first to come, looking fresh, well-rested and completely mistress of her house and the situation.

'Good morning, all,' she said. 'Thank you, Marion, I will have a glass of orange-juice. The house is quite disorganized, I am afraid, but you all look quite collected and comfortable. How are *you*, young man?'

'Simply splendid, Madame, thank you,' said Sashie. 'I have seldom slept better.'

'We call that room of yours the Governor's Bedroom, from the old days of horses and carriages, you know.'

'Oh, I *see*!' said Sashie. '*That* accounts for the space!'

Madame held him firmly with her eye. 'I meant the days when distances were *actual*,' she explained, 'and not reduced by motor cars, when the return journey between King's House and Paradise could not be accomplished in a single day. The horses, of course, were housed in the stables.' She took a sip of juice from her glass. 'Marion, where are Ian and the boy?'

'I don't know, Madame.'

'Oh, well, we can wait a little for them. We have plenty of time. I understand from the Commissioner that he would prefer we all stayed here until his men find that boy Denholm. One should try to co-operate with the police, I suppose. The Commissioner is a fine officer, but hampered by the stupidity of his local men. And Beattie Denholm is behaving extremely badly – not replying on the Instrument like this.'

'Are you sure she is at Mount Melody?' Twice asked.

'Certainly! Where other would she be? Of *course* she is at Mount Melody and she also knows that I am trying to speak to her on the Instrument. She was a Poynter of Blueclear, you know – very odd people. They have this failing of refusing to speak to people when they are annoyed, even their own brothers. Although why *Beattie* should be annoyed passes my comprehension. After all, it was not *my* grandson that tried to shoot *her* guests, but that's the Poynter family all over. Quite unreasonable.'

With the sun streaming in through the long windows that had

been so black the night before and Madame's calm, decisive voice laying down her firm views, all that had happened only a few hours ago seemed to recede into the lurid, blood-stained history of the island. In a visionary way, I could see Sir Ian, five years hence, telling some new arrival like myself the story of 'the night o' the shootin' on Paradise.'

'Are the police at Mount Melody now?' somebody asked.

'Yes,' Madame said. 'Ian and I both insisted, too, that the Commissioner should go up himself. I told him that it was quite useless sending a coloured corporal or two to deal with Beattie Denholm – not the thing at all. I would not co-operate with such people myself and I am a great deal more reasonable than Beattie Denholm.'

A short, strained silence followed this announcement which was so much in character as to be almost caricature, and then Madame turned to me.

'Although it was very trying for you and Mr de Marnay, Janet, it is really a blessing that this thing happened last night. I understand from Ian that this wretched young man should have been treated for drunkenness long ago and that Beattie was being thoroughly obstructive. We are now in the position to force her hand,' she ended with malicious relish.

'Yes, Madame,' I said. 'Quite.' – and as Sir Ian and Sandy came round the corner of the verandah, I thought to myself that Madame, in her own way, was as much of a human menace as Mrs Denholm.

' — an' I could borrow that Cranston cissy's fiddle, my boy!' Sir Ian was saying.

'Yes, sir. An' I would use Aunt Maria's mandoline – it's older-fashioneder than my guitar.'

'An' here, listen, I've thought of a chune!'

'What, sir?'

'You know that thing – London's burnin'! Fire! Fire! . . .'

'Gosh, sir!' said Sandy with deep appreciation.

They paused by the breakfast-table on the verandah and, following Madame, we all went out to join them.

'Well, Ian, we've been waiting for you. Good morning, Sandy. Janet, will you sit there? Miss Davey – you there beside Mr Yates. Marion, you here, please. Please sit down, gentlemen.' She took her chair at the end of the long table and after we were all seated she rose again in her own place and looked round at all of us. 'Before we begin breakfast,' she said, 'I wish to thank all of you here for the delightful entertainment last night for which you were responsible. Events being what they were, and I need hardly mention that they were beyond *my* control, only Edward and I, I think, of the people here present heard His Excellency's delightful speech of thanks. I think he spoke truly when he said that all my guests and the people of the Estate had a most enjoyable evening and I have to thank you all for the hard work that made it possible. And now, Mr de Marnay, I wish to convey to you my personal apology and an apology on behalf of all Paradise for the unfortunate injury you uffered. I assure you that such a thing has never occurred in my house before and I sincerely hope that such a thing will never occur here again. I wish to say, too, that I deeply appreciate the way in which you co-operated with us in keeping the disastrous occurrence a secret from my other guests. It would have been a deep embarrassment to me had the Governor on the one hand and the working people on the other come to know that one of my acquaintance had attempted to murder a guest of mine in my own house. On behalf of all of us here at Paradise, therefore, I offer you my apologies, Mr de Marnay, and also my sincere thanks.'

Through the coma which this oration had induced in me, I heard the mischievous voice of Don say: 'Hear, hear! Speech, Sashie, speech!'

Sashie, in his place at mid-table, rose and bobbed a curtsy at Madame who blinked at him as if her brain could not believe in her own vision and, as if to convince herself that he really did exist, she stared with concentration at the bandages and the slung arm. 'He *must* be human!' I could hear her think. 'He got shot and bled and they had to bandage him!'

'As a rule, don't you know, Madame, my sweet,' Sashie began coyly, 'I talk all the time, but *all* the time, but I never *say* anything, if you see what I mean, because, you see, I never *really* can find anything to *say*. As for you apologizing and things like that, it isn't really at all necessary – *quite* the reverse. It was all rather fun, really – although I was scared quite witless at the time – being shot at like that by that simply furious young man, for people like me always making a point of *not* going to grouse parties or even the movies or *any* places where they have *guns*, so frightening. The only thing I am annoyed about, but really very annoyed indeed, is that he burst my bladder — '

Madame's eyes widened and moved from Sashie's chest to somewhere in the region of his lower abdomen.

' — I say, don't take me up in error, dear lady! *Nothing* to do with the Flags of All Nations! Quite the reverse! My big balloon on a stick, you know. Look, it is a ruin!' Dramatically, from under the tablecloth he pulled the wilted remains of his bauble. 'And it was such a beautiful, symbolic balloon! Madame, I beg of you, would you arrange to buy me a new bladder? Given that, all will be forgotten and I shall bless you from the bottom of my heart.'

Sashie sat down and for a long moment Madame stared at him in wondering silence while he stared back at her, his satyr-mask quite expressionless.

'Rob,' she said at last, in a voice faint and far away for her, 'please arrange to import – I believe they are obtained from dollar sources – a suitable replacement bl – balloon for Mr de Marnay. . . . Ian, ring the bell for breakfast.'

It took a little while for all of us, after what had transpired, to decide that any conversation of any kind was safe or decent, but, naturally enough, Sandy was the first to recover.

'I'll tell you a thing!' he said as he attacked a plate of cereal.

'What?' we said, almost with one voice out of relief that the semi-stunned silence had been broken.

'Sir Ian an' me's just been discussin' next year's play!' If we were bemused before, we were stricken utterly speechless now.

'Yes, by Jove!' said Sir Ian. 'We're goin' to have a kind of combination of Macbeth an' Nero an' Cleopatra!'

'No!' said Sashie. '*Do* go on!'

'Classical stuff, ye know. After all, we're gettin' pretty good at the job now an' might as well have a worth-while play, dammit.'

'Do you feel that Macbeth, Nero and Cleopatra would be worth while?' Don asked in an awed voice. 'I've never heard of it. Don't you mean Antony and Cleopatra or Caesar — '

'Certainly it's Caesar! *Nero* was their Caesar! *All* their emperors were Caesars – you learn that at school! But we're pickin' on Nero because o' the fiddlin' an' burnin' the place down an' everything.'

'Ian, I will *not* have the place burned down! Nor will I have any more varlets and – and Articles and shooting! You will choose some decent, Christian theme — '

'But, Mother, this is *full* o' Christians, dammit! Ye have to have Christians to throw to the lions!'

'Where are you going to get lions? The nearest lion to here is in Africa!' said Rob sourly.

198

'Old Ezekiel's mule is so hairy that it looks jolly like a lion, sir!' said Sandy. 'An' we could dress Cadence in that tiger skin that Sir Ian shot in India!'

Rob gave up for the moment, but Don was rash enough to say: 'What fascinates me is Cleopatra! Who are you going to have as the Serpent of old Nile?'

'*Not*, surely, Miss Poynter?' Sashie enquired.

'Don't be stoopid, Sashie!' said Sir Ian. '*You* would be Cleopatra!'

'We'd have to get him a asp for his bosom, Sir Ian,' said Sandy.

'Sandy, eat your food and shut up!' said his father. 'Besides, neither of you could remember a tenth of the words of a play by Shakespeare, apart altogether from — '

'*You're* thinkin' o' Shakespeare!' said Sir Ian. '*We* ain't goin' to do Shakespeare! Missis *Janet* will write it for us.'

'Me?' I squealed. 'Not on your life! I want no more to do with varlets — '

'Now, now!' he told me. 'Don't you go gettin' like that! There weren't any varlets in Nero's time, ye know – just slaves an' thanes an' the odd eunuch or two. Whole thing's perfectly simple – got it all worked out already. First Act – Macbeth an' Cleopatra meet an' hit it off at a party where they're throwin' a few Christians to the lions. Second Act – the ghost o' What'sisname tells Nero that his wife is carryin' on with this fellah in the kilt an' he an' Macbeth have a bit o' joustin'. Third Act – Nero kills Macbeth when he's in bed an' Birnam Wood comes to Dunsinane an' Cleopatra gets goin' with her asp an' Nero plays the fiddle an' burns the place down. Splendid endin', don't ye think? Perfectly simple. All ye have to do is write it down.'

It was too much. I could not speak. I felt that nothing save a miracle could prevent my becoming embroiled in another nightmare of a play and that the jungle of the fantastic was once more sucking me in, its tendrils wound about me, choking and submerging me.

'I daresay something can be done with it,' said Don, which was the truly tactful way of closing the subject, but he was too mischievous to leave it at that. 'If Nero killed Macbeth, though, wouldn't that make him a regicide?'

'What's wrong with that?' Sir Ian asked. '*All* the Caesars were regicides! You couldn't *be* a Caesar unless you killed the one that was Caesar already! That's what that play Friends, Romans, Countrymen is *about*, dammit!'

'I see,' Don said humbly.

'Well, that's settled,' Sir Ian now said with smug satisfaction, mopping his lips with his napkin and smiling round at us all. 'I must say, I enjoyed myself last night, in spite o' that fellah an' his shootin' an' carryin' on. *Every*body enjoyed themselves. An' everything turns out for the best, like I was sayin' to Mother. Didn't know what I was goin' to do about Beattie an' that boy an' her power complex an' everythin', but after Cardew's been up there an' knocked some sense into her, we'll get the boy off to the States an' make a job of him.'

We continued to sit around the table, long after the servants had cleared away the breakfast things, for there was nothing else to do. The sun climbed, the heat increased and I found that my feeling of near-hysteria of the early morning was evaporating as if the degree of mental tension which is the precursor of hysteria were too much effort here in the hot, languorous shade of this tropical verandah.

'I'll tell you a thing,' Sandy said at one point, 'tomorrow's Christmas,' and he twanged a languid note or two of a carol from his guitar. Christmas Day. And this was Christmas Eve and my thin dress was sticking to my sweaty back and the police were hunting for a drunk homicidal maniac and I did not care. Given another few months of this, I thought, I shall be as mentally lax and flaccid as any native. Nothing will move me. But even as the thought crossed my mind, I saw the Police Commissioner's big car with its white-uniformed corporal at the wheel turn in at the south gate and come round the sweep to the library door immediately below us. I was sitting bolt upright in my wicker chair, my sweaty hands stuck to its arms, when his head and broad shoulders came into sight at the top of the verandah stairway. He stopped at the top of the stairs and stood looking at us.

''Morning, all,' he said.

''Mornin', Cardew,' Sir Ian said. 'Been up there? Found them?'

'Yes,' he said slowly. 'We found them – all three of them.'

I saw Madame's plump little body stiffen as she became even more erect in her chair. 'Where, Commissioner?' she asked.

'At the bottom of the Rio d'Oro Gorge.' We all stared at the big, pink-faced man across the hot silence. 'The boy is badly damaged, but they say he will live. The girl is only concussed, they think.'

'And Beattie? Mrs Denholm?' Madame asked.

200

'Mrs Denholm is dead, Madame.'

'Poor old Beattie,' Sir Ian said quietly and then: 'Oh, well, could be for the best, I suppose.'

Chapter Thirteen

SASHIE, SANDY and I were sent round to Guinea Corner in Madame's Rolls within half-an-hour of the Commissioner's arrival on the verandah and as I sat down on a chair in my own drawing-room I was grateful that I had not been called upon for any major role in the next activity that was being planned at the Great House of Paradise.

'Well, well,' Sashie said, pushing the stick of his bauble into a pot of ferns in the corner, 'here we are, my sweet – the women, the children and the maimed for a passive part only, thank Heaven. You and I have had overmuch of this hurly-burly already. . . . Would it be in order to ask the good Clorinda for a little iced lime-juice?'

'And a little gin with it wouldn't come amiss,' I said. 'Sandy, please go and ask the kitchen for gin and lime-juice and ice and whatever you want for yourself.'

'All right. And I'll tell you what – I'll take my guitar to the kitchen an' play to Cookie, an' you an' Mr Sashie can have a nice quiet sit-down.'

'That's very thoughtful of you, Sandy.'

'He is a singularly likeable child, that,' Sashie commented while I mixed drinks for us. 'At his age, I am sure I was more than objectionable.'

'He has a very remarkable mother,' I said.

Sashie looked at me over the glass I handed to him. 'Paradise is rich in remarkable people,' he said. 'Not the least of them is that old tartar Madame who took such undoubted command of us all, including that very large, stolid Police Commissioner with the enormous feet.'

In spite of the shocking events of the last twenty-four hours, I found myself half-smiling as Sashie's words recalled to me the scene on the Great House verandah when Madame rose from her chair, took up her bunch of household keys and clasped her plump little hands over her plump little stomach.

'Yes. Poor Beattie, but, as you say, Ian, everything may be for the best.' She then turned to Mr Cardew. 'Commissioner, I have known Mrs Denholm for over sixty years. She was a friend and neighbour of long standing and it is my privilege to arrange for her funeral. How soon will your necessary formalities be over?'

'The funeral could be arranged for tomorrow, Madame.'

'Very well.' One by one, she turned towards us, giving us our orders. 'Rob, Twice – and you also, Mr Candlesham – will be good enough to arrange the funeral formalities from the Estate office. Marion, you will inform the ladies of the Compound that I require cake and sandwiches for about two hundred and fifty people for tomorrow afternoon and that I shall be grateful for their assistance. Janet, you will take Mr Sashie, Sandy, Miss Davey and Mr Yates to your house and the ladies of the Compound will be informed that they may place their children and their nurses in your charge until this evening and during the day tomorrow if they so wish. Ian and Edward, you will come down to my office with me and make the necessary calls to our friends on that Instrument for me. And – Commissioner?'

'Yes, Madame?'

'Can you inform me how one causes an announcement to be made from the island wireless station?'

'I could arrange it for you, Madame, when I go down to the Bay, if you will give me a note of what you want said.'

'That is very kind. Please come down to my office, Commissioner.'

Her firm little heels tap-tapped away along the verandah and down the stairway, the men following in Indian file behind her, the Police Commissioner bringing up the rear. The sight of her upright, stiff little back filled me with shame for my near-hysteria of the morning and for my present inertia and, without words, I nodded to Sashie, Sandy, Dorothy and Bertie who followed me to the waiting car that brought us to Guinea Corner.

It was late afternoon before I saw Twice again, when he came on to the verandah where Sashie and I were watching the Compound children playing Musical Chairs on the lawn, under the guidance of Dorothy and Bertie, to the sound of Sandy's guitar.

'Tired, Twice?' I asked.

'Not too bad. . . . Don and Rob not back yet?'

'No. Where are they?'

'Up at Mount Melody at the family burial-ground. They said they'd come here when they came back – shouldn't be long now.'

'So everything is – arranged?'

'Every last thing. Marion even has all last night's crockery out of the hampers and the tea-tables are laid. Oh, well.'

'Get our good Twice a drink, darling,' Sashie said to me. 'It is all very efficient and – very depressing.'

The Compound wives began to arrive now to collect their children, but everybody was tired and listless and had little to say, and, shortly after the last of them had gone and Dorothy and her Bertie had gone for an evening walk, Marion, Don and Rob arrived, accompanied by Sir Ian.

'Well, that's that,' Sir Ian said. 'Poor old Beattie! Well, Missis Janet, we all might as well have a tot.'

The light had begun to fade and in a few moments it was pitch dark and the crickets and frogs were setting up their frenzied evening chorus from the garden. In a corner of the dining-room, where we had gone to pour the drinks, Twice said to me: 'Listen, can you remember what you were dreaming about last night when you were talking all that stuff about water on the ceiling?'

'Lord, no! Why?'

'I've had the creeps all day. I had to take the mobile crane up the gorge to get those two cars out for the police. They – they were both lying upside-down at the edge of the river, with the water flowing through them – flowing across their ceilings!'

'Twice!' I stared at him for a moment, horrified, and than I made an attempt at a laugh. 'Don't be absurd!' I stammered. 'Here, drink this for the love of Pete! Your nerves are getting the better of you – not that it's any wonder!'

'No, I'm all right, but – well – it's *queer*, isn't it?'

'Coincidence is always queer!' I said, but unconvincingly, for I myself felt unconvinced and scared. 'Come on, let's go back to the others.'

The party had moved from the verandah into the drawing-room and they were gathered round the wireless set out of which the muted voice of a news announcer was coming into the room.

"The announcement,' Sir Ian explained. 'It's due to come through just after the news.'

And after a moment he increased the volume and the impersonal voice with the slight American accent said: 'We have been asked to announce the arrangements for the funeral of Mrs Beatrice Denholm of Mount Melody who died in a tragic motor accident last night – Mrs Beatrice Denholm of Mount Melody. The Cortège will leave the Great House of Paradise at two pm tomorrow, two pm Christmas Day, for the Denholm Family burial ground at Mount Melody where the service will be held at three pm. As announced in the news, the Rio d'Oro road between Paradise south gate and Mount Melody will be closed by order of the Police Commissioner to all traffic not attending the funeral between the hours of one-thirty pm and five pm. We will now repeat the arrangements for the funeral of Mrs Beatrice Denholm of Mount Melody — '

There was a click as Sir Ian turned off the radio and in the silence the nonchalant, uncaring chorus of frogs and crickets outside – that night voice of the island – seemed monstrously loud.

'Oh, well, poor Beattie,' Sir Ian said again.

'Has anyone heard anything about the young people?' Marion asked.

'Edward went down to the hospital with Cardew, me dear. The girl's conscious and they're quite pleased with the boy. Funny thing, when a fellah's drunk, ye can't kill him. The girl was lucky, though – she was thrown out and caught in the bush. Old Beattie was drivin' an' hadn't a chance.'

'Do they know what happened?' somebody asked.

'Oh, yes. The girl told them the whole story. She an' Beattie missed the boy sometime about nine o'clock an' they knew he had been drinkin' so they set out to look for him. *He* was on his way *up* the gorge after his shootin' match with Sashie here, goin' like blazes, of course, an' he went slap into Beattie's Cadillac on one o' these blind corners an' they both went over the edge. The girl even remembers flyin' through the air. She must have hit her head on a rock or somethin'. But she's all right. There's real Denholm stuff in that girl. An' maybe this'll teach that brother o' hers a lesson. Don't suppose they'll stay here. Hope they don't. No future in a mountain place like Mount Melody these days. Fine old house, of course.'

'It's a creepy old hole!' Marion said, rising and laying aside her glass. 'Sandy, Rob, it's time we went home. . . . I wouldn't live at Mount Melody for all the sugar in St Jago!'

Sandy was standing between Twice and me as his mother spoke. 'My mother's quite right,' he said. 'Me, I wouldn't live at Mount Melody neither, not for *any*thing!'

'Don't be stoopid, boy! It's one o' the finest old houses in the island!' Sir Ian barked.

'I'll tell you a thing, sir,' said Sandy gravely.

'What, boy?'

'You won't hardly believe this, but it's true!'

'*How* true, Sandy?' I got in my question.

He turned his big eyes up to me. 'As true as my name's Sandy Maclean, Missis Janet. . . . One day Sir Ian an' me went up there an' Missis Denholm told me to wait in the drawin'-room an' gave me some magazines to read. An' listen, ye know what? The ceilin' in there – it *moves*!' He looked round at us all. 'As sure as my name's Sandy Maclean, that ceilin' in that drawin'-room moves all the time!'

'Oh, tommyrot, boy!'

'Sandy is quite right!' I said, almost shouting the words. 'He's quite *right*! That ceiling *does* seem to move – the water of the Rio d'Oro is reflected on it all the time and it seems to ripple and flow like running water!' I turned and smiled at Twice with a great upsurge of relief and then turned back to the boy. 'You're quite right, Sandy! It's one of the weirdest, uncanniest things I've seen since I came to the island and I wouldn't live there for anything either!'

There was a ripple of liquid, falling notes from the guitar and '*There* you are, see?' said my friend Sandy.

THESE ARE PAN BOOKS –

Doris Leslie
THE PERFECT WIFE
Nineteenth century England with its frivolities, dissipation and political crises – the colourful setting for a best-selling historical novel that tells of the little back-street milliner who climbed to Mayfair and married Disraeli. (3/6)

Anne Duffield
THE INSCRUTABLE NYMPH
A sensitive drama of sorely strained loyalties set in Canada in the summer of 1940. The destinies of an English Major and his youthful Norwegian ward are strangely linked. (2/6)

Rumer Godden
THE GREENGAGE SUMMER
Brilliant novel of emotion and suspense – set in the Champagne country of the Marne – by the author of *An Episode of Sparrows*. Recently filmed. (2/6)

Rumer Godden
CHINA COURT
An intimate portrait of five generations playing out the drama of their lives in the same beautiful house. 'Brilliant' – *B.B.C.* (3/6)

PICK OF THE PAPERBACKS

Joy Packer
THE HIGH ROOF
Set in the enchanting Cape Peninsula, this delightful story, with all its social and racial distinctions, explores the intimate human emotions of three women and the men they love. (3/6)

Joy Packer
VALLEY OF THE VINES
Vivid with colour, brimful of excitement, a best-seller by any standard. 'Only the born teller of tales can provoke this feeling. An admirable and irreplaceable talent' – *Sphere*. (3/6)

Lloyd C. Douglas
MAGNIFICENT OBSESSION
Tells of a young playboy's determination to follow in the steps of the brilliant surgeon whose life has been sacrificed for his own. (3/6)

Morris West
THE DEVIL'S ADVOCATE
Winner of the James Tait Black Memorial Prize for the best novel of the year. 'A fanfare of critical trumpets has heralded the approach of *The Devil's Advocate*,' said the *Observer*, 'and for once one is not disappointed.' (3/6)

THESE ARE PAN BOOKS

Marjorie G. Lowe
JESS
The fiery historical romance that kept five million women in suspense for nine weeks when it was serialised by *Woman* as 'Romany Gold'. Introduces a new novelist whose flair for telling a really satisfying story should rapidly win her wide popularity. (3/6)

Peter de Polnay
MARIO
The realism of *Children of the Sun* and the tenderness and sensuality of *The Roman Spring of Mrs Stone* combine in this moving novel of Florence. Mario is a penniless, ragged pimp, a helpless tool of corruption in a city of palazzos and hovels, elegance and vice. (2/6)

PICK OF THE PAPERBACKS